WEREWOLF QUARRY

WEREWOLF QUARRY
THE ORIGINS STORY OF MONSTERS™ BOOK TWO

MARTHA CARR

MICHAEL ANDERLE

This book is a work of fiction. All of the characters, organizations, and events portrayed in this novel are either products of the author's imagination or are used fictitiously. Sometimes both.

Copyright © 2023 LMBPN Publishing
Cover Art by Jake @ J Caleb Design
http://jcalebdesign.com / jcalebdesign@gmail.com
Cover copyright © LMBPN Publishing
A Michael Anderle Production

LMBPN Publishing supports the right to free expression and the value of copyright. The purpose of copyright is to encourage writers and artists to produce the creative works that enrich our culture.

The distribution of this book without permission is a theft of the author's intellectual property. If you would like permission to use material from the book (other than for review purposes), please contact support@lmbpn.com. Thank you for your support of the author's rights.

LMBPN Publishing
PMB 196, 2540 South Maryland Pkwy
Las Vegas, NV 89109

Version 1.00, February 2023
ebook ISBN: 979-8-88541-161-5
Print ISBN: 979-8-88878-195-1

THE WEREWOLF QUARRY TEAM

Thanks to our JIT Readers

Jackey Hankard-Brodie
Jeff Goode
Dorothy Lloyd
Diane L. Smith
Jan Hunnicutt

Editor

SkyFyre Editing Team

CHAPTER ONE

"Okay, listen." Halsey Ambrosius reached into the tote bag resting on her lap and pressed her lips together. "If you get caught with any of this stuff, I'm gonna need you to swear an oath."

Propped upright in his narrow recovery bed, her cousin Brigham stared at the bag and smirked. "You mean like not to throw you under the bus?"

"At the least. You'd also need a reasonable explanation for the contraband in your possession, so I'd suggest finding a reliable scapegoat. Who's not *me*, by the way."

Brigham laughed and readjusted his position. "Perfect. If anyone asks, I'll say it was The Burger."

Halsey snorted as she reached farther into the bag on her lap. "And if anyone asks *him*, he'll probably believe he's really done it."

"Oh, the *irony*..." Brigham shoved his elbows into the pillows behind him and smacked his lips as she withdrew one large Tupperware container. The opaque green plastic made it easier to hide what she'd brought him. Which would have been immediately confiscated if any of the healers and nurses in the medical wing got a whiff of what was inside.

Halsey leaned over the container and shot a wary glance at the door to her cousin's recovery room. So far, the coast was clear. She popped open the lid, and the room filled with the mouthwatering scent of still-hot pizza.

Brigham's hazel eyes lit up, and he stared longingly at the green case. "You didn't."

"I totally did. What irony?"

"Huh?"

She pulled out a stack of napkins and slowly moved them toward her cousin without handing them over yet. "About hypothetically blaming The Burger for bringing you three melty, insanely greasy, perfectly topped slices of freshly-out-of-the-oven—"

"Just…" Brigham swiped at the container, glared at his cousin, then lurched as far forward as he possibly could. "Gimme that."

This time, Halsey let him snatch the container and snorted. "It would've made sense if I'd brought you a burger…"

His eyelids fluttered as he inhaled over the open Tupperware, and his groan of pleasure almost made her laugh out loud. He settled back into the pillows and set the container in his lap. "A burger would've been great, too. Don't get me wrong. But *this*? This is the kinda thing that shows a guy you really care, you know?"

"Which The Burger wouldn't have done, by the way." She couldn't help but smile as she watched her cousin lift the first slice of pizza to his mouth, take a massive bite, and lose all sense of time and space. Grease dripped back down onto the other pieces. "Plus, I'm not a fan of being ironic."

Brigham chewed slowly, swallowed, then looked at her with wide eyes.

Yep. He's still in bed, but man, he already looks so much better.

Two weeks ago, Brigham had hardly been able to open his eyes at all. The left one had been swollen shut. His lips had been split and bleeding, and he'd been covered in bruises as he was raced through the estate house on a gurney. Which, honestly, were nothing compared to the internal bleeding and two fractured ribs.

If he'd been anyone else, he wouldn't have been able to sit up like this for at least two more weeks if he was lucky. Being an Ambrosius elemental came with a whole swath of benefits, and not only with elemental magic, weapons, or on the battlefield.

Halsey reached into her bag one more time and produced a crisp, ice-cold, sweating can of blonde ale appropriately called Monster Bash. Her cousin was taking his second bite of pizza when she cracked open the beer can.

The snap and ensuing hiss made him look up, and his jaw dropped. "No shit. Are you *trying* to kill me right now?"

"I don't know. Depends on how quickly you can get your head back in the game."

He chewed, eyed the beer, and muttered, "Uh-huh."

"'Cause I'd call *this* ironic." Halsey raised the can and pointed at it. "You know, almost like it was made for *us*."

"Hal."

"But now…"

"Oh, come on." He swallowed thickly, looked like he was about to start drooling, then shot the recovery room door another cautious glance. "Fine. You. The Burger. Irony. You know, because Owen's the only one who'd straight-up volunteer to take to the fall for breaking the rules, and you're the only one who's actually breaking them. Now, what the hell are you gonna do with that beer?"

Her mouth popped open in feigned shock and insult. "Okay, first of all, I'm not *breaking the rules*. I'm only… bending them in a way that's generally frowned upon." She thoughtfully lifted the can to her lips and took a long, glugging pull.

Brigham's shoulders slumped. "Dude."

"Second," she continued, pretending not to notice his reaction while she messed with him. "Owen's not getting blamed for anything else I've done or might still do in the future. Which also isn't technically breaking the rules."

"I get it, Hal."

"I only want you to see that there's no irony." She took another long sip, then smirked and waved the beer can around like she had no idea he wanted it. "I could be anywhere doing anything right now. Yet I'm here. Bringing you all your favorite things that medical won't let you have…"

"You *are* trying to kill me."

"Quit being so dramatic." With a snort, Halsey set her just-for-fun beer on the side table next to her chair, then pulled another one out. Her cousin eyed her warily as she cracked open the second can, but his eyes lit up again when she offered him the drink. "You know I always got your back."

"While being a jerk about it the whole time." Brigham reached for the beer, then quickly took it so she wouldn't have a chance to change her mind. "I'm flattered."

"You should be." Grinning, she withdrew another container of pizza and opened it so they could eat their contraband lunch together. "You're the only person in the world I'd ever do this for."

"You mean you don't screw with everyone like this? Huh. You know what? Somehow, that doesn't make me feel special." He took a tentative sip of his favorite local beer, swallowed, then knocked it back again and drank like he hadn't had a drink in weeks. Which, as far as delicious adult beverages were concerned, was technically true.

Halsey enjoyed her own hot, greasy pizza and watched him with a knowing smile. *If this doesn't put him in a good mood, nothing will. He sure deserves it, though.*

After Brigham finished enjoying his first good chug of beer since before he'd been sent to the medical wing on the brink of death, he leaned back and closed his eyes. He looked ready to fall asleep with a beer in one hand and pizza in the other. Then he let out a long, heavy sigh and nodded. "I take it back."

"Oh, yeah?"

"I totally feel special right now."

"You're welcome."

For the next five minutes, they enjoyed their medically unapproved lunch in relative silence, punctuated by Brigham's occasional sigh or groan of approval as he wolfed down all three slices. He chose to savor the beer a little more slowly. While drinking it, he pushed his cousin for the thousandth time in the last two weeks toward the conversation she wasn't ready to have yet.

"So. They haven't assigned you a new partner yet?"

Halsey widened her eyes and finished chewing her mouthful before responding. "Nope. They haven't even tried. Even if they did, that would only be another rule for me to break. Sorry, pal. You're stuck with me."

"You mean you're stuck with *me*." He raised his eyebrows and gestured around the recovery room that had been his temporary home for the last two weeks. "I have no idea when I'm getting out of here, and nobody will tell me a damn thing."

"Because it doesn't matter." She tried to laugh, but it came out flat and forced. "If you're not going anywhere, I'm not going anywhere. Plain and simple. Listen, you put yourself out there for the Clan. You did your job, and you got hurt. It happens to everyone."

"No, it doesn't."

"Brigham, our family has an entire *medical wing* on their headquarters estate. Pretty sure that wouldn't be a thing if you were the only monster hunter to get tossed against a few trees by overly aggressive ogres."

"When you put it like that, I *am* the only one."

"You know what I mean."

"And you know what *I* mean." He sipped and fixed her with a knowing stare over the rim of his beer can, waiting for her response.

Halsey didn't want to respond.

I can't talk to him about how my dad and I rushed into that cemetery and killed nine ogres at once by chopping off their hands. *Not when I came back from that mission without a scratch, and he's...been here the whole time.*

"Hal."

"What?" She looked sharply at her cousin, then downed the rest of her beer. It felt like the only thing she could do.

"I hate to break it to you, but you're not the only person who's come to visit me in here."

"Good. Otherwise, I'd probably have a few sets of teeth to bash in." They both chuckled without enthusiasm, but neither mentioned the disparity. When it came to hunting monsters, Halsey was the best the Ambrosius Clan had. When it came to starting physical fights with family members, she was generally the first one to back out.

Brigham shifted again. Halsey knew where this was going. She also knew her cousin wouldn't let this go.

"That means you're not the only person who's been feeding me updates over the last two weeks," he added casually, completely ignoring her attempt at a joke.

"Ah." She pointed at him. "But I'm the only one who's been *literally* feeding you, too, right?"

"Okay, Hal. Let's cut the bullshit." Brigham's words emerged friendly enough, but he'd stopped paying attention to his beer and simply held it as the dripping condensation left a ring in the bedsheets. "You've been avoiding this since day one."

Halsey cleared her throat. "Actually, I think you gained consciousness again on, like, day three…"

"I know you and your dad went after those ogres and finished what Cadence and I couldn't. Honestly, I would've given almost anything to see that."

"Yeah? Like what?"

Brigham snorted and shook his head. "Quit trying to change the subject."

"Why?" She folded her arms, sat back, and tried to look like she didn't care about this conversation and only participated out of concern for her cousin's wellbeing and recovery. "Forget the ogres, Brigham. Everyone else has."

"That's a load of crap."

"I'm here for *you*, cuz. Not the monsters. Not even nine ogres, okay? Right now, the only thing you need to focus on is—"

"Ha! You too?" When Halsey fixed him with a blank, clueless look, he shrugged. "Everyone and their actual mother have been telling me what I *need*, Hal. You're the last person I expected to pull that shit on me. Especially now."

Halsey stared at him for what felt like an incredibly long time, then broke into a wry smile. "You sound like your mom right now. You know that, right?"

"Hey, I never said she's *always* wrong."

"No, of course not. Only when her attempted guilt-trips are successful."

He grinned like she'd given him a compliment. "So I made *you* feel guilty?"

"Yeah, don't push it." They both laughed, and this time, Halsey didn't feel as pressured to have this conversation. More than that, she didn't feel the need to protect him anymore. *He's sitting up on his own. Moving around. In a lot less pain, probably. You fed him pizza and beer for crying out loud. Quit treating him like a kid.*

Still, she couldn't bring herself to dive into one hell of a story and what it meant for the Ambrosius Clan elementals and their monster-hunting militia. What it meant for all the elemental families in the world, and their magic, and the monsters, and everything in between.

Fortunately, Brigham was as skilled with diplomatic relations as Halsey was with monster-hunting. Including with his own cousin and partner.

"You realize it's been like pulling teeth with you, right?" he finally asked, which made her laugh because it was so out of left field.

"Not sure what you're referring to..."

"The whole story, Hal. 'Cause yeah, I've had tons of visitors. They only gave me the bare minimum and kept saying to ask Halsey, which is a different torture on its own. Like the whole thing's some kinda...massive infection, and everybody's so scared of making me sick, they won't even go there."

Halsey snorted. "Oh, but you want *me* to infect you? That's real heartwarming, dude. I'm flattered."

"Well, maybe you're the only one of us with any real immunity to this thing. I trust you more than anyone else, too. If anybody's gonna come in here and *not* infect me with the truth, it's you."

She stared at him, wondering what she could possibly say to make any of this go down easier. Nothing came to mind yet, so she went with, "That's a terrible analogy."

Brigham chuckled. "Yeah, but it feels right. Now I'm wondering why you won't *tell* me. It's not like I didn't already know you're a badass with an ax. Or...any other weapon that fits your *mood* for the day."

"I don't have moods."

"Sure." He sipped his beer, both to steel himself against

the news everyone else had known for weeks and because he'd missed the taste so damn much. "Hit me, Hal. I'm not pissed that you and Aiden took care of those ogres after I couldn't. Of course you did. And unless I seriously fucked it up before you guys got there, or somebody died..."

"No." Halsey shook her head. "Nobody died. Not if we're talking about people, at least." His eyes widened in curiosity, but she still faced a block in her conscience. She didn't want to bring her bedridden partner the kind of news that might have given several Clan Council members minor heart attacks.

Brigham had been her top concern since the day he'd been rushed to the medical wing, minutes after she'd been called into an emergency Council meeting with one week left in her month-long suspension. It felt wrong to do or say anything to jeopardize his recovery.

Even after being seriously injured and kept under close watch by healers and family members, Brigham Ambrosius wasn't one to give up easily. Halsey knew he'd keep pushing her for the truth he couldn't get from anyone else, and that only made it worse.

I want him back on his feet before we face all the insanity waiting out there in the world. Or maybe I want a break.

That last thought felt like a punch to the face. It told her she was done trying to keep her cousin safe and not dwelling on the hard, dangerous, potentially deadly work ahead of them. She had to start talking, whether she liked it or not.

"Okay, so no *person* died," Brigham prompted, spreading his arms. "Come on, Hal. You're dragging out the suspense here."

"I…" She sighed and shook her head. "I don't want you to beat yourself up about any of this, okay?"

"Ha. No, I had a few slobbering, pea-brained monsters take care of that for me."

"You know what I mean. You and Cadence went in there with everything you had, and you did your job. Except your *job* didn't bother to prepare you the way you deserved.

"Huh." The corners of Brigham's mouth turned down in consideration, then he laughed. "Well, *I* could've told you that. And *you're* gonna tell me everything 'cause now I'm really interested."

"Yeah, I bet." Her cousin's good mood and unfailing sense of humor were infectious. Halsey let herself laugh with him as he finished his beer and nodded for her to keep going.

She told him everything he'd missed, from the night he was injured, and Halsey was sent after the ogres in his place up to the present. After she finished, she steeled herself for the inevitable explanation of what they were facing now. Even though it wasn't pretty.

CHAPTER TWO

"Beyond that, I don't know much more." She finished with a shrug. "For now. I only hope the Council doesn't decide to crawl back into their dark hole and pretend they can't see what's happening."

Brigham stared blankly at her before he clenched his eyes shut and grimaced. "Their *hands?*"

"Yeah."

"You had to chop off nine ogres' hands. Why their *hands?*"

Halsey bit back a laugh. "To kill them. I explained that part somewhere in the beginning."

"Yeah, but that doesn't even make sense. Why not put the rune somewhere that's hard to get to? Like an armpit, or…the back of the head or something?"

"*That's* the thing you're hung up on?" This time, she did laugh. "Nine ogres with blood-magic runes on their hands. The same runes that are painted in our family's records about blood humans, by the way. Plus, Meemaw storming into a meeting like she owned the place and basically telling the entire Council they're idiots for not seeing what this is. The Blood Matriarch's back, we have proof, and things are gonna get even weirder from here on out. And you're confused about *hands?*"

"Right? I know. It's insane." Brigham inhaled through his nose and ran a hand halfway through his hair before the movement jarred his still-recovering injuries, and he grimaced. "I mean, yeah. Good work, Hal. You found the proof they needed, and you and Meemaw rubbed it in their faces. That's awesome. But…the *hands…*"

"Okay, well, I didn't come here to talk to you about your sudden obsession with them. Should I go?"

He looked at his palms, shuddered a little, then shook his head. "No, you're staying. We're not done."

"Of course not." Halsey pulled out two more beers from her bag before shooting her cousin a questioning look. "Want another?"

"Brought the whole damn case in your giant purse, huh?"

"You know what? Sneaking a six-pack in here felt like too much. I was right on the money with four, though. Even *you* can't tell what's in there until I pull it out."

"Then hand it over."

They both checked the door before she dished out the last two beers, and they tried to quietly crack them open. Brigham enjoyed the first few sips of his before getting back to business, and Halsey was glad to have a break from talking. Even if it only lasted twenty seconds.

"So, weird crap's happening to monsters," he mentioned. "We already knew that. The Council didn't wanna believe a word of it, and I admit I was there too. Until the whole wyvern thing."

"Which was weird."

"Definitely weird." He pointed at her, then paused for another long pull of beer. "Blood runes on some of the dumbest monsters we've seen. All the legends and speculation, backed up by your pile of ogre hands and Meemaw's perfectly timed scroll. Man. Leave it to Meemaw to charge in at the last second."

"It wasn't the last second for her," Halsey clarified. "She wasn't even a little surprised when I told her what we found in Ireland. Actually, it seemed like she was waiting for someone else to show up and say they believe in the legends like she does."

"When did you talk to her about all that?"

"While you were out throwing ugly rocks at wyvern nests, and I thought I still had a full thirty days of suspension to suffer through."

"Wait. Hold on." Brigham sat up straighter, tilted his head, and frowned. "She agreed with you from the beginning?"

"She said that if *she'd* seen what we saw—the werewolves, the silverback alpha, the open silver coffin washed up in the seaweed on the beach—she would've thought the same thing. She told me to be careful, but the whole 'because the Mother of Monsters might be out there right now' part was implied."

"Well, damn. Now I feel like a real asshole for not having your back on that one."

She thought he was joking and laughed until she realized he wasn't laughing with her. "Why? You didn't do anything wrong."

"Not officially. I told you to cool it on the Matriarch talk *until you had proof*, though. Then I went off on a bunch of missions that went exactly the way you thought they would, and you had to stay here. Everybody else kept brushing it all off until I came back looking like a hundred and eighty pounds of ground beef."

"I...wouldn't say *that's* what you looked like."

"It's what I felt like. Trust me." They both chuckled. Brigham drank more beer, and now that he'd lost his interest in ogre hands, the wheels in his mind started turning again. "Boy. I bet every member of the Council felt like an idiot after that meeting. Hell, they *punished* you for being smarter than the whole family put together. Then they had to call you back to save the day before you got to rub it in their faces. Please tell me you rubbed it in."

"I mean..." Halsey shrugged. "I had a little fun with it."

"Hell yeah, you did. Good."

When he grinned at her, he looked so much like the Brigham who *hadn't* been nursed back from the brink of death, Halsey almost forgot they were still sitting in the medical wing. They could have been hanging out in the greenhouse attached to her little cottage on the property or in Brigham's apartment closer to town. They could have had so many fewer problems, concerns, and frustrations to think about instead. Two cousins and best friends hanging out together over pizza and beer, and nothing more.

Until his smile faded into a confused frown, and he opened his mouth again.

"Why did it take you a whole two weeks to tell me *that*?

I was expecting all kinds of doom and gloom here. I'm kinda feeling a little disappointed now."

She quickly sipped her beer to buy herself time, but she had to say *something*. "I didn't want to overwhelm you with all the crazy new facts."

"Hal. Have you met me?" He spread his arms but didn't look as amused as the gesture suggested. "I can do crazy. The only thing that overwhelms this guy is a pack of nine ogres who won't go down, and you bringing beer but not to share."

"Yeah, those were both pretty obvious."

"Watch it." He pointed at her, then stared as he slowly sipped his beer. "For real, though. Do you see me freaking out right now? No. Is the thought of you and your dad chopping off ogre hands together a totally mind-blowing experience? You bet. I knew from the beginning that things were gonna get weird. Not *that* weird, and not with a bunch of blood runes involved, sure. I'm not overwhelmed, though."

"No. You're not." Halsey pressed her lips together, lowered her beer can, and muttered, "That might be because I haven't told you *everything*..."

"Oh, *now*." Brigham started to throw his hands up, then remembered the drink and barely managed not to spill it. "What happened? They *did* assign you another partner, didn't they?"

"What? No. I'd never let that happen."

"Then what? You're being stationed halfway across the world without me 'cause I can totally walk, but the healers haven't cleared me for battle yet?"

"Brigham. It's not anything like that." After taking a

deep breath, Halsey shook her head and tried to look calm. Clearly, he was starting to freak out now.

"Well, you sure as hell waited long enough to give me the news."

"See? This is what I was trying *not* to do. You need to keep resting and relaxing, not worrying about this stuff. I'm only making it worse."

Brigham snorted. "I'm fine. You're stalling."

"It's about Meemaw, okay?" She didn't mean to shout, but the sharp echo of her own voice made her recoil.

Her cousin stared in mute, wide-eyed expectation. "Is she still... I mean, she didn't have some kinda—"

"No. Definitely not. I'm starting to think there isn't a lot that can actually hurt her, if anything. No, she's fine. Physically."

He grimaced and shrank into himself as he sank into his pillows. "Uh-oh. What are they saying she did this time?"

"That's the thing." Halsey wrinkled her nose and studied the top of her beer can, hating to even think about this. Yet he deserved to know, even if it didn't directly have anything to do with him. "They didn't bother coming up with an excuse. No crazy story. No attempt to justify why Greta Ambrosius doesn't get a seat at the family table anymore."

"Don't forget, 'It's better and safer for everyone this way.' That one's a real gem."

"Right? Like the Council thought we'd keep believing that crap past fifth grade." With a bitter laugh, she shook her head and tried to think how to tell him what happened that didn't make it sound more insane than the first part of her story. "Point is, they didn't have any excuses this time. They took her at her word when she showed up with that same blood rune on a legitimate historical record. They had to start listening to her. How could they not? Still, they didn't like it, so they kicked her out."

"Wait, *again*?" Brigham cocked his head, and his frown deepened. "How does that even work?"

"Not off the actual Council, obviously. Only out of the estate house."

"Like…right after your giant mic-drop and the two of you proving them wrong?"

"Not exactly." Halsey knocked back more beer, wishing she'd forgone subtlety and brought a whole six-pack. "She stuck around here for a few days after that. Didn't go back to her house. It was, like, meeting after meeting with the Council. At least, it felt like it. They did take her seriously. I know that much. Then I guess she started telling them what they needed to *do* about it, and they got fed up fast."

"Okay. So they told her to go home and let them handle running the Clan the way they want to." Brigham shrugged. "Nothing they haven't done before."

"Yeah, but this time they made sure she won't be able to get back in."

They stared at each other, and Halsey hoped he'd guess what that meant so she wouldn't have to explain in detail. Unfortunately, the truth was too unbelievable. It had been even for her.

CHAPTER THREE

The punchline to her unintended joke seemed to whiz right over Brigham's head. "What does that even mean?"

"It means magic, Brigham. As in the Council came up with a way to physically keep Meemaw *out* of the estate house. No more interrupting emergency meetings with the proof she's been trying to convince them of for a while. No more backing *me* up. No more calling her own meetings. No more Greta Ambrosius on the premises. Period."

"Holy shit." His blank expression morphed into horror and disgust when the implications sank in. "They can't do that."

"They already did. Last week. I only found out about it because my dad gave me as much of a warning as I was ever going to get, and I'm pretty sure he flipped the other Council members the middle finger for saying something. To me specifically."

"Oh, *man*... What did he say?"

Halsey clenched her jaw, stared at the far wall, and lowered her voice in an impersonation of Aiden Ambrosius. "'You have support in a lot of different places, Halsey. And I'm glad. Really. But there's a time and a place. That was the last time your grandmother will be storming into the Council room to back you up.'"

She pulled a face at the memory of her dad's coarse, emotionless words in direct opposition to the remorse and distaste on his features as he said them.

Brigham shook his head. "That doesn't mean they kicked her out *magically*. Or even permanently."

"Do you honestly think Meemaw would say, 'Okay, no problem. I'll stay out of what used to be my own house and my own Council room because all of you said so'? She didn't two weeks ago. From the sounds of it, that wasn't the first time she'd stormed in to deliver unexpected information that threw a wrench in the Council's gears." Halsey shrugged, knowing how insane this sounded and that it was absolutely true. "I have no idea what those other times were, and nobody's gonna say a thing to me. Plus, I overheard Lawrence and Wallace talking about it in the halls."

"As in specifically saying they magically locked her out?"

"Pretty much. If you ask me, they took it way too far this time." Halsey slugged more beer and had to practically force it down.

"No kidding." Brigham did the same, though he looked about to be sick. "Damn. Lawrence actually signed off on the whole thing? My mom. Your dad. Florence and Beatrice. They did this to their own *mom*…"

"Meemaw was *everyone's* Council leader. Hell, she trained everyone on the Council and more than half the militia herself. She's got her own spot on the property now, but before they kicked her off the Council, the estate house *was* her house. Like it's all of theirs now."

"Well, shit, Hal." He raised his beer can in a silent toast and shook his head. "Makes more sense now why you didn't throw this at me the second I could hear it. I'm still not freaking out, but you're right. This sucks."

"Yeah, sorry to burst your recovery bubble." She toasted him back, and they drank again. "Things have been tense and weird around here since then. So when you get released from constant bedrest and seriously crappy food, we have a lot of work to do."

Brigham looked surprised. He briefly considered whether or not to down the rest of his beer, then did so. After he stuck the second empty can next to the first in the Tupperware container, he sighed. "First, we figure out what's really going on out there. Find the Mother of Monsters and come up with a good plan to get rid of her. Then we get Meemaw back into the big house. Maybe even back on the Council, right?"

"I say we do it *before* all this with monsters and the Matriarch gets sorted out. If she even wants to be back on the Council at this point. I seriously don't get why they keep ignoring everything she says and *still* end up dumping all the blame on her. I mean, I know everybody thinks Greta Ambrosius lost her mind or whatever. At least, they pretend that's what they think. She's not crazy, though. Not even a little."

"Yeah, you two are almost in the same boat, aren't you?"

She fixed her cousin with a playfully dubious frown. "What's that supposed to mean?"

"You know…everyone thought *you* were crazy when we got back from Ireland. Except you're not. Obviously."

"Hey, thanks."

They laughed, then Brigham's smile settled into a getting-down-to-business line. "Okay. We know what's going on out there. We know what's possible, or at least that the impossible is starting to happen now. The Mother of Monsters is *probably* back, and we need to make sure it's for a limited time only. What else you got?"

"Um…that's it. You know everything I do."

"No, seriously, Hal. What else did you find out while I've been in a coma and-or imprisoned in this shitty room?"

"Nothing."

He shot her a deadpan stare, blinked quickly, then laughed. "Nice try."

"Thanks. 'Cause I'm serious." It took her cousin a moment to realize she meant it as Halsey stared at him to drive her point home faster.

When Brigham finally believed her, he looked more upset by this than by the Council magically banning Greta from the estate house. "You mean you haven't done shit since I got here?"

"Great." She tossed a hand up and let it fall back onto her lap. "If I'd known coming to visit you every day for the last two weeks, whether or not you actually remember it, held absolutely no value, I wouldn't've bothered."

"Well, that's what I *expected* you to do—"

"So you would've been totally fine without the pizza and beer today."

His face fell into a frown. "I mean, that was today."

"Or the lasagna on Friday."

"Nah, that was delicious."

"Or those chocolate chip oatmeal cookies you begged me to bake for a year straight when you were twelve. Total waste of my time."

"Come on." Brigham's shoulders sagged.

Halsey tapped a finger against her lower lip as she gazed at the ceiling. "Oh, *and* that can of Spam. Which is super disgusting, and of *course* no one in medical would even consider letting you eat that crap. Yet your partner was over here trying to save the day. Trying to be a good best friend because she *thought* bringing you all the weird shit you love but can't have would make your days easier and *maybe* get you back on your feet faster—"

"Okay, okay. Stop. Jeez." He scowled and shook his head, looking thoroughly scolded. "I take it back, all right? It wasn't worthless or a waste of time."

She turned her head and leaned her ear toward the bed. "And…"

"And…I'm happy as hell you stuck around. There." Brigham folded his arms, tried to look pissed, but chuckled anyway. "Damn, Hal. You almost gave me a heart attack."

"By threatening to take away your unapproved snacks? Funny."

He smirked before shaking his head again. "Seriously, though. I bet you've been driving yourself crazy waiting for me to wake up and pull myself back together. Don't get me wrong. I'm glad you've been here this whole time. Still, you could've at least started looking into this mess we're gonna have to clean up eventually, and I totally would've understood. Why didn't you?"

Halsey briefly entertained the idea of coming up with something witty, sharp, and right up her cousin's alley. Yet she'd spilled the beans on everything else, so the truth was the only way to go here. "When I was on mission probation for a month, *you* could've grabbed any other monster hunter in the Clan and said you wanted them as your new partner. Hell, we both know the Council would've made it happen in the blink of an eye to get you away from Halsey and her crazy ideas, right?"

He snorted. "I *am* good at saving your ass."

"Sometimes." They shared a laugh, and she looked at her almost-empty beer can. "Point is you could've left me in the dust, but you didn't. Yeah, you took other missions, but when you couldn't figure out why the monsters were doing things they definitely weren't supposed to, you still asked *me*. Even though I was in limbo. I wasn't gonna leave you here to waste away, eating terrible food and not laughing."

"Well, shit." Brigham scratched the side of his face and shot her a sheepish smile. "You know, I had this whole speech planned out for when you told me you'd been going off the grid on your own until they let me outta here to join you. About how you have to go through the proper channels to find proof and use the right procedures to get the Council and the rest of the Clan invested in this war. How if that still wasn't enough to convince them, *then* you could go rogue. And I'd be damned if I let you do it alone."

Halsey pressed her lips together and tried not to laugh. "That was actually sweet."

"Yeah, I know." He shrugged. "Not really my thing, right? Brigham the Clan clown, getting all sappy and sentimental and shit. Gross. Glad you didn't start screwing around on your own, though, 'cause then I'd have to *tell* you all that. It'd only make things messy."

"Right. Saved us both the awkwardness by *not* doing what everyone apparently expects from me."

A massive grin spread across his face. "Only me. I'm pretty sure everyone else expects you to sit quietly and keep following the rules. Even now."

"You say that I've been talking about the Blood Matriarch and legends coming true for years."

"It kinda feels like it."

They chuckled. Halsey felt like a massive weight had been lifted off her shoulders after telling her cousin everything she'd been sitting on for two weeks. For no reason, apparently.

"Okay. Now that you know, the focus is on you getting better so you can get out of—"

The doorknob rattled and turned, then the door opened. One of the resident healers on the Ambrosius Clan estate stepped inside.

"Nurse Perry!" Brigham grinned and quickly lowered the evidence of his unapproved meal out of sight. "You look stunning as ever. How was your break?"

"Not long enough." The woman in her late sixties with gold-rimmed glasses attached to a glittering pink and lime-green lanyard around her neck scowled as she walked into the room. Her scowl deepened when she saw Halsey sitting in the visitor's chair with an open food container and an open beer can in her lap. "Let me guess. You forgot to bring him a straw?"

"What?" Halsey gaped at the woman, then quickly tried

to cover up her surprise with a fake laugh. "No. Absolutely not." She raised the beer in one hand and pointed at herself with the other. "This is mine."

"Honestly, Nurse Perry," Brigham added, his beaming smile unchanged. "I'm shocked you'd even think something like that."

"Uh-huh." The healer readjusted her glasses, then picked up the electronic tablet on the other side of her latest patient's bed and scrolled across the screen. "Something wrong with your arm today?"

"Uh...not that I know of."

"Why is it dangling off the side of your bed like you forgot how to move it?"

"Ha-ha. Oh, *this* arm? I was stretching it out, you know? Not a lotta room on the side of the bed when it's so narrow." He failed miserably at completing a subtle toss of the empty Tupperware container holding two empty beer cans.

Halsey had no idea what he'd intended, but she reacted quickly when the green plastic container clacked across the linoleum floor and slid toward her with a scratchy whisper. The beer cans were harder to mask when one of them toppled out and rattled in a skittering twirl toward her. She kicked the Tupperware aside, so it vanished behind her giant tote bag on the floor. As Nurse Perry looked up from her tablet, Halsey smashed a foot onto the rolling beer can.

If it had been Brigham's shoe, he might have been able to hide it all. Yet a sliver of aluminum peeked out from beneath the sole of Halsey's boot. She flashed the healer a broad, gleaming smile that matched her cousin's.

Perry peered over the rim of her glasses before Brigham

whipped his hand up from the side of the bed and wiggled his fingers to draw her attention. "See? Perfectly fine. Better than fine, actually. This arm right here? This is a specimen of Ambrosius prowess. There's more magic in the pinky of *this* hand than all the—"

"Save it," the healer muttered as she returned her gaze to the tablet.

Neither cousin moved as they waited for Nurse Perry to either lose it on them or write the whole thing off and leave the room. Brigham hadn't even lowered his hand.

I feel like we're in a wax museum. As the exhibit. 'Recalcitrant Ambrosius Cousins Caught in the Act.'

It was a funny thought, but Halsey didn't dare laugh.

Brigham's tight swallow filled the silent recovery room. "So. What's my favorite healer gonna tell me we're looking at today?"

"You don't give up, do you?" Perry didn't look up as she typed, poked, and scrolled away.

"No, ma'am. I'm a fighter. Literally. As in, that's my job. Somebody's gotta keep the world safe, so I don't have the luxury of giving up on *anything*. Know what I'm sayin'?"

Halsey snorted and closed her eyes.

She's about to break his ribs all over again if he doesn't stop.

"Well." Perry finally looked up and scanned Halsey with a pinched grimace. "Fortunately for the world, that's not far off the mark."

"I was talking about everything, by the way," Brigham continued, his nervousness showing itself in the way he couldn't stop talking. "Fighting. Hunting things nobody else will ever see. *Healing.* I don't give up on that either, lemme tell ya. You can count on me to keep going. Before you know it, I'll be ready to get outta here. When that happens, Nurse Perry, you come and let me know. 'Cause I don't give up waiting for good news, either."

The woman returned an unamused gaze, her face completely expressionless, and raised an eyebrow. "Like now?"

He burst into fake, nervous laughter, but it abruptly stopped when he realized what she was telling him. "Wait, what? Now as in…"

Perry sighed. "As in this very second. The present moment. Not before, not after. Right now." She looked back and forth between the cousins, then rolled her eyes. "I'm releasing you from your remarkably quick and efficient recovery period. Try not to break yourself all over again right off the bat."

"Ha. You hear that, Hal? I'm fucking free!"

Halsey pumped a fist and let out a soft yet enthusiastic "Yay."

The healer rolled her eyes, dropped the tablet where it belonged, then turned and headed out of the recovery room without another word.

Brigham didn't seem to notice as he whipped the sheets off his lap and spun his feet to the floor. "Now get me the hell outta here. Good work with the can, by the way. I don't think she suspected a thing."

CHAPTER FOUR

Two hours later, they'd packed up Brigham's things, and he'd taken forever to say goodbye to all the healers who'd helped him in the last two weeks. He'd insisted on doing that despite multiple protests from Halsey *and* the healers. Finally, they got him into one of the spare ATVs from the gardening supply shed. Halsey drove, of course.

He only made one joke about riding behind her with his arms around her waist as they rumbled and bounced across the rolling hills of the hundred-and-eighty-acre property. After that, he concentrated on riding the thing without jostling himself, so there was no more conversation.

Until they were five minutes from the cottage Halsey had claimed as her official home once she'd turned eighteen and left the estate-house nest, as it were. Brigham clearly recognized where they were going. He slumped his chin onto his cousin's shoulder, jamming it painfully into the muscle there every time his jaw moved. "Did you get lost, cuz?"

"Ow. No."

"You sure? This is *not* the way off the property, and last I checked, that's where I live. Unless somebody pulled a dick move while I was in health-prison and got me a new place."

"Not that I—hey." She swatted his face away from her shoulder as the ATV rumbled up the next rising hilltop before the descent into the cottage's cozy little valley in the middle of open fields. "I haven't heard anything about your apartment or any other spot. Not like anyone would tell me anyway, but they can't take over for you like that unless you're…you know. Dying."

"Did anybody think I was?"

"Not really."

"Okay. So why are we going to *your* place?"

Halsey's eyes widened, though fortunately, he couldn't see a thing from behind her. "I don't know, man. I figured you'd want a shower and some more food before driving another hour back to your place. There's more beer in the fridge, too, by the way."

"Huh." Brigham propped his chin on her shoulder again, then burst out laughing when she swiped at him and actually made contact this time. "You should've told me that. I've been daydreaming about my own bed the whole time."

"Maybe you should stay a while at my place. You know, for *observation*. If you're already daydreaming on the back of an ATV…"

"Relax, Hal. I don't have to pay attention right now. *You're* driving."

Halsey laughed and looked at him over her shoulder.

"Not all the way to your apartment. And definitely not on this thing."

He clicked his tongue. "Come on. That'd be fun."

"Says the guy who wouldn't be driving an ATV on a highway for an hour. No."

"Fine…" His warbling groan was supposed to sound irritated but ended up reflecting the sarcastic humor with which Brigham Ambrosius did almost everything. "I guess I'll resign myself to another meal with you. And more beer. As long as we get to take it into the greenhouse."

"Why? You don't like the rest of my house?"

"Don't go puttin' words in my mouth, cuz. I like your house fine. The greenhouse, though… That's *ours*."

Yes, it is. Not only mine, not only Brigham's. That place belongs to all of us who made it. I hope he likes what we did to it.

It took a lot of effort not to grin like a lunatic as the top of her eggshell-blue cottage with the green front door came into view. The Clan's healers had released her cousin sooner than anyone anticipated. While none of them had known when Brigham would be cleared for active anything, Halsey and her other cousins had prepared as much as possible with such late notice.

Except when it came to Jasper's stupid olive-green Jeep.

Oh, come on…

"Hey." Brigham pointed in front of them, which wasn't necessary. "Did you get a new car or something?"

"Yeah, Brigham. I got myself a Jeep for fun." She playfully slapped his arm to get it away from the side of her face, but her cousin clamped onto her shoulder instead to screw with her.

"Wow. That's so not like you. When'd you pick *that* up?"

"I don't know. Sometime last week." She managed to keep a straight face and pretended to focus on driving to her cottage. *There's no way he doesn't hear my sarcasm right now. No way. Unless his pain meds still haven't worn off...*

"You know," Brigham began in a thoughtful voice. "I can't imagine you driving anything else but *this*."

"An ATV."

"Totally."

"Dude." She snorted and shook her head. "It's not even mine."

"Fits you better than that Jeep, though."

"Great. Thanks."

Halsey wanted to scream at Jasper for leaving his obnoxiously loud vehicle's front bumper poking conspicuously from behind the small stand of pine trees beside the cottage. *How hard is it to park out of sight when this whole property is off-road? Hell, how hard is it to double-check that nobody can see the stupid thing when they pull up?*

As if he didn't already have her attention, Brigham repeatedly tapped her shoulder and added, "Hey, doesn't Jasper have one kinda like that?"

"No way."

"Yeah. I'm pretty sure he's got one *exactly* like that."

Halsey scoffed and kept facing her front door, though she couldn't stop glaring at the front of the Jeep. "You don't know what you're talking about, dude. Jasper's is, like, way darker. I think it's more forest-green than olive-green, honestly."

"Uh-huh." Brigham was suspiciously quiet before he removed his hand and shrugged. "Hell, what do I know, right? I've been outta the loop for two weeks. That's way more time than your thirty-day suspension 'cause you were still, you know. Conscious."

"Twenty-two days, actually." She shot another quick smile over her shoulder. "But who's counting?"

"Not me, cuz. That's for damn sure."

Halsey skidded the ATV to a stop along the dirt driveway. She shifted to watch Brigham as he jostled around on the back of the seat. "Can you handle getting off this thing on your own?"

"Please. Hopping on, riding for half an hour, then jumping off. That's my thing."

She wrinkled her nose as he slowly but successfully swung one leg over the back of the vehicle. "We're still talking about ATVs, right?"

"What?" Brigham faltered on his grounded leg and looked sharply at her, then burst out laughing. "Got me. Why do I have to pick one?"

"I don't wanna know." She shook her head and faced forward, so he didn't feel like he was being stared at and scrutinized and also to glare at her front door. *I swear, if those bozos left any other condemning evidence, I'm going after every single one of them. Personally.*

The ATV wiggled when Brigham finally made it onto the dirt and hauled his duffel bag along. He didn't wait for Halsey to get off the thing before he headed for the entrance, gazing around like he was seeing the place for the first time. If he noticed the slight limp in his right leg, he didn't mention it.

Neither did she.

He released a low whistle and shook his head. "Man. Feels like I haven't been here in years."

"It's been more like a month, I think." She hurried to catch up with him and almost lost her cool when the neon-orange siding of yet another conspicuously parked vehicle caught her eye. "Or five weeks."

Trying to be subtle and actually succeeding, Halsey flicked her fingers toward the bushes beside the poorly hidden vehicle. They rustled when her magic brushed against the life force inside them, then four branches moved up, down, and to the side to effectively hide the bright orange.

As long as he doesn't start searching the bushes, I guess we're fine. So far.

"Nothing's changed, though," she quickly added as she hopped up the front porch stairs. "Promise."

"Except for the new Jeep." Brigham stopped at the front door and cast a curious look over his shoulder. "Right?"

"Right. Totally."

The front door squeaked when her cousin pulled it open, then they both stepped inside, their footsteps thumping across the hardwood. Halsey shut the door behind her and took a quick inventory of everything in her house that had probably been touched by at least seven different people. Recently. "I mean, how much could I do to one place in five weeks?"

Brigham ran his hand along the surface of the half-wall countertop jutting out from the kitchen on the left and shrugged. "You? The chick who snagged our *clubhouse* as her actual house because she didn't wanna spring for anything new?"

"That's not why I—"

Her cousin chuckled, waved her off, then checked the

fingertips he'd run across the counter. "You don't like change, Hal. Everybody knows that. Which is weird, seeing as you're the one advocating for changing the whole damn militia, top to bottom. Or is it bottom to top with us? Is there a difference?"

Good work, Brigham. Say it loud enough for everyone in the back, why don'tcha? She didn't have an immediate reply to such a useless question, so she ignored it and tried to redirect both the conversation and her cousin. "Want a beer?"

He faced her with his trademark grin as she made a beeline for the fridge. "*Do I?*"

"You got it."

Brigham's duffel bag thumped onto the kitchen counter. He dropped his elbows beside it and propped his chin in his hands. "Hey, were you serious about the shower?"

"Uh...yeah." She pulled the fridge open, then paused to shoot him a crooked smile. "Why? Was it funny?"

"No, I... It's weird, actually." He rubbed his neck and gazed around her kitchen as Halsey took her sweet time grabbing two beers. "I think the last time anyone took care of me, like *really* took care of me when I needed help, was Meemaw."

"Oh, yeah?" *Don't get cozy, cuz. We're not spending all night in the kitchen.* Halsey shut the fridge with her hip and carried the beers toward the counter. They were bottles this time, which she'd specifically chosen because they took longer to open. She wanted her cousin to get frustrated enough to take their usual routine at her house to the next stage. Which definitely wasn't here in the kitchen.

"Yeah." Instead of staring at the drinks like he normally did, his hazel eyes centered on her face. "Remember that time we were practicing earth magic down at the quarry, and I broke my arm?"

"Flying rocks. Yep." She set the beers on the counter but didn't move to offer him one yet. "We called her 'cause she was the only person who wouldn't chew our heads off for *unsupervised activity.*"

Brigham snorted, his gaze softening as he stared off into space. "And we made her promise not to tell my parents while they were out of town or even when they got back."

"On a mission," Halsey corrected with a nostalgic smile. "Weird how we didn't know that's what 'out of town' meant back then."

"Right? And I thought we were smart. Well, at least *I* was, anyway."

"Very funny."

Brigham absently reached for a bottle, and Halsey didn't try to stop him. "She didn't say a word about any of it, though, did she? She nursed my arm and fed me rabbit soup and popsicles for three days."

Halsey wrinkled her nose.

"No, listen, it was amazing. My parents still don't know a thing about it. Nothing. Meemaw was the shit."

"She still is." For the first time since they'd left the estate house, Halsey was fully invested in the conversation. *She is the shit. Today. Right now. Yet our family still treats her like a half-wild dog that breaks all the vases and The Good China every time she comes into the house.*

"True that." Brigham tilted his bottle toward hers and frowned. "You forgot to open these."

"Shit. Sorry." She pretended to scramble around for a bottle opener, opening and closing all the wrong drawers at random.

Instead of doing what she wanted him to do, her cousin stayed at the counter, patiently waiting for her to open their drinks before they took off for the greenhouse like he probably assumed they would. "Anyway, it's been a long time. I know we're partners and everything, Hal. And I know I'm your best friend. Pretty easy to do when I'm your *only* friend…"

"You're on a roll today with the Halsey burns, aren't you?"

Brigham chuckled, but it was distracted and not like his usual carefree self. "We hang out all the time, obviously. Which is cool and all…"

"Okay, dude. Say what you're trying to say." She hopped on her tiptoes to open the overhead cabinet doors and pretended to look for a bottle opener there.

"Aw, hell." He slowly ran a hand through his hair and looked supremely uncomfortable. "I only wanna make sure you're cool with this. Picking me up from medical and taking me back to *your* place for a shower, food, and beer is basically uncharted territory, you know?"

She gestured toward the other side of the cottage. "I've got a pull-out couch, too."

"That's what I mean. None of it's new, but put it all together 'cause I got pancaked by a couple of ogres, and it feels weird. Like… I don't know. Like I *need* you or something."

"Yeah, but we both know you don't. So it's fine." *Why won't he leave already? This is getting ridiculous.* Halsey had checked her kitchen drawers two and a half times by now, but her cousin had chosen this opportunity to get sappy because he didn't like depending on his own partner for support instead of monster-fighting backup.

"Maybe *you* need *me*, though," Brigham muttered. "Last I remember, the bottle opener was in *that* drawer."

"Nope. Can't find it."

"Okay, shit. Lemme get one of my lighters—"

"You know what?" Halsey gestured toward the back of the house with her bottle. "Don't worry about it. I'll handle these. Why don't you go back and put your feet up?"

"Hal, my feet've been up for two weeks."

"So another five minutes won't hurt." She fixed him with a warning stare, then nodded toward the sliding wooden door along the far wall of the living room. "Go on, git."

His eyes widened, and he leaned away in mock alarm. "Damn. You sound way too much like Charlie when you're trying to be bossy. You know that?"

"Well, it runs in the family, cuz. Now go, so I can figure out what—"

A loud creak rose from the back of the house, followed by a heavy crash and snap that could only have been a tree branch. Halsey definitely heard somebody cursing under her breath behind the sliding door. For a second, she thought the branch crashing might have covered up the voice enough for Brigham not to hear.

She was wrong.

Her cousin stiffened, met her gaze, and whispered, "You heard that, right?"

"What?" *I look so clueless right now. Damn it, I'm gonna wring their necks!*

"There's something going on here." He raised a finger to his lips and nodded. "I'll take care of it."

"What? No. Brigham, come on."

He'd already spun on his heels and marched confidently away from the kitchen counter toward the back wall. As he passed the long dining room table, his gaze landed on the array of weapons Halsey had laid out a few days before to go through her regular cleaning routine. Closest to the edge was her trio of throwing axes, one of which Brigham snatched without hesitation like he actually knew how to use the thing.

He kept walking and shook the ax above his head without turning around. "You shouldn't leave this shit lying around, cuz. *Anyone* could take it and cause some serious damage."

Oh, shit.

Halsey grabbed the beer bottles, raced around the end of the counter, and hurried after him, trying not to give anything away. "Hold on. Those aren't yours."

"Neither is that." He pointed the ax blade at the back door.

"Hey, stuff breaks out there all the time. Totally normal. Maybe put that thing down before you hurt yourself, okay?"

"Oh, I'm gonna hurt someone, all right," he grumbled and kept storming toward the sliding door.

Well, I guess we'll still get the intended effect.

She grimaced and hurried after him, sparing two seconds to lock onto the aluminum bottle caps with her magic. They popped off in quick succession and clinked onto the floor, rolling and spinning. Another perk of coming from an elemental family specializing in alchemy. When she wasn't pretending she'd lost her bottle opener.

"Brigham, maybe we should—"

She didn't have time to say anything else because her cousin threw open the door like there was a fire and swung his arm back, the ax glinting in the light that streamed from the other side.

Halsey held her breath.

CHAPTER FIVE

"Surpri—"

The ax flew from Brigham's hand, whistling as it spun end over end.

"Whoa, shit!"

The *clunk* of the ax head burying in solid wood on the other side of the greenhouse cut through every other sound before the greenhouse erupted in chaotic noise.

"What the hell, Brigham? Are you trying to *kill* somebody?"

"Shouldn't play with her toys, bro."

"Huh. Looks like somebody didn't actually need two weeks in medical."

"Dude, we spent all this time setting up this kickass surprise, and he almost chopped Nick's head off. Why are we even here?"

Only half the exclamations were intelligible. The rest echoed through the wide-open sliding door to bounce around Halsey's living room walls.

She stepped up next to Brigham and handed him an open beer. "Surprise, cuz."

He absently took it without looking away from the eight other Ambrosius operatives from Brigham and Halsey's generation filling what they lovingly called the greenhouse. "You gotta be shittin' me."

"Hey, Hal," Nick called from the back. "How about telling him we're on *his* side, so he doesn't try killing us again."

The others laughed with less frustration, and Nick reached for Halsey's ax buried in the trunk of the massive oak in the far corner of the magically cultivated room.

She watched his first failed attempt to rip the ax free, then narrowed her eyes and willed the oak's trunk to tighten around the blade. "You're on *his* side, huh? Here's the thing, Nick. I'm not even sure y'all are on *my* side."

"The hell we ain't," Charlie barked and laughed before taking a giant swig of the beer in his hand. "Look at us. We came all the way out here to show up for *his* recovered ass. Last-minute, too."

"Yeah." Nick grunted as he tugged on the ax handle again. "You didn't give us a whole lot of time." He pulled again with both hands, but the blade didn't budge despite the creaking of the tree trunk that held fast under Halsey's magic. "Damn, dude. Hal been giving you throwing lessons or what?"

"We had almost three hours," Cadence pointed out from the other side of the room as she headed toward Brigham and Halsey. "It's not like you guys put more effort into this than buying a crapload of beer and drinking a quarter of it while we waited."

Their other cousins sniggered. Nick, Charlie, Owen with his big meaty head and goofy smile, Otto, Aldous, and Jasper. Even Brigham's brother Rupert was there, sitting on a tree stump at the back behind the enchanted fountain that kept the place cool despite it technically being outside.

Halsey met Cadence's gaze and smiled.

Yep. Two weeks later, and you can hardly tell she got her fair share of an ogre beating too. At least she knows what it takes to throw a surprise party.

Cadence stopped a few yards from Brigham and raised her drink toward her temporary partner for a mission that had ended so badly. At least for her and Brigham. "Good to see you're finally out of there."

Brigham had already been staring at their gathered cousins. His eyes widened further when he met Cadence's gaze. He leaned toward Halsey and murmured, "You did all this?"

"If by 'all this' you mean sent a text and told everybody to get their asses down here while you were schmoozing with the nurses, then yeah." She clapped his shoulder and gave him a gentle shake. "We're *all* glad you made it through that one."

"Huh." When it sank in that his cousins were throwing him a getting-out-of-recovery party and there was nothing dangerous hiding in the greenhouse, Brigham broke into a cheesy grin and raised his fresh drink. "I *knew* that was Jasper's damn Jeep out front."

Everyone cracked up laughing.

Cadence turned toward the cousin in question with a mock frown. "Yeah, nice going, Jasper. I told you that thing stuck out like nobody's business."

"What? No way." He sniggered, then shrugged. "So sue me if I can't get the trees to do what I want like *some* of you."

"*Or* move the damn car and quit making the trees do all the work!" Otto shouted to another roar of laughter.

After a silent toast, Brigham clinked his beer bottle against Halsey's, and they shared a knowing look before drinking together.

Now I have my partner back. Might as well enjoy a little R&R. Then we'll get to the hard work of finding the Mother of Monsters and stopping her before this turns into the last great war all over again, and we kick off the next Ice Age...

"Speech!" Rupert shouted through the noise. "Speech!"

"What the hell?" Brigham laughed along with everyone else. "This is *my* surprise party."

"So say something, bro."

"Aw... Thought I wasn't gonna wake up and missed my voice that much, huh?"

His brother flipped him the middle finger, getting another round of guffaws.

"Yeah, you know what?" Aldous interjected. "Forget it. Brigham talks too much, anyway. We should all head out now and save ourselves the torture." He jokingly started to walk across the greenhouse toward the sliding door, waving his drink for everyone to follow. "Come on—"

"Oh, no." Cadence whirled and pointed at him. "You're not going anywhere." Before she finished speaking, thick tendrils of vines snaked across the greenhouse floor to curl around Aldous' legs and root him to the spot.

If he hadn't been magically held in place, he would have fallen flat on his face. Instead, his torso surged forward while his legs stayed, and he flailed his arms to regain his balance. His drink sloshed all over the ground and those standing closest to him. He looked up in annoyance. "Cadence, it was a *joke*!"

"Wasn't very funny."

"Looks pretty hilarious to me," Rupert shouted, and Owen The Burger's donkey-like braying joined him.

Jasper watched the vines tighten around Aldous's legs and chuckled before taking another drink. "Nope. I definitely can't do that."

"I said speech!" Rupert called again.

"Fine. Okay! Jesus." Brigham chortled as he spread his arms.

This was what Halsey had wanted when she'd sent out a last-minute invitation to this little get-together. The complete opposite of what the two of them felt during their recovery room chat. If anyone deserved to have a good time being the center of attention right now, it was Brigham.

"Speech, huh? Let's see." He took a long drink of his beer, stalling to mess with everyone who'd quieted down to hear him.

Several people groaned, and someone muttered, "You drink *after* the toast…"

Brigham thrust his beer into the air and cleared his throat. "To the morons who helped build this place as kids, who only come back as adults when someone almost dies."

Halsey gaped at him and fought back a laugh. Some of their cousins couldn't do that much, and the greenhouse filled with stifled sniggers and forced coughs.

"To my partner." Brigham swung his bottle toward

Halsey with too much enthusiasm and almost smacked her in the face. "She didn't actually save my life or anything, but she sure as hell merced the asshole ogre that tried to end it."

"Oh, come on…" Playfully rolling her eyes, Halsey drank her beer before the toast finished, which garnered several joking groans.

"To the Ambrosius Clan Council!"

When Brigham didn't add anything to that, the greenhouse fell silent. The relatively young elementals who'd grown up together, trained together, and fought monsters together looked confused, but nobody said a word.

Brigham's face lit with sheer glee as he continued his so-called speech. "I have no fucking idea what they're doing, and I doubt they do, either. To our leadership, who gives us orders without considering that shit's getting real out there and they might have to do something about it. Can't say I blame them, but they did almost get me killed."

The whole time, he spoke with his signature beaming grin, his hazel eyes sparkling in the sunlight streaming through the leaves and branches that made up the greenhouse walls and ceiling. His smile slightly faded before he finished with, "And to Meemaw."

The cousins stared at him in mute shock, drinks halfway raised. None looked excited about the way their guest of honor had turned his surprise party into a familial-politics statement.

Nice one, Brigham. You're about to get yourself tossed into the crazy Ambrosius basket with Meemaw and me.

Halsey grabbed her partner's shoulder and spoke to

break the tense silence. "And *that* is why Brigham doesn't make speeches. To Meemaw!"

She thrust her beer in the air. Fortunately, they were only waiting for someone else's lead to follow that wasn't Brigham's.

"To Meemaw!" everyone echoed, including the man of the hour, and they drank.

"All right." Still grinning, Brigham patted his stomach and looked around the greenhouse. "We got beer, speeches, and a little bit of magic…"

His gaze settled on Aldous, who had bent over trying to untangle the vines around his ankles and calves with his hands as he muttered, "I hate this."

"Still, it's not a *real* party without grub," Brigham continued. "Whoever's got it better cough it up right now!"

"Got a treat and a half for you, dude." Rupert lifted an enormous, bright red shopping bag. "We brought friggin' *Bojangles*."

"Now that's what I'm talking about!"

Brigham headed toward his brother to help lay out the massive number of chicken-biscuit sandwiches, hash browns, and sweet teas on the metal patio table in the center of the greenhouse. Most of the other guests made their way toward the food as the conversation picked up again. Everyone was ready and willing to forget the odd statements their newly recovered cousin had made in honor of his surprise party. Fortunately, Brigham didn't bring it up again.

Aldous was still magically tied to the dirt floor by the vines that wouldn't give up. He tugged at them, then noticed Cadence a few feet away, watching him silently. He dropped the vines and glared at her. "Do you mind?"

"Not at all." She stuck a hand on her hip and smirked. "I'm actually enjoying this."

"Come *on*." With a heavy sigh, he straightened and spread his arms as he looked around the greenhouse as much as possible. "Can anybody else here get these things to loosen the hell up? Not you, Jasper. You can't even get a branch to listen to you."

Jasper chuckled as he passed the guy magically bolted to the floor. "Wasn't even gonna offer, man. Don't you think you should figure out how to get yourself unstuck, though?"

Aldous pointed at him. "Don't."

"At least it's not as bad as that time he got himself stuck in that vampire coffin," Otto mentioned. "Remember that? We had to call in Clara and Jack to help drag him out without alerting the whole damn nest that we were there."

Fresh laughter filled the greenhouse, and Aldous clenched his fists, quickly turning red in the face. "Not helping."

"*They* did, though. Hey, maybe we should've invited them, too."

"No." Brigham spun and sawed a hand across his throat. "The twins don't come to real parties unless they're throwing it. We'd have more Bo-Berry Biscuits in the dirt than our mouths. Uh-uh."

"Forget the damn twins," Aldous bellowed.

"Hey, Aldous." Charlie flicked his hand toward the perpetual fountain eight feet away, and a spray of water shot from the burbling column to splatter his cousin's face and chest. "You need to cool it."

The other guests practically fell over laughing while their eternally stuck-in-something cousin wiped the expression off his face and stood there, dripping and blowing water droplets away.

Halsey laughed with them, but a fuming Aldous in the background didn't make a fun party.

She reached for the vines around his ankles as she headed toward the table. The plants' life force responded to her magic in an instant, slowly recoiling until Aldous had enough room to angrily kick them off the rest of the way.

Cadence rolled her eyes when she saw that someone else had released him. She looked up and met Halsey's gaze, and they shared a knowing smile.

Best way to throw a party is to act like nothing's wrong. Even if we most likely have another massive war ahead of us. Aside from Brigham's speech, I think we're doing a damn good job.

CHAPTER SIX

Despite its rocky start, the "Glad You're Not Dead" surprise party for Brigham was a massive success, all things considered. Granted, the qualifying standards for successful Ambrosius cousin parties were low. Beyond beer, speeches, and food, the only other requirements included no blood spilled, no personal property smashed, and no interruptions from parents. Many of whom were also Council members.

They heartily consumed the beer and food. The greenhouse remained intact and even received minor additions of greenery and magically-induced flower buds opening up courtesy of Cadence, who was revisiting the greenhouse for the first time since Halsey moved in five years ago.

Most importantly for Halsey, the festivities drew to a natural and satisfactory ending three hours later, which left plenty of time for everyone to do whatever they'd planned for the day but abandoned to celebrate their cousin's return to active militia duty.

The cousins filtered out of the greenhouse and through

Halsey's cottage in a steady stream. Each took a moment with Brigham to hug him, clap him on the back, offer a firm handshake, and generally let him know they were there to support him. They also expressed their gratitude that ogres maddened by ancient blood runes hadn't succeeded in smashing the life out of him.

Nick was the last to leave, which surprised Halsey until she and Brigham walked him to the front door.

"Glad you're alive, my man." He clapped Brigham's back and leaned toward him as if the cottage was still full of people, and he didn't want anyone to overhear. "Though if you're gonna make speeches like *that*, maybe give a shout-out to the guy who almost got his head chopped off 'cause you were rearin' to play hero again."

Brigham shot him a crooked smile before reaching for the doorknob. "Not my fault if y'all can't figure out how to put the 'surprise' in surprise party."

"Dude."

"Thanks for coming." Brigham opened the door, and Nick stared at him before bursting into laughter.

"Yeah, all right. See ya, Hal." He waved and nodded at her.

Halsey jerked her chin in return. The last of her afternoon guests waltzed out of her cottage, across the porch, and back to wherever he'd come from when he'd gotten her group text.

Brigham's crooked smile lasted until he shut the front door again. Then it morphed into a grimace as he turned and leaned against the door with a heavy sigh. "Damn."

"Whoa." Halsey scanned him, wanting to rush over in

case he fell. That was exactly what he looked like he was about to do. "You okay?"

"Yup." He pressed a fist against his chest and wrinkled his nose. "One too many spicy chicken biscuits, I think. Or three."

He's lying through his teeth. Brigham doesn't get heartburn, and he doesn't stop at three biscuits, either.

She wouldn't call him out on it yet, because he'd been holding it together like a champ through the entire party. She hadn't even noticed.

"Right. Go sit down for a sec, then. I'll get you some water."

He released a wry chuckle and straightened. "How about another beer?"

"Sounds like beer and Bojangles are the dangerous duo that got you into this."

"Huh. Listen to you. Could've been a healer in the med wing." Brigham only took one step toward the couch before his strength faltered, and his grimace returned full force.

Yeah, that's not heartburn. That's pain.

Halsey pointed at the couch. "Sit."

"Yup." His face paled as he hobbled over, and she hustled into the kitchen to pour him a glass of water.

She tried to ignore his sharp inhale and grunt of discomfort as he lowered himself onto the couch cushions, pretending to be too busy to notice much. *Crap. This was supposed to be good for him, not make it all worse on his first day back.*

When she returned to the living room, Brigham was leaning back with his head tilted up, his feet propped in front of him, and his eyes closed. The pained grimace was gone, but his face still lacked most of its color.

He took long, slow, deep breaths without moving. He didn't say a word, either, which was probably the biggest tell that he was in a lot more pain than anyone had guessed. Including his best friend.

Instead of sitting on the couch beside him, Halsey perched on the coffee table and nudged his outstretched legs with the back of a hand. "Here."

He blinked, dropped his gaze, then accepted the water with a smirk. "Thanks, Nurse Halsey. You're the best."

"Definitely cut it out with the nurse crap." They shared a light laugh as Brigham chugged the water down. When he finished, he slumped against the couch cushions and sighed.

Halsey fixed him with an empathetic frown. "I wish you'd said something."

"And send all our guests packing the second they got here? Please."

"They were all here for at least an hour before we rolled up."

"Fine. The second *we* got here."

She took the empty glass from his loose hand in case he passed out on the couch. He looked exhausted, and he had every right to be. "They would've understood," she insisted.

"They were ready to party, Hal. Who am I to crush their dreams because I'm a little under the weather?"

"Under the weather, huh?" With a wry chuckle, she set the glass on the coffee table and sighed. "First of all, you're the guy who found himself in the middle of a nine-ogre shitshow without sufficient preparation or intel from the

Council and still made it to the other side. So, you know, that kinda gives you the right to say anything you want at your own party."

"Ha." Brigham's eyelids drooped, and a lazy smile spread across his lips. "Yeah, but I already did that."

"*That's* right. With your little speech and that super-classy toast to the Council."

He clicked his tongue and pointed at her. "Bingo. Seriously, what else could I say after that? I'm a tough act to follow, even for myself."

Halsey giggled at his weak jokes and didn't bother trying to make him "take this conversation seriously." She knew he was. The only time Brigham Ambrosius *didn't* make jokes was when he felt confident about absolutely everything, and that was rare. It was rare for Halsey, too.

Anyone who was completely confident and felt invincible was asking for trouble. Maybe even more so as part of the Ambrosius Clan. Their family had skills most regular humans didn't know about and likely never would, but that didn't make them infallible and unstoppable.

If any Ambrosius elemental had forgotten that recently, Brigham was a stark reminder for all of them.

Halsey gave her cousin a moment to settle into something resembling comfort, but she couldn't let this go without him hearing it. "They would've left, you know. They would've understood. You *just* got out. Now I'm realizing I probably jumped the gun on the whole surprise party thing. You were bouncing around the med wing like a squirrel on energy drinks, and I assumed you could handle everything else. I'm sorry."

His eyelids were only half-open when he looked at her,

and though his smile was equally tired, he was all there. "None of this is on you, Hal. Don't beat yourself up about it."

"Oh, I'm definitely not." They laughed, and she crossed one leg over the other before pursing her lips in consideration. "I guess I'm trying to say that if you need to take it easy for a little while longer, that's totally fine. Nobody's gonna judge you for it. You're a badass."

"Yeah. I know." Brigham's eyebrow twitched up as his smile widened. "Let's be real, though. I've been taking it easy for two weeks, and I'm sick of it. Besides, we have a bajillion things to do in the immediate future, right? Might as well party like it's…literally any other year while we can. It helped not to think about anything remotely related to the Mother of Monsters for a while and kick back like we used to. You know, before adulthood reared its ugly head and tricked us into believing that being a legal grownup means nobody has any damn fun anymore."

"That *has* been weird to watch." Halsey nodded and mulled over their dozens of cousins and second cousins and extended family who'd lost the spark of fun since officially graduating from militia training and taking their positions as bona fide monster hunters. "Sometimes it feels like we're the only ones who still care about fun."

"Except for today." Brigham snorted. "Perfect storm for knocking everybody off their so-damn-serious high horses. You know, I think *they* might've needed that more than I did. Loads of fun all around. You did good."

"Well, thanks. Still." She shrugged and tried to act more casual than she felt. "Don't feel like you have to hold it together for anyone else if you're not feeling it, okay?"

"Hey, trust me. I got to let a whole bunch go today, too. If my extremely sophisticated and tasteful speech didn't make everyone run away screaming, I don't think anything could've gotten rid of them. Even if I'd said something about feeling like a bowl of Jell-O. I can already hear Rupert telling me to lie down and sleep it off while everybody else enjoys themselves."

"Huh." Halsey glanced at the ceiling, then jutted out her bottom lip and had to concede. "Actually, yeah. Your brother would totally say that."

"See? I'm the operative who *lived*, Hal. Ain't nobody got time to tell me what I can and can't say in my own party speech."

"Come on. Did you really say that?"

"You know I did."

She laughed and shook her head. "What was up with that speech, anyway? I get the first two. Morons and me." When Brigham choked on his own chuckle, she smiled with him. "All that about the Council, though? And Meemaw? That was a little on the nose, don't you think?"

"Of course it was. *Something* has to be right now, doesn't it?" He shifted to nestle into the couch cushions and stretched his legs farther as he folded his arms. "You've been giving the Council the good ol' middle finger since Ireland. Technically without breaking any rules. I'm your partner, Hal. I had to back you up."

"Right." Halsey raised an eyebrow as she realized what her cousin's motives had been. "You can't get enough of the shock factor. That's what this is."

"Hey. A guy has his vices."

"Everybody's been tiptoeing around you for the last two

weeks, and you wanted them all to know that you know. Subtle."

Brigham's smile flickered in and out as he tried to play it cool but was too pleased with himself. "Subtle's my middle name, cuz."

"Right. Spelled C-A-R-A-T-A-C-U-S."

"I don't know. It's French or something."

"Not even close."

As they sniggered together, she realized how hard he was fighting to keep his eyes open. *Now I'm beating a dead horse.*

"Hey, feel free to stick around as long as you want. The couch is yours. I don't mean only for today, either." Halsey grabbed the empty water glass and stood from the coffee table. "If you need more stuff from your apartment, say the word."

"I appreciate that, but don't you have better things to do?"

"What?" That made her laugh until she realized what he was implying. "Dude, I already told you. I'm not starting any of this hunting-for-answers and proving-the-legends stuff until you're ready to go. Not doing it without you. For now, it looks like we have plenty of time. Plus, there aren't any scheduled missions for the foreseeable future. I guess that's kind of a small win wrapped up in all this crazy."

That momentarily made Brigham perk up. "What, the Council put a hold on 'em or something?"

"Or something, yeah."

"Why the hell would they do that?"

Halsey laughed bitterly. "I wanna believe it's because

they feel like shit for sending you and Cadence out to get your asses whooped, but I can't help feeling that gives them too much credit."

"Oh, come on."

"Seriously, though? I think they're scared. All of them. Even my dad."

He wrinkled his nose at the thought of Aiden Ambrosius, the largest, fiercest-looking, one-eyed, heavily bearded Ambrosius elemental with more muscle than any three other operatives combined, scared of anything. "That's…huh."

"I mean it. I found their proof. My *dad* helped me find it and bring it back. He stood right there when I dumped a bunch of ogre hands on the table in front of everyone. He knew what I was gonna tell them, but he didn't say anything. Definitely scared."

"Because they believe you," Brigham muttered.

"Yep. And they have no clue what to do with it." Halsey exhaled sharply, shrugged, and plastered on a fake smile. "If anyone asks, the whole Clan has *me* to thank for freezing all accounts, missions, and militia action until further notice."

"A.K.A. until you and I bring more proof and spoon-feed them exactly what we have to do next."

They stared at each other. At that moment, Halsey knew he'd meant every word of his promise to her in the recovery room. No way in hell would he let her do this alone. "That's a pretty accurate assessment," she agreed. "Except *we* aren't doing anything until you can spend three hours sitting upright without looking like you're gonna pass out."

"There's that nurse in you again."

"Shut up."

He chortled as she passed him and headed for the kitchen. Craning his neck as much as his almost-healed injuries would allow, he called after her, "I'll be fine, Hal. Rearing to go in no time."

"Uh-huh."

"Hey, there's at least one good thing about two weeks in the med wing. Got some *pretty nice* painkillers in my bag, if you don't mind grabbing those and a bit more water. And then? Well, you're gonna have a hard time getting rid of me."

Halsey smirked, detoured to his duffel bag, and muttered, "Can't wait."

CHAPTER SEVEN

Brigham slept on Halsey's couch through the rest of the evening until 8:00 the next morning. When he finally woke up, he almost lurched upright before the dull pain in his ribs reminded him to take it easy. He inhaled through his nose and closed his eyes. "Oh, man... Am I dreaming right now?"

"I don't think so," Halsey replied from the kitchen as she worked over the stove. "Hard to tell with you sometimes."

"Funny." He turned on the couch to stare at her. "Please tell me that's bacon."

"Yep. Very—ow! Shit. Hot bacon. What the hell? It keeps—ah!"

"Lemme guess." Brigham tilted his head and watched her jerk away from the pan before tentatively diving back in. "You haven't poured out any of the grease since you started."

"What? How is that—ow! Nobody ever told me anything about pouring out the grease!"

"Maybe because you've never cooked bacon before."

"You don't know anything about what I have and haven't cooked, thanks." Halsey reached for the bacon strips with her tongs and flipped one over. Another spray of piping-hot grease splattered her forearm. "Screw this."

"Grab a coffee cup or something. Dump a little out and keep going. Simple as that."

"Yeah." She snatched an oven mitt from the drawer beside the stove, shoved it onto her hand, and went after the bacon again. "Says the super helpful guy sitting *on the couch*."

"Hey, you told me to take it easy."

"I…" With a frustrated growl, she flipped a few more strips, turned down the heat, then clacked her tongs together. "I need to focus."

"So you *do* want me to keep sitting here while you burn yourself to a fleshy crisp, or…"

"*Or* you could finish setting the table while I work on *these* fleshy crisp—ah! Jesus. I'm never making bacon again."

Brigham released an exaggerated sigh and rolled his eyes. "This is why we've never been roommates."

"You're not helping."

"Fine." He pushed off the couch, ruffled a hand through his hair, and swayed a little when he stood. "Quick pit stop first."

"You do you, man. I'll stay here and torture myself over this damn stove."

"Yep."

Halsey laughed after she heard the bathroom door shut and the water in the sink start running. *At least I didn't start yelling about it until* after *he woke up. He can't blame me for interrupting his beauty sleep.*

She didn't manage to figure out how to pour out the extra grease before she finished cooking the stuff, but she did have all the strips on a plate and cool enough to eat by the time Brigham emerged from the bathroom with fresh clothes and a mostly genuine smile.

When she turned with the bacon plate in one hand, and a covered dish of cheesy scrambled eggs in the other, her cousin's expression told her something was wrong. "What?"

"Nothing." He tried to shrug it off, but his flaring nostrils and faint sneer overrode his attempt at a casual expression.

"Brigham."

"It's all good, Hal. I'm not a complainer, and I'm not starting now."

She glanced at the covered dish and puffed out her cheeks. "Crap. You still like cheese eggs, right?"

"Love 'em."

"Then say it already."

"You, uh…" Brigham stuck a thumb over his shoulder. "Your bathroom's a little…you know."

"No." It hit her in the next second, and her eyes bugged. "*No…*"

"I think so, yeah. We all know Hal's a badass, but I don't think you're capable of something like *that*."

"Damn it." She slid both plates onto the dining room table, where she'd cleared off a space big enough for them to eat together alongside her array of monster-hunting weapons. "That's it. Owen is officially banned from this cottage."

"Could've been Aldous, too, honestly."

"What? Come on. The guy can't tap into flora magic to save his life, but he'd never stoop *that* low. The Burger's the only one who doesn't have enough brain cells to know the difference."

"True…"

Halsey sighed in frustration and spun back toward the kitchen to finish preparing their breakfast. "Not gonna let it ruin my day. Yet. You want coffee?"

"You get another bottle of that fancy-pants creamer?"

"Yup."

"Then hell yes, I want coffee." He joined her in the kitchen and grabbed plates and silverware while she poured them each a giant mug of fresh, steaming-hot coffee before grabbing the extras from the fridge.

After they settled at the table, Brigham slid aside her specially built hand grenades to clear more eating room, then they dug in.

"Hey. Not bad for a bacon noob."

"Don't call me that."

"Want me to hold your hand next time?"

"Either shut up and eat or keep running your mouth and take your plate outside."

Brigham burst out laughing over the rim of his coffee mug. "Where the hell did this head-of-the-table mama-bear shit come from?"

Halsey wouldn't look at him as she shook her head and shoveled a forkful of eggs into her mouth. "That's not what I'm doing."

"That's exactly what you're doing. You sound like Meemaw and *my* ma smashed together and coming outta your mouth at a family picnic—"

Unfortunately, she hadn't swallowed her mouthful before she tried to hold back a laugh and ended up snorting eggs all over her plate.

"Whoa!" Her cousin grinned, spread his arms, and leaned back in his chair. "Never mind!"

"Ow…" Halsey swiped a giant handful of napkins and wiped up the mess before blowing her nose several times. "You can't do that when people are eating, man."

"Why not?" Still grinning, Brigham watched her as he lifted a piece of bacon to his mouth. "It's funny as hell. Now neither one of us can say we have perfect manners, so I've reset the playing field."

"You mean the game board?"

"Come on, Hal. With us, it's the same thing." As she kept blowing her nose, his smile faded. "Okay, for real. You all right?"

"Other than feeling like someone pulled my brains out through my nose? Yeah. I am *peachy*." After a final nose-blow, Halsey checked to make sure she'd cleaned up the whole mess, then met her cousin's gaze.

It only took three seconds before they burst out laughing.

After that, it was easier to eat and talk at the same time, especially when Brigham turned the conversation to something other than jokes and Halsey's less-than-stellar bacon-cooking skills. He started it with, "So I've been thinking."

"Uh-oh."

"Nah, hear me out. The way you told it, sounds like

you've been way too busy the last few weeks worrying over little ol' me to do much when it comes to our job and shit."

"Very nice."

"Thanks." He wiped his mouth with a napkin in an attempt to look poised. Then he dropped the napkin onto his empty plate, folded his arms on the table, and leaned toward her. "Anyway, now that I'm *back*..."

"At about eighty percent."

"Damn it, Hal. I'm not talking about hopping on the ATV and booking it into the jaws of our family's mortal enemy, who's supposed to be buried in the ocean, dead, or both right now. I'm trying to make you a proposition here."

Halsey snorted, then quickly tried to cover it up by burying her face in her coffee mug. "Right, right. Totally my bad. Sorry."

"Uh-huh." After inspecting her with the same expression usually found on their Aunt Beatrice's perpetually pinched face, Brigham cleared his throat and tried again. "I'm thinking we start with that scroll."

"Hmm. I assume you're talking about the one Meemaw slapped every Council member across the face with, right? Because I..." She chuckled at her cousin's scrunched face as he tried not to laugh. "I'm afraid I wouldn't know about any *other* scroll."

Brigham produced a grating, squeaking sound. If his face hadn't already gained its color back during breakfast, it sure did now. "Yep. The, uh... Ha! The slapping scroll. Which should be the only identifier we need for the thing, because that's amazing."

"Well, it definitely will be *now*."

"To be clear, though, we're talking about the scroll with

the same blood rune you and your dad found on those ogre assholes."

Halsey smirked and stared at her coffee mug. "Actually, the runes were on their hands."

"Stop. Please..." His laughter bubbled up in the form of sputtering snorts between gasping inhales. "You gotta stop, man. You're killing me."

"Okay, okay. Sorry."

"No, you're not." He fixed her with a mock-warning stare and took his sweet time slurping down coffee and scrutinizing her before he got himself under control again. "My question for you is this. Do we have any idea what that rune means?"

Her smile deteriorated as she considered how to answer that. "Well, the Council hasn't been gung-ho about showing me much of anything lately, and I'm banned from the library until Charlemagne kicks the bucket. Which could be decades, honestly. So...off the top of my head, we know the rune invokes blood-magic strong enough to make ogres hang out together and dig up human *graves* for dinner instead of the usual smash-and-grab with somebody's baby."

He grimaced in disgust. "Aw, dude. That's messed up."

"Everything we do is messed up, Brigham. It's part of the job."

"Yeah, I know that. It's just...*babies*?"

Halsey spread her arms. "That's what ogres *do*."

"Man. You know I love you, cuz, but sometimes..." Brigham snorted and trailed off.

"Sometimes what?" Her last piece of bacon crunched noisily between her teeth as she stared at him.

"Sometimes I feel like I don't know even know you. You're the only one of us who has a serious problem *killing* the things we go after on a regular basis. Yet you have no issues sitting talking over breakfast about ogres stealing babies like it's some dude robbing a Lucky's."

She couldn't help but laugh at that one, too, before coming up with a response that felt particularly appropriate. "Way to put me in a box, but you're missing a few details. I could sit here all day *talking* about killing monsters and not have any more problems with it than talking about ogres stealing babies. But I promise you it isn't any easier for me to actually steal a baby than to take the lives of the supernatural creatures we're sent out after. That's the difference."

"Hmm." Brigham raised an eyebrow and squinted with the opposite eye, his lips pursed as he considered. "Yet you don't seem bent outta shape about snuffing out nine ogres in one night."

"Eh. That's also different."

He laughed and sat back in his chair. "How the hell is that different?"

"All *I* did was cut off their hands. They took care of the rest on their own. Hell, we could even blame the blood rune for killing them. Or whoever put it on them. I didn't technically do it."

"No. They puked so much that the last thing to come up was the spark of life, right?" Brigham folded his arms and stared blankly at the tabletop. "Helluva way to go."

Halsey raised her mug and nodded. "Helluva way."

For the next few minutes, they sat in silence. Brigham seemed deep in thought about something, possibly rethinking the extent of his cousin's abilities to compartmentalize between action and talk. Halsey watched him from the corner of her eye as she sipped the last of her coffee.

That got him thinking. Not that it was even on *the priority list at the time, but I wish someone had taken a picture of me and Dad walking down the back hall together the next morning. I can tell Brigham about it all day, but a picture says a thousand words, right?*

Finally, he thumped a hand on the table and looked up with renewed determination. "I really went far out there for a minute. My bad."

"Happy to wait while you work on firing up that big old brain of yours. You know, after you went so long *not* using it."

"You..." Wearing the goofiest scowl, he shook a finger at her. Then his regular grin returned, and he winked. "...*are* a peach. Thank you very much."

"No, no. Thank *you*." She laughed and kept waiting.

Any minute now. He's gonna have a bright idea that either gives us what we're looking for or kicks off a massive domino effect that gets us to the same place. Then I get to run with that idea and beat back the monsters with a bolt-action rifle, an ax, or my bare fists if I have to. No surprise we make the perfect team.

Halsey drummed her fingers on the table as her cousin stared into space without moving.

As long as he doesn't take this long simply to think *now every time we need a new plan. Seriously, I thought he'd skipped the head injuries that night...*

"All right." Brigham nodded as he came out of brainstorming mode, and she sat up straighter in her chair. "We need to figure out what that rune means first so we know what to expect. Hell, we might even have to reverse-translate blood runes as we go. Don't ask me why I'm calling it that. These things come to me, and *I* know what I mean, so that's all we need."

"Mm-hmm." Halsey pressed her lips together and waited for him to say something that sparked at least one next step that sounded more productive than anything she'd come up with on her own so far.

"Even if I walked in there alone and asked nicely with my best manners, the Council's not gonna tell me a thing because I'm your partner. No offense."

She pointed at him. "Facts."

"They sure as hell won't let me take a look at that scroll, either. *If* Meemaw actually handed it over, which is a big if. We need to go straight to the source."

"Of…the few-thousand-year-old scroll detailing blood humans and their worst magic?"

"Hey. So you *have* seen it!"

"Only the part with the blood rune on it." Halsey shook her head. "I'm speculating about the rest of that particular magical historical record."

"Fine. Obviously, going straight to *that* source is one thousand percent impossible. Unless you've found some way to communicate with our great-great-great-great-great-great-whatever and haven't told me about it yet. No? No elemental séance? It's cool." Brigham pursed his lips, then thumped the table with a fist. The blow rattled several weapons but fortunately didn't disturb any of them enough to make them more dangerous than they already were. "Then we'll have to go with the only source we *do* have access to."

With a surprisingly academic, stuck-up expression, he thrust a finger in the air and concluded, "The Mother of Ambrosius."

Halsey fixed him with a deadpan stare. When he didn't continue, she dropped the expression and sighed. Her shoulders slumped in defeat. "Seriously?"

"What? She's *our* Matriarch."

Halsey lifted the coffee mug to her lips and muttered, "Whole lotta extra nothing to say, 'Let's go talk to Meemaw.'"

"Hey. It's a good idea."

"Oh, I know it is."

Brigham frowned and leaned away from her. "Why do you look so pissed, then?"

"Because it's a good idea I already had on my own. I thought you'd have something better."

Brigham scooted his chair down the length of the table and stopped when he was close enough to sling an arm around her shoulders. Halsey didn't fight it as she stared at the ceiling.

"That's the thing about starting over in a magical war nobody knows anything about," Brigham told her. "Equal playing field. You and me, Hal. We're on the same page."

"Okay. Fine." Laughing, she shrugged out from under his arm and pushed away from the table to stand. "Let's get our *same pages* together and go."

CHAPTER EIGHT

Fortunately, there was no real return time for Halsey's impromptu ATV rental from the gardening garage. Even if there had been, she was more than willing to stretch it so she wouldn't have to endure walking for miles across the Ambrosius Clan property in the late-morning heat at the end of July. Also, so Brigham wouldn't jeopardize his fresh recovery with a strenuous hike like this one.

They piled onto the ATV and raced across the rolling hills and open fields of their enormous family property, this time headed northwest toward Greta Ambrosius' little bungalow tucked away beside the river. Halsey slowed when she reached the unforgettable spot by the riverbed. She swept the area for any sign of their grandmother's augmented golf cart whizzing across the open land, but Greta wasn't around. Not half a mile out from her home, at least.

Even when they pulled up in front of the house, there was no sign of the woman who made a habit of always greeting guests or intruders the second she was aware of them. Sometimes before they were aware of *her*. Halsey caught a glimpse of the souped-up golf cart parked in front of the greenhouse being used as a storage shed for random junk, but everything else was perfectly still. Way too quiet.

If something happened to her, we would've known by now. Right? I mean, if the Council still goes to the trouble of keeping her out of 'their business,' they'd at least track her enough to if anything goes south. They'd be stupid not to.

Brigham dismounted the ATV easier this time, though he still limped slightly on his right leg. When Halsey didn't climb off after him, he faced her and cocked his head. "You good?"

"*I'm* fine." She scanned the front of the house and couldn't shake the feeling that something massive had changed since the last time she'd visited her grandmother. Not in a good way, either. "Does it feel too…peaceful here to you?"

"What?" He laughed. "This is Meemaw's house, Hal. It's always peaceful."

She frowned at him, but her cousin had already spun to head for Greta's screen-less front porch. Confused, Halsey hopped off the ATV and turned to peruse the rolling hills in front of her grandmother's private plot on the massive property she owned.

Always peaceful at Meemaw's house? Do we have *the same grandmother?*

The last time Halsey had been here, during her mission probation, Greta's house had felt so much more alive. The woman's odd experiments were everywhere. She had projects scattered all over the yard, and she'd talked nonstop about things that didn't make sense until Halsey seriously thought about them. She'd been busy. Not to mention they'd worked together to fight off a swarm of garden gnomes that had broken all natural laws by letting two elementals see them in broad daylight before they'd engaged in more mischief than they were worth.

This, though? It was the same house on the same property, but it felt like someone else's home. It could have belonged to anyone else's grandma—a Meemaw that Halsey didn't know.

The gentle tap-tap-tap of Brigham's knock pulled her back to the present. She hurried across the front yard featuring beautifully pruned hedges and a tiny fishpond with a wooden crane bobbing its head in and out of the water. Birds twittered in the surrounding trees. Cicadas droned from every direction. In the distance, the background rush of the river's gentle summer current filled the air.

Halsey realized she was hearing all these things for the first time.

Because Greta Ambrosius wasn't in either of her side yards building something ridiculous, zooming across the open fields on her golf cart, or sounding an alarm to alert her and everyone else to trespassers on her property.

The front porch screen door creaked when she opened it and clacked shut behind her.

"Huh." Brigham peered through the window beside the entrance, but the lace curtains made it impossible to see much of anything inside. "Maybe she's taking a nap or something."

"At ten o'clock in the morning?"

"She's old, Hal. Old people take naps."

Yeah, so do twenty-four-year-olds newly released from a magically fast two-week recovery. You don't see me defining him *by that.*

Brigham knocked again, and they waited in tense silence. At least, it was tense for Halsey.

"Something's wrong," she murmured.

"Dude." He turned toward her with a crooked smile. "It's a talk with Meemaw. What's with all the doom and gloom?"

"You seriously don't see how weird this is?" She swept an arm to indicate the plot of land given to Greta so she could "live comfortably" after her days on the Ambrosius Council had come to an abrupt end.

Her cousin looked around and smiled like he expected her to deliver the punchline to this complicated joke any second. "I don't see anything."

"Exactly. That's the point. This isn't...normal."

"Uh. We're still talking about Meemaw, right?"

"I mean, it's not normal for *her*."

Brigham laughed and shook his head. "Okay. I appreciate you trying to get me back into the mission groove, but we're not on a mission, Hal. This is—"

"I'm one hundred percent serious." Halsey scowled. "All this. The quiet. The calm. No noise or crazy magic or flying around on a golf cart. This seems totally okay to you?"

He finally realized she wasn't joking, and the smile disappeared from his face, replaced with a deep frown as he studied her. "You feeling okay?"

"Don't."

"Well, now *I'm* serious, Hal. You get enough sleep last night?"

She rolled her eyes and turned away from him to stare at the door, shaking her head.

"Hey, I get it. You went through some shit too. We both know that. Taking out those ogres with your dad right after hearing about me almost being an Ambrosius slushie. Then two weeks of waiting for me to get better and get the hell out of medical. Wondering if I *was* gonna get out. Hell, I know I did. You spent the whole time *not* telling me what's been happening in HQ, which I also get. That's a lot of stress, man. It's probably not easy to pop back into go-mode after spending all that time on edge, worried, and sleeping like shit. Am I right?"

"That has nothing to do with this."

"It's all connected, cuz." Brigham clapped her shoulder and nodded. "I spent a lot of time watching this show on TV when I was in medical. They talked about that pretty much the whole time. Physical, mental, emotional. Spiritual, even. It's all one big crazy soup mixed together, right? Mess with one, you're messing with all the rest. Like a domino effect."

Halsey turned her head to meet her cousin's gaze. "So it's Domino Soup now?"

"What?" He chuckled and ignored her odd question. Apparently, he was on a roll now. "I'm saying it's normal. For things to feel weird and off right now because you spent so much time getting used to *not normal*. It'll take a minute. That's cool. I'm here, cuz, and I got your back no matter what."

"Thanks…"

"Hey, what are partners for, right?" His hand slid off her shoulder so he could knock on Greta's front door one more time, still oblivious to the source of his cousin's confusion.

She decided not to say anything else about it, including trying to explain what was *actually* concerning her right now. It wasn't worth the effort. Especially when his little monologue was backed with good intentions despite sounding like all the other platitudes Halsey had gotten from their family over the years. A mix of condolences for her losses and warnings not to stray too close to "the crazy side of the family."

He doesn't think I'm crazy, though. Only...what? Overly exhausted and delusional?

It was easy to shake off the misconception, but she couldn't help tacking on a half-joking comment because that *did* feel normal. "Sounds like you found a whole new path to enlightenment in recovery, huh?"

Brigham grinned. "I had time to think about some shit. I'm still me, though."

Halsey snorted. "Well, thank the gods for that, right?"

He turned toward her and muttered from the corner of his mouth, "You know, way back before we had electricity, airplanes, credit cards and shit, I bet all the regular humans thought *we* were gods."

"Okay, now you're getting ahead of yourself."

"Hey, it's possible…"

Before their conversation could do a complete one-eighty in that odd direction, the doorknob jiggled softly before turning, and the cousins faced forward again.

Greta Ambrosius opened the door, squinted, then broke

into a massive grin. "*Well.* If it isn't my two favorite grandkids."

Brigham returned the smile and eyed their grandmother. "I bet you say that to all of us, don't you?"

"Mostly you, sweetheart. Come on in. Come on. What a nice surprise." Greta stepped aside and waved them into the house. "What's the occasion?"

"You mean missing our Meemaw isn't enough of a reason to stop by on a Thursday morning?"

"Ha! Come here." Greta flittered her hands as he stepped inside, then pulled him into a giant, grandmotherly hug with lots of pats and a quick, noisy peck on the cheek. "So good to see you. Halsey?"

"Huh?" Halsey tried to wipe the baffled look off her face, but she'd failed at that a few too many times today.

Greta chuckled as she looked around Brigham to scan the front porch. "If you feel better standing out there, I won't judge. I promise I don't bite. Plus, I just pulled a fresh tray of cookies out of the oven, if that's enough of an incentive to walk through the door."

"They smell amazing." Brigham inhaled deeply to accentuate his point. He sighed happily and let Greta lead him toward the kitchen at the back of the house. "I hope you made a lot."

"You have as many as you want. If you eat 'em all, we'll make more."

"Meemaw, I like the way you think. Any chance there's some milk in your fridge to go with?"

"Refilled on groceries yesterday. It's all yours."

"Oh, man. You're the best."

As her cousin's and grandmother's voices faded away

across the house, Halsey stood on the front porch gaping at what she'd witnessed.

The woman who'd greeted them looked, sounded, moved, and even smelled like Greta Ambrosius. At least, her house did. She had the same silvery-white hair cut in a bob halfway to her shoulders. The same shimmering blue eyes and brilliant smile that took off at least fifteen years, even with all the laugh lines. Anyone else who knew Greta would have said this woman was her, through and through. No doubt about it.

That is not *Meemaw.*

"Halsey?" Greta called out. "Shut the door behind you when you decide to come in. Tightly. There's no AC bill, but I do like to keep the place cool."

Halsey swallowed thickly, ripped herself from her hesitant confusion, and stepped into her grandmother's house. The door closed behind her with an easy pull. She scanned every inch of the entryway and the front living room.

It looked exactly the same as the last time she'd visited three weeks ago. Nothing had changed, not even the feel of Greta's elemental magic that permeated almost everything. The smell of freshly baked cookies was a new addition and completely innocuous. Yet somehow, cookies had become a major red flag as well.

Meemaw doesn't bake cookies *on the off chance her grandkids might stop by. She doesn't bake cookies at all. I definitely didn't tell her we were coming.*

Laughter rose from the kitchen, and Halsey wrinkled her nose as she headed that way.

Whatever she's trying to pull, she better get to the punchline soon and cut out all this granny crap.

CHAPTER NINE

When Halsey walked into her grandmother's kitchen, Brigham and Greta were already sitting at the table. The chocolate chip cookies were heaped in a giant pile on a plate in front of Brigham, and he'd gotten himself a glass of milk to complete the perfect snack. They were still laughing about something as Brigham jammed almost an entire cookie into his mouth before he looked up and saw Halsey enter the kitchen.

"Dude, these are *so* good," he enthused around his mouthful, shaking the last of a cookie for emphasis. "Hal, you need some of these."

"Okay." Still suspicious but willing to play along for now, Halsey approached the kitchen table and took a seat beside her cousin.

"Oh." Greta smiled and stood. "Milk for you too, sweetheart. Don't get up. I'll be right back."

Halsey reached for a cookie from the dwindling pile as she watched her grandmother grab a glass from the pantry and walk toward the fridge. *Sweetheart? Since when did she start calling me, or anyone, sweetheart?*

Completely oblivious beside her, Brigham tore into the cookies like he'd finished running a marathon. He alternated between gigantic bites and gulping down more milk.

Halsey wasn't thinking about chocolate chip cookies when she nibbled her first. After that, she couldn't *not* think about them. "Whoa."

"I know, right?" Brigham raised his milk and smiled, his lips lined with crumbs. "Nobody does these like Meemaw."

"Ooh, now my ears are ringing." Chuckling, Greta crossed the kitchen with two glasses of milk. "You sure know how to flatter an old lady rattling around in her house all day."

He shrugged. "And *you* know how to make the best damn cookies in the world—"

"Language, Brigham. You know better than that."

"Whoops." He smiled sheepishly. "Sorry." He mock-grimaced at Halsey before digging into the cookies again.

Halsey had forgotten about the half-eaten treat in her hand because now her grandmother had gone too far. "*What?*"

Greta paused beside the table but didn't set a glass in front of Halsey. "What's wrong, honey? You're looking a little wan."

Halsey looked between her grandmother and her cousin, feeling like her head was about to explode. "Okay, *what* is going on right now?"

Brigham set down his glass and came up for air. "I think she's stressed out."

"No. That's not—"

"Aw, sweetie." Greta tilted her head and fixed her with a sympathetic smile before placing a glass of milk down for her. "That's completely normal."

"See?" Brigham nudged Halsey with his elbow and reached for two more cookies. "Told you."

"No. Hold on." As she laughed at how ridiculous this was, she hoped this *was* something she could laugh about later. If it was real, if this woman was Greta Ambrosius at her core and she *wasn't* faking a thing, maybe Halsey actually was going crazy. "You guys…planned all this. Right?"

"Hal, Meemaw *always* has cookies," Brigham replied. "As soon as you walk in the door. We even talk about this."

She gawked at him and wanted to punch the cookie out of his mouth.

With her own glass of milk in hand, Greta sat across from them and dropped two cookies onto a plate for herself before lifting one to her lips. "Halsey, honey, why don't you tell us *your* version of what's going on? Maybe I can help."

"Not if you keep *this* up."

"What's that?"

Halsey stared at her grandmother, then gestured around the kitchen. "This. All of it. Cookies and milk. *Sweetheart*. You told Brigham to *watch his language.*"

He sniggered and pointed at her with a cookie. "Old habits, right?"

"No. Not old habits. Those are *all* our habits."

Greta bit into her cookie, chewed slowly, and watched her granddaughter with calm, loving, understanding eyes. She didn't say a thing.

"There's nothing crazy going on outside," Halsey

continued. "This is a normal house. In the middle of nowhere. And you. You're in a... What is that, a muumuu?"

Her grandmother looked down at her long housedress in a floral pattern of light colors and smiled. "Thanks for noticing. I just got this one. You like it?"

Halsey's jaw dropped. She smacked Brigham's arm. "Help me out here, huh?"

He'd crammed another cookie into his mouth and stared at her while he chewed noisily. "No idea what you're talking about, cuz."

"Seriously?"

"Honey, have you been getting enough sleep lately?" Greta asked with genuine empathy and concern.

Brigham choked down his mouthful. "That's what *I* said."

"Okay." Halsey slumped in her seat and shook her head. "I give up."

"Have a cookie, sweetheart." Her grandmother nodded as she bit into her own. "It'll help."

She didn't want a cookie. Or milk. Or any of this "sitting in Meemaw's cozy kitchen like normal people" crap. *This is insane. This isn't her. None of this is real, but* I'm *the one who sounds crazy. And Brigham seriously can't tell the difference.*

Despite her thoughts chasing themselves around her mind in circles, she did as she was told and ate her cookie. She chewed angrily for a moment, but the cookies themselves were undeniably real.

Damn it, he's right. These are the best cookies ever.

This whole thing made her feel like a complete idiot or the butt of a practical joke drawn out way longer than her cousin's usual pranks. Still, she kept eating and even sipped her milk to wash it down. She slowly settled into feeling more comfortable in her grandmother's kitchen, the three of them enjoying cookies and milk around the table in silence, like they'd been doing this every Thursday for years.

In that contented silence, Halsey wondered why Meemaw couldn't be both things at the same time. A wild, crude, hilarious mentor eighty-three years young some days, and a sweet old grandma baking cookies and shuffling around in a muumuu and day slippers on others. Halsey was a lot of different things too. A cousin, a daughter, a best friend, and a militia partner. One of the Ambrosius Clan's top monster hunters who had serious ethical issues with actually *killing* those monsters. At the same time, she was probably the Clan Council's biggest pain in the ass right now. Or at least tied with Greta.

She looked at her grandmother one more time as the woman reached for another cookie to put on her empty plate. *Wait a minute. Is that how it started with* her? *Everybody else acting like they had no idea what she was talking about? Like the way* they *were handling things was the right way, the most natural thing in the world...*

The revelation was startling enough for Halsey to open her mouth, but Greta beat her to it with her own conversation starter.

"Not that I'm complaining," she proclaimed with a knowing smile. "I can't shake the feeling the two of you didn't drop by for cookies and milk."

"Don't forget the excellent company," Brigham added as he pointed at her and winked.

Halsey was overwhelmed by the urge to smack her cousin across the back of the head. She fixed him with a tight, sarcastic smile instead. "I don't think I've seen you kiss ass this much since our final training exams."

He sniggered and leaned back, another cookie poised in front of his mouth. "What can I say? It's one of my many gifts."

She ignored him and fixed her attention on Greta. "Actually, Meemaw, we stopped by to ask you a few questions."

"We did?" A clump of crumbs spilled from Brigham's mouth and onto his plate. Halsey didn't have to say anything before he remembered why they'd come out here in the first place. "Right. Getting down to business already, huh? Yeah, okay. I gotcha. Entering serious mode..." He finished chewing, swallowed, and brushed his hands off over his plate as he nodded. "Now."

Greta smiled sweetly and waited as if she had absolutely no clue what might be coming.

As if she and Halsey hadn't dropped a massive bond of enlightenment on the Council before they'd magically locked her out of the estate house for her troubles.

After making sure one more time that her cousin was ready to focus on this conversation, Halsey began. "We have some questions about the scroll."

Her grandmother blinked, looked between her grandchildren, and kept smiling. "What scroll?"

This time, Brigham picked up on the strangeness of her reaction and chuckled uncertainly. "Uh...the one you brought to the Council two weeks ago. You know, to help Hal prove that something's screwy with the monsters out there now. Blood rune on the scroll. Blood rune on a bunch of ogre hands…"

"Nine ogres acting like a bunch of ghouls who couldn't actually stomach their unburied dinners," Halsey added.

"Right." He pointed at her. "That, too."

Greta's smile faded. At first, it looked like she'd drop the façade and engage in the conversation. Instead, she pushed her chair back and stood. "Sorry, kids. I'm afraid I don't know what you're talking about."

She picked up her empty cookie plate and milk glass before turning from the table to head for the sink.

When Brigham and Halsey shared a glance, she was relieved to see the same confusion on his face. *Okay, good. It's not only me anymore.*

Brigham wrinkled his nose, stuck a thumb toward their grandmother, and whispered, "What's with *her*?"

"I *know*." Halsey nodded and hoped that now he understood why she was getting so frustrated. "That's what I've been trying to say."

Dishes *clinked* in the kitchen sink, followed by the faucet running as Greta busied herself washing one plate and one glass.

Brigham frowned and leaned closer. "Okay, well… You didn't make up that whole story about the runes and them kicking her out and stuff to make me feel better or something, right?"

"Dude, that is *not* a real question."

"I mean…" He started to shrug, but when he caught her warning glare, he stopped and shook his head. "No, you're totally right. I was only testing you."

"All right. How about less testing and more helping me out here?"

"Yeah." Brigham squinted and followed Greta with his gaze as she moved from sink to dishwasher and back. The woman was clearly taking as much time as possible, and she hadn't turned back once to look at them. "Looks a lot like she's hiding something."

"No kidding." Halsey kept her voice low and joined her cousin in watching their grandmother move at a snail's pace. "We need to get her to start talking about that scroll. I don't know how she got her hands on it, but it was definitely a secret weapon at that last Council meeting. You're right about needing to know what that blood rune means. Then we can take it from there."

"Perfect plan, cuz." Brigham snorted. "Exactly what I was thinking."

"Great. So…" She gestured toward Greta, prompting him to do what Brigham Ambrosius did best.

He didn't look happy about diving into a strategic conversation with their grandmother to extract the information they needed. In fact, he looked like he'd never done anything like that in his life. "So…what?"

"Do your thing," she whispered with more force this time.

"My thing? Why do *I* have to do it?"

"Seriously? Because the Meemaw we're dealing with now is clearly the one *you* know and love."

He clicked his tongue and rolled his eyes. "Oh, come on. You love her too."

"Of course I do. Except I only know how to talk to the Greta Ambrosius who tries to boil me alive with security measures and blows up garden-gnome dens for fun."

Brigham's eyes bulged as he whipped his head toward her and hissed, "Are you *on* something right now?"

"Says the guy with two giant bottles of painkillers in his duffel bag."

"Hey, those are prescribed and necessary—"

"Ask her, Brigham."

"This kinda thing takes a certain level of precision and planning, Hal. I can't—" He stopped abruptly and plastered on a beaming grin as the refrigerator door closed, and Greta walked briskly toward the table. "*Hey*, Meemaw. Whatcha got there?"

"You're out of milk, honey. Figured I'd bring the whole thing over and let you help yourself." She set the half-gallon carton on the table, then lowered herself into her chair with a chuckle. "Otherwise, I'll be walking back and forth all morning."

Grinning for real now, Brigham reached for the milk. "You are literally the best—"

Halsey kicked his shin under the table, and he stared at her with his hand still outstretched toward the milk.

"I'm *thirsty*, Hal. Sometimes a guy needs a little more milk with his cookies before he starts to *dig in*. You feel me?"

She wanted to grab the carton and chuck it at his head so he'd start taking this seriously. Instead, she smiled as sweetly and fakely as Greta and replied, "Then drink your milk, cuz."

Brigham struggled to maintain a satisfied expression as he snatched the carton, sat back down, and refilled his milk glass nearly all the way to the brim. He crammed another cookie in his mouth, barely chewed it, and proceeded to glug the entire glass without pulling it away.

Greta and Halsey stared at him. While their grandmother chuckled as if watching her grandson enjoy himself was the greatest thing that had ever happened to her, Halsey was neither fooled nor amused by her cousin's stalling tactics.

Wow. Somebody's on a mission to prove his point.

Halfway through the giant glass of milk, Brigham met her gaze and raised his eyebrows in a silent challenge as he gulped away.

She snorted and shook her head.

The empty glass clinked on the table, and he exhaled a massive sigh before wiping his mouth with the back of a hand.

"Still thirsty?" Halsey muttered.

He pressed his lips together to hide a grimace and clapped a hand to his stomach. "Nope. That hit the spot."

"Whenever you want, honey," Greta assured him. "You come on by and help yourself to absolutely anything."

Halsey would have kicked her cousin's shin again, but he took the moment as an opportunity to do what they'd come here for.

"How about a little information?" he asked.

"Of course." Greta sat back in her chair and spread her arms. "I'm an open book."

After completely avoiding us the first time we asked? I don't think so.

"Great." Brigham grabbed another cookie but didn't eat it this time. "Hal and I wanna know what other kind of blood runes are in that scroll you brought to the Council and what they mean. We're gonna ride this ride all the way to the top, Meemaw. Right now, you're the only person we know with the knowledge to get us there."

Greta stared with the same vapid, cookie-cutter-granny smile she'd been wearing all day and didn't say a word.

Apparently, that was all it took to cut through Brigham's outer shell of businesslike conversation. "Plus, you're pretty much the only person who's willing to talk to us about this. We need your help."

CHAPTER TEN

Greta gazed at them for an unreasonably long time until Halsey wondered if something irreparable had broken inside their grandmother. At last, the woman took a slow, deep breath through her nose, settled her gaze on Brigham, and wiped the smile off her face. She looked like a completely different person.

"Sorry, kid. That one's a lost cause."

"Wait, what?" Brigham glanced at Halsey, then scooted closer to Greta and her strange response. "Hold on. What do you mean it's a lost cause?"

"I mean, I'm not sitting here watching you stuff a few dozen cookies in your face only to discuss something I have no intention of talking about. Not gonna happen."

Halsey bit back a laugh. Even if she'd let it out, it felt a lot more appropriate now.

Her cousin stared at her in confusion and pointed toward their grandmother. "Is *she* okay?"

"*She* is fine," Greta interjected. "She also heard everything you've been saying for the last ten minutes. So we're clear, there's nothing wrong with any of us at this table. As long as you quit trying to drag us down a road that doesn't exist."

"Huh?" Brigham stared at his uneaten cookie as if that were the source of his confusion. He swallowed and placed it on the empty plate in front of him. "What does that even mean?"

"It means don't ask. 'Cause you won't get an answer."

"This is…" Brigham narrowed his eyes, then slumped back. "What's going on?"

"I'll tell you what's going on. The two of you put together are more than this old lady can handle. Plus, you ate a shit-ton of cookies."

"*Meemaw!*" His eyes were wider than ever, and he almost choked on the real surprise of hearing his grandmother curse. Probably for the first time.

Halsey cackled and received a scathing glare from her cousin. "I am *so* relieved right now. You have no idea."

"Well, consider that a temporary reprieve from…whatever you were trying to do here." Greta tossed a vague gesture that swept aside the entirety of their interactions this morning. "I'm tired, girl. I'd be surprised if you weren't too. And *you.*" She pointed at Brigham. "What are you doing, diving into this crap *the day after* you got out of that recovery bed? Give yourself a break, for crying out loud."

"I have no idea what's going on here," he murmured.

Halsey sighed in relief, then grinned at her grandmother. "I really thought there was something wrong."

"There *is* something wrong. You, me, and this entire damn family have been cheated out of an excellent opportunity to do what we do best and meet a whole wave of new challenges head-on. We've been overrun by a bunch of uptight, butt-hurt *protocol*-pushers who'd rather tie the status quo in a pretty little package then set fire to the whole damn thing because it doesn't work anymore. Which totally sucks." After snatching another cookie, Greta slumped back, chomped an irritated bite, then folded her arms and chewed angrily.

Following her outburst, Brigham looked ready to be sick again. This time, it wasn't the leftover pain from his injuries. "Who are you, and what have you done with my Meemaw?"

That got Greta to smile for real. She leaned forward and held his gaze as cookie crumbs spilled from her lips. "More than you could possibly imagine, kid."

"*What?*"

Greta smirked at Halsey. "Didn't you tell him *anything?*"

"Sorry, Meemaw," she replied with no small amount of sarcasm. "I didn't realize you've been playing Little Old Granny his entire life. What did you want me to say?"

"Huh." After another chuckle, Greta inspected Brigham and nodded. "You're shocked. I get it."

"Shocked? That's an understatement." He blinked with no expression. "Times a thousand. What *is* this?"

"This, young monster hunter, is what happens when a Clan that's been running things as a family for thousands of years has been on the path to division for way too long. You're too young to remember much about how it started, and I honestly do *not* have the time and energy to start rehashing that tar pit of an ugly past right now. Hell, I might never have it."

Brigham slanted toward Halsey and whispered, "Meemaw's using bad words."

"Meemaw already told you she can hear everything you're saying," Greta replied. "She would appreciate all three of us refraining from referring to each other in the third person. Eyes over here, kid." She slapped the table, then pointed at her own eyes.

Whether he wanted to do as she said or was too shocked to consider anything else, Brigham straightened, met his grandmother's gaze, and nodded obediently.

Halsey snorted.

"Have I ever told you you're a tough nut to crumble?" Greta asked her.

"Once or twice. Probably in different words."

"Great. I told you again, then. Except I'm tougher. Harder. Crankier. Crazier, too, depending on who you ask."

Brigham clicked his tongue. "Nobody thinks you're crazy, Meemaw..."

"Of course not. They know I'm sane as a bat. They only *want* to believe I'm off my rocker so they can do...whatever they damn well please. Isn't that right?"

Halsey grabbed another cookie from the few left on the plate and actually enjoyed eating it from start to finish. "Does that mean you'll tell us about the scroll and the blood runes now?"

"Absolutely not. Don't ask again."

The look her grandmother gave her said everything there might have been to say. This topic of conversation was closed for discussion. Indefinitely.

She stuck her neck out for me two weeks ago. For the entire

Clan, honestly. She got kicked out of HQ like a wild dog because of it. Can't blame her for wanting to lock that up in the past. At least for now.

Halsey decided to try a different tactic. "What if we take a look at it for ourselves?"

Greta's only reaction was to raise an eyebrow.

The suggestion seemed to spark a whole new level of brainstorming for Brigham as he sat up straighter and didn't look nearly as worried. "Yeah. You know Hal and I can get what we need from that thing on our own. We always do when we put our heads together."

"Huh. Looks more like bashing your heads together, but okay."

"Ouch." He recoiled, then laughed and turned toward Halsey. "And she—"

Greta slapped the table. "Did you not hear me the first time?"

"What? Oh. Sorry." Frowning because he had no idea how to interact with this new-to-him version of his grandmother, Brigham opened his mouth, paused, then met the woman's gaze again. "And you say mean things."

"Come on, kid. Hitting you in the face for fun is mean. Stealing your lunch and breaking all your toys is mean. If you think the *truth* is mean, you might as well call it quits on your partnership with Halsey and go join the yuccups in their high-horse Council chairs."

"The what?"

Halsey shook her head and muttered, "Just roll with it."

"Okay..."

Greta scoffed. "*Mean.* That's like calling a bee mean for stinging you when you weren't paying attention. Or calling the rain mean for falling out of the sky and ruining your outdoor artwork without asking permission first. Or calling a swarm of vindictive garden gnomes mean little shits for screwing with your preconceived notions before they tear up your entire yard."

"Holy shit." Brigham grimaced before she'd finished. When he got no reprimand from his uninhibited grandmother, he looked at Halsey. "That really happened?"

"Yeah. Do you think I've been lying to you about everything?" She addressed Greta again. "That was totally different, though. Those gnomes were mean as hell."

"No, you're right about that one. I still have dreams about giving those little shits a piece of my mind."

"I think we gave 'em a pretty good run, though," Halsey suggested.

"We did, didn't we?"

While grandmother and granddaughter shared a knowing smile, Brigham looked between them and shrugged. "Okay. Everything I thought I knew about everything is changing. Not only monsters, apparently."

"Don't sell yourself short, my boy." Greta pointed at him. "Each of us has always been who we are. What everybody else does or doesn't know about it depends on how generous with our own truth we happen to be. There's your food for thought for the day. Take it with you. Chew on it a little. Don't worry about bringing it back. I've got plenty to go around. Come back tomorrow if you have any other questions, all right?"

"Uh…right. Thanks." Brigham frowned and pushed out of his chair, clearly ready to take his grandmother's ad-hoc dismissal as the end of their visit because now he was in unfamiliar territory.

"Brigham." Halsey shook her head and tried not to laugh. "Sit down."

"She told us to come back tomorrow, so we—*oh.*" His grin returned, and he plopped into his seat and pointed at Greta. "You're *good.*"

"No idea what you're talking about, but I always accept compliments." The woman's amused, calculating smile was at complete odds with her words. Then again, when Greta Ambrosius opened up enough to be herself, what she said and what she meant generally opposed each other, anyway.

Which Halsey had already known. Now her partner knew it, too.

I can't believe he's seeing this for the first time. He spent his whole life thinking she was only a grandma, *even as an Ambrosius elemental.*

Now that Brigham had picked up on their grandmother's honed deflection tactics, he was ready to engage with his full focus. "You never answered my question, Meemaw. Can we take the scroll and figure it out for ourselves?"

Greta laughed and slapped her hands on the table. "If you think I'd let my two favorite grandkids get their hands on a piece of parchment paper with blood-magic written all over it and probably sewn into the fibers of the thing, you're as crazy as I am."

"Wait, but you're not crazy. Right?"

"Then don't give it to us," Halsey added, loving the back-and-forth between her favorite family members but still aware of the work that lay ahead of them. "Bring it out here. We can go over it together. *You* can supervise *us* if it makes you feel better. So you know we're not doing anything stupid."

"Halsey." Greta's shrewd smile softened into something a lot more grandmotherly, and this time it was genuine. "None of this is about me *feeling better.*"

"At least let us make a freaking copy of the thing," Brigham blurted. "If you counter that with a copout like 'I don't have one of those fancy printers all you young people are using these days,' let me remind you that I scored the highest marks for penmanship in Charlemagne's courses. I have no problem pulling out fifty notebooks and a whole box of pens if I have to. What do you say?"

After he finished his final-offer outburst, the kitchen fell silent except for the constant tick of a clock somewhere in the house and a violent twittering of birds before they took flight. When Halsey looked at her grandmother, the woman was staring at her with wide eyes.

They both burst out laughing.

Brigham sat back with a self-conscious smile. "Well, that's one way to win a room."

"'You *young people?*'" Halsey shrieked through her laughter.

"Like I'm eking out the rest of my days in a damn nursing home!" Greta added before howling again. "Don't even get me started on *Charlemagne's courses.*"

"Brig, you were—" Halsey slumped over the armrest, nearly hyperventilating to catch her breath. "You were the...the *only* one who took those courses."

Her cousin's grin widened. "Doesn't mean I wasn't still the best."

"His *courses!*" Greta screeched before slapping the

tabletop several times. "Did my brother offer something on How to Make A Librarian's Big Head Even Bigger?"

Brigham sniggered. "I mean...probably."

That made her scream with laughter all over again, then all three of them were at it together.

When they finally managed to calm down, with Greta taking longer than either of her grandchildren, the tension that had been swimming around them since Halsey and Brigham arrived finally eased.

Greta wiped tears of laughter from her eyes, chuckled again, and sighed in complete satisfaction. "Whew. You know, in the last three weeks, I've laughed more and been more pissed off than I have in *years*. Can't help but think there's something to that."

Brigham stuck a thumb toward his cousin and muttered, "Or it's all Hal's fault."

She stared at him in mock insult. "I thought we were partners, man."

"Uh-huh. You ever think maybe that's *because* it's all your fault?"

Halsey had nothing to say to that. She rolled her eyes and prepared to steer them back toward the conversation that mattered most. "Seriously, Meemaw. We really do need—"

"A different plan. Sorry, kiddo. The scroll's off the table. For you, for me, for anyone with half a brain and elemental magic who's remotely interested in preparing for the biggest, bloodiest, deadliest battle this family's seen in thousands of years. I can't help you there."

"Wait a minute." Brigham shook his head. "If everything you said is true, and apparently it is, we should all be helping each other out. Preparing. Learning. Even if that means diving into a few mini-lessons on blood runes, right? At least then, we'd have a little knowledge about what we're up against."

"She means she doesn't have it," Halsey murmured.

"Huh?"

"The scroll. She doesn't have it."

"I thought she stormed into the Council room and slapped it down in front of all the...*oh*."

Greta sniggered. "Is that what you told him?"

"It's what I know about what happened."

"Fair enough." The woman squinted at Brigham. "I see those gears turning in your head, kid. Keep 'em turning, only in a different direction, okay? Charlemagne's not letting *anyone* into the library if it carries the potential of leaving the slightest blemish on one of his precious records. I can tell you right now that Lawrence has already put a security hold on anything that might help you two put this puzzle together on your own. Not that there was much left in there after I was done with it."

"No way." All the humor had left Brigham's face, and he looked more concerned than he had throughout the entire conversation. "You mean he's censoring the family library?"

Greta shrugged.

"Hold on. No. He can't do that. What happened to the pursuit of knowledge? To freedom of understanding? To Clan militia being a family that shares everything we have because we're the only people in the world who can do what we do, and *we have magic*?" He glanced between Greta and Halsey, growing more frantic by the second. "That's not how this works."

"It's how Lawrence wanted it to work, kid." Greta gestured in concession. "The Council either agrees with him or is too scared to put their foot down. Either way, you've hit a dead end with your search here."

"That's fucking insane!"

"Yup." The woman pursed her lips. "Now you're breathing like a freight train on steroids in my kitchen, Brigham. Some might even call it fuming. Go ahead. Take a minute. Let it hit you however it needs to hit. Trust me, this ain't the end."

Surprisingly, he didn't take any of his grandmother's words as insulting or condescending. Instead, Brigham did what she'd suggested. In under ninety seconds, he'd brought his anger and frustration under control again. He ran a hand through his hair and sighed at Halsey. "Dude. I am so sorry I didn't trust you and believe everything you were talking about from the beginning."

That took her by surprise, and she chuckled reflexively. "It's fine—"

"No, it's not. I feel like I've been living in a goddamn conspiracy my entire life, and you were the only one who saw through it."

Greta cleared her throat, and he shot her a sidelong glance. "Okay, yeah. You and Meemaw were the only ones who saw through it."

"I think my dad might be on our short list too, actually," Halsey added. "Only because he fought the ogres with me and saw the blood runes with his own eyes. You know, on the hands when they were attached to the bodies."

"That was really enough to convince him?" Greta asked.

"Plus the fact that he couldn't choke out a single ogre on his own by doing his normal Aiden-hulking-out thing. That was probably the kicker for him."

"Anything threatening your father's sense of purpose as an elemental instead of a new seat on the Council? Yeah." Greta snorted. "That'd be a hell of a thorn in his ass."

Brigham sniggered at the odd expression. After that, it seemed like no one else had anything to say. At least not anything that would have benefitted the conversation. Now that they'd been turned down, Halsey and her cousin were out of ideas.

Greta's eyes narrowed, along with her sly, knowing smile. "I think I can offer you two something better than a dumb piece of parchment that's been stuffed on a shelf and collecting dust longer than my brother."

Here we go. This is where it finally starts to get good.

Halsey glanced sideways at her cousin, and he smiled before they both gave their grandmother their undivided attention.

CHAPTER ELEVEN

"If I were you," Greta began slowly, drawing out the suspense like she was telling a ghost story instead of giving practical, crucial advice to her grandchildren. "I'd quit trying to look for answers in the places you've always found them before. Right now, the place of *your* beginning is in a renovation stage, as it were. Obviously. Closed for remodeling."

Brigham's wide-eyed excitement faded into a frown. He tried to hide by pursing his lips and nodding like he followed her.

Halsey didn't understand her grandmother's words any more than he did, but she did know Greta would get to the point eventually. It was a matter of how long she wanted the process to take.

"If it were *me* riding the front lines of this thing, I'd go back to the beginning. To where it all started."

Brigham popped his lips. "You said our beginning is closed for business."

"I'm not talking about you, kid."

He looked at Halsey for an explanation he didn't expect to receive, but she'd figured out what their grandmother was trying to tell them. "I think she's talking about Ireland."

"What? That wasn't the beginning of anything, Hal. That was a successful mission with a few weird coincidences that... Oh. Damn it, how come I'm always the last to put these things together?"

"Because you're the first active hunter to see the world through your cousin's eyes," Greta replied. "As they really are. In that sense, I'd say you're ahead of the curve on this one." She smirked, settled back in her chair, and patted her silver bob. "Like me."

"None of this here at home would've happened if Ireland didn't turn out the way it did," Halsey added. "Werewolves acting like lunatics, the silverback alpha, the creepy silver coffin. We brought back what we saw and expected the Council to have a helpful opinion about it."

Brigham snorted. "Fail."

"It makes sense that we'd find more answers where all the weird changes started."

"It sure does." Greta's smile flickered in and out as she studied her grandkids. "That's a good enough idea that even the Council can't shoot it down. *If* they have the balls to take a good idea and run with it."

"Ha. Fail again." Brigham folded his arms and frowned at the cookie crumbs on his plate. "We don't have to tell them about this, do we? I mean, even if *they* don't have the balls, you know they're gonna try to take ours to keep us from bringing back more proof of what they don't want to accept."

"What a colorful analogy," Greta mused before popping the second half of a cookie in her mouth.

Halsey chose to ignore the way he'd worded his description of the potential potholes in this plan. "You're right. They'd never approve of it. If you and I decided to take a fun little vacation on our own without making it a public thing, though…"

"Yeah, okay." His eyes lit with understanding. "I see the light at the end of the tunnel. So…what? You, me, and an all-expenses-paid-out-of-pocket trip to the Cliffs of Moher?"

"Change Moher to Dublin, and you have yourself a deal." She shrugged. "Before you got used as a human ax by a blood-cursed ogre, we were thinking about going to the warehouse in Dublin anyway, right?"

"Now *that's* a colorful analogy."

Greta snorted and crammed another cookie in her face so she wouldn't further interrupt their brainstorming.

Halsey ignored both of them. "We could check out the warehouse ourselves."

"You really think we'll find anything out there? If Patrick had no idea what happened to the coffin and none of his guys had anything to add, what the hell's left for *us*?"

"Don't get me wrong. Patrick's a good guy, and he's good at his job. He's not one of us, though."

Brigham pointed at her. "I think you mean he's *magically stunted*."

"Sure. Don't call him that to his face, and I think we'll be fine."

"Okay, then. We're going back to Ireland." He frowned and scanned the kitchen. "Definitely not looking forward to that international flight, though. Oh! I'll do you one better, cuz. We check out the warehouse. Play elemental detective or whatever. And I'll reach out to the Havalon Council. See if anyone out there's willing to talk to us about a little craziness and a lotta monster. Couldn't hurt, right?"

Halsey grinned, liking the idea more by the second. "When you can't get what you need from your own family…"

"Bother someone else's."

Greta shrieked laughter that made both her grandchildren jolt in their seats before they faced her and waited for her outburst to subside.

"It wasn't *that* funny," Brigham muttered.

"You two!" Greta chortled and shook her head, gasping for breath.

"Hal, you sure this whole thing isn't one big joke?"

"Don't ask me that again."

"Fair enough."

Their grandmother finally settled down so she could explain why she thought they were so funny. As it turned out, her amusement had nothing to do with them.

"Yes. Go. Reach out to the Havalons. Great idea."

"And a funny one, apparently," Halsey added.

"A huge kick-in-the-face surprise for *everybody*." Greta howled with laughter again, then shook a finger at her granddaughter. "You're way too young to remember the last time any of the elemental families banded together to accomplish anything. Both of you. Ha! Believe me when I tell you, even what they accomplished didn't make a pretty picture. So much *competition*. And for what? There are only three families now..."

"So..." Brigham squinted at her. "You *don't* think it's a good idea?"

"That's the opposite of what I said. I think it's an excellent idea. *If* they're willing to talk to either of you."

Halsey shook her head. "Why wouldn't they be?"

"Who knows?" Greta cracked up all over again, and it started to look like she'd spend the rest of the morning and most of the afternoon in this state.

Halsey was already forming a plan. Which, of course, would be improved when she and Brigham hashed it out without one eccentric grandmother interrupting every time they said something good.

Ignoring Meemaw, Halsey grabbed the last cookie and raised an eyebrow at Brigham. "We need to have our story straight when we meet up with the Havalons. *If* they agree to meet. We have to be convincing, too."

"Should we pack a few severed ogre hands in a leak-proof bag or something, then?" The way her cousin smiled made it clear he was only half-joking.

"Nah. Better stick with the pictures and a story this time."

"Not that I'm trying to tell y'all how to handle your business," Greta cut in. "This feels like it bears saying, though. First, you've got plenty of time for this. I don't see the Council coughing up new missions for you anytime soon, and definitely not together. Plus, I'm guessing Brigham hasn't officially been cleared for field duty yet."

"I'm recovered." He puffed out his chest and struck the

manliest pose possible with a cookie in hand. "And you would be correct."

"Well, then, they won't come after you for how you go about this. Still, remember that it's all on you. I do mean *all* of it."

Halsey began to thoroughly enjoy the last cookie. "Such as?"

"Such as the fact that if this isn't a pre-approved, Council-ordered monster-hunting mission, everything you do is on your own dime, kid."

The cousins shared a knowing look, then Brigham held his cookie out and nodded. "I'm pretty sure we can handle that."

Halsey chuckled and bumped her cookie against his. Neither paid attention to the rain of crumbs falling onto the table. "I don't doubt it for a second."

It took them another day and a half to plan the next steps for a visit to Ireland, this time *not* on official Ambrosius Clan business. The flight from Fort Worth to Dublin International could not be considered fun, but it got the cousins to the Emerald Isle on time and in one piece. Which was really all that mattered.

By the time they checked into their hotel off Temple Bar, jetlagged and disoriented, they were ready to hit the ground running and tackle their to-do list. First, they took the time to shower, freshen up, and make it look like they'd been here adjusting for a few days. Plus, Brigham was overly excited about ordering room service for lunch.

After lunch, they headed to the Ambrosius Clan's Dublin-based acquisitions warehouse, situated off the docks with all the other freighter warehouses along the Dublin Port. Even in late July, the thick fog rolling into the harbor off the ocean almost completely obscured the docks. However, when the young elemental team entered the warehouse property with a full array of questions and conversation topics already planned out, the place looked empty.

It sounded empty, too.

Brigham's eyes narrowed as he scanned the shipping yard beyond the warehouse. "You told him we were coming, right?"

"Of course I told him. He said he'd be here whenever we wanted to come by, day or night. Then I told him what time we were coming."

"And he confirmed it?"

"Dude." Halsey glared at him. "Not my first rodeo. Not even my first rodeo in Ireland."

"Yeah, yeah. I know. I still had to ask."

"No, you didn't."

"Hey, lemme tell you something." He pointed at her as they walked across the parking lot behind the warehouse, where only four cars were parked in the first few spaces. "Since the night I got side-swiped by a flabby-ass ogre with a pistachio-sized brain, it's been hard for me to figure out what's real or not."

"Yeah. Welcome to my life." They both laughed as they approached the warehouse's front entrance, and Halsey didn't bother trying to emphasize that she hadn't been joking. She'd been questioning the reality of things for a while now. Months before the Ireland mission with Brigham. Until recently, she'd wondered if all the subtle jabs and not-so-subtle insinuations from the Council and the rest of her family had carried any weight.

Until recently, she'd wondered if they weren't correct when they claimed to worry about the state of her sanity and some biological propensity to follow in her mother's footsteps. And Greta's.

Yet she knew more now than she had then. She had undeniable proof that the changes she'd seen coming down the pipeline were real, valid, and incredibly important for the trajectory of the Ambrosius Clan. Maybe even the entire world, regular humans included. Although the Council and most of her family had chosen to ignore that until the last second.

Don't get ahead of yourself, Halsey. This isn't about being the "chosen one" or saving everybody and everything singlehandedly. You happen to fall ahead of the curve, like Meemaw. And Brigham now, apparently.

Everything they did had to be one step at a time. By the book, even though the Ambrosius Clan Council had clearly reinvented the definition. Right now, the step was talking to Patrick Graham face-to-face and getting an in-person look at the facility from which the heavy silver coffin had been stolen.

The coffin Halsey knew belonged to the Mother of Monsters, no matter what anyone else said.

The fact that the coffin had been stolen from one of the most secure warehouses in Dublin without a shred of evidence left behind only supported her theory. Now, it was time for two of the Ambrosius Clan's best monster hunters to start hunting something else.

If they could get a lead on it.

The warehouse's front door was locked tight, as it should have been, though Halsey tried the handle anyway. Then she looked at the security camera mounted on the wall three feet above the door and smiled. "Guess who…"

"Really?" Brigham snorted. "You think they're gonna let us in with your face and random—"

"Hey, Hal." Patrick's deep voice crackled through the exterior intercom, and Brigham flinched. "Yah're right on time. Not that Ah'd expect n'ethin' less from ya. Cam on back."

The buzzer sounded, followed by several metallic clicks and the sharp boom of the automatic locks disengaging.

Brigham raised an eyebrow at the camera, waved, and muttered, "Did he always have that accent?"

"As long as I've known him. I think it tends to disappear when he's scared." Halsey grabbed the handle and pulled the door open. "Or pissed."

"Huh. That seems like the opposite of what everyone else would do."

"Well, Patrick Graham is not everyone else."

"Fair."

The door opened easily, and the elemental duo stepped into the dimly lit acquisitions warehouse that had housed, stored, and shipped countless artifacts and items from around the world to the Ambrosius Clan's Texas headquarters. Unless, of course, the Council told Patrick and his team to store something for an indeterminate length of time to keep an eye on it.

Either way, the Dublin warehouse could have been considered the Ambrosius Clan Museum for all the rare, magical, semi-magical, or merely suspicious objects taking up space within its walls on a regular basis.

Patrick Graham stood there to greet them with open arms. "Oy! Wid ya look wa' the ca' dragged een. Ah didn't naw fer real if ye were comin ar' nah."

"We're here, all right." Halsey laughed and approached the man in his late forties who fit the American perception of "authentic Irishman" to a tee. Flaming red hair, green eyes, pale skin, and a cardigan in the middle of summer.

He wrapped her in a crushing bear hug like they'd been greeting each other this way their entire lives. For Halsey, that was technically true.

Brigham stood back and folded his arms, smirking as his partner and her favorite normal-human Ambrosius employee hugged.

When they released each other, Patrick beamed. He ran a hand through his hair, then turned toward the long hallway stretching down the center of the warehouse. "Ya wanna peek at ware yer disappearin' box was, aye?"

Halsey nodded. "That's it."

"Brigham." Patrick extended a hand, still grinning, and they shared a firm shake.

"We'd also like to see your security systems, if you don't mind," Brigham casually added as they released each other's hands. "Main doors, bay doors, anything in between. Camera footage from the night the coffin went missing. If you still have it."

"Aye…" The man's joy faded, and he held Brigham's gaze a moment longer before looking to Halsey again. "I keep all the footage 'round five years after the fact. Like it says in our contract."

Great. Now he thinks we're here to accuse him of not doing his job.

"Not that you and your crew would've done anything to the camera footage or didn't look it over enough that day," Halsey added quickly to defuse Patrick's growing confusion and irritation. "It's in case there's something only an Ambrosius would take any interest in. We know you guys are doing top-notch work out here for us. You always have."

Fortunately, Brigham caught on to her intentions and tried to help drive the point home. "We definitely don't need to start with camera footage. Not at all. Drop that to the bottom of the list."

"Uh-huh." Patrick crossed his arms. His smile morphed into a dubious frown, his bright red eyebrows drawing close together. He nodded at Halsey. "Did Aiden happen to say anything else about it after I called you with the news?"

"My dad?" She shook her head. "No. Nobody said a word."

"Nary a speck?" Patrick tilted his head and scanned the warehouse hallway behind them. "I would've thought the first missing piece of inventory in several decades might raise a few red flags. I was all prepped and ready to have that conversation. 'Cause I do take full responsibility for all of it. Don't know how it happened, but I know my lads had nothing to do with it, either way."

"We know that too, Patrick," Halsey replied. "Hands down. Nobody's questioning the work you do or the integrity of your team."

"Then..." The man looked away and cleared his throat, which was as much embarrassment as he was likely to show. "Why didn't anyone ring me up? Besides you, o'course. It's usually the spick-and-span record with one little blemish that brings the holy hellfire rainin' down on a man and all the lads workin' for him. Honestly, I've been waiting for that for the last few fortnights and change."

Despite the acquisitions manager's obvious discomfort, Brigham sniggered and shoved his hands into his jeans pockets. "Trust me, man. The Council's had a lot more on their plate than one washed up, disappearing casket they never gave a shit about in the first place."

"Aye?" For some reason, that confused Patrick more. After another glance around, he leaned toward the cousins and lowered his voice. "Even once ya told 'em what it can do?"

Halsey and Brigham exchanged a quick glance, then she laughed uncertainly. "What the *coffin* can do?"

"O'course. All that shimmerin' and shudderin'. Now, I won't say this in front of anyone else, but that thing gave me the willies. And that's after half me life spent pickin' up and watchin' over all manner o' strange objects your family contracts. Includin' that slaverin' beastie head a few years back. The one with all the horns and that purple goo drippin' down its—"

Brigham interrupted with a sigh. "Yep. That'd be the bonnacon."

"Aye. I thought *that* was the strangest of 'em until ya rang me to come fetch that box out in Moher. And if we're all bein' honest..."

When he raised his eyebrows and didn't say anything

else, Halsey realized that was supposed to be a question. "Completely honest, Patrick. We're not holding back. You don't have to, either."

Brigham drew an X over his chest with an index finger. "Cross our hearts and hope to...I mean... Well, you know."

She frowned at her cousin, and he shrugged.

"Well, then," Patrick continued. "Since we're bein' honest, I'll go ahead and tell ya right now that I'm glad the thing up and vanished. I'd bet my right foot most of the lads are, too, though they'd never say a thing about it. Neither will I, after this."

The cousins nodded slowly, then Halsey cleared her throat. "Neither will we. *And*, since we *are* being honest, we should probably tell you our family has no idea we're here."

"Aye?" The man's bushy red eyebrows shot straight up, and he jumped on the opportunity to sweep the creepy-coffin talk under a rock and focus on this new discovery. "Nary a one of 'em?"

"Greta knows," Brigham offered. "She'd probably tell you this was *her* idea, but all she did was remind us it was our idea first, so..."

"Greta." Patrick's full grin returned. "She's one who'd ne'er say a thang about i'teither. So it's the two o'yas pokin' about an yer awn?"

"Yep." Halsey inhaled deeply and shrugged. "Contrary to popular Ambrosius belief, we think there was something off about that casket. There's something even *more* off about it vanishing out from under *you* without a trace. Disappearing from the beach where we found it would've been one thing, but you've got the best security in the country here. Maybe even in the UK. Who knows?"

Patrick chuckled. "As evidenced by naught a soul arund havin' any idea tha' all they tink is superstition actually exists. Right'ere under thar noses, aye?"

"Aye," Brigham echoed, then chuckled and shook his head. "I mean, obviously. We'd appreciate it if this didn't get back to the Council or any other Ambrosius who might come sniffing around. If you know what I mean."

"Not that anyone else is remotely interested in this," Halsey clarified. "Let alone enough to come all the way out here to see for themselves. The three of us and your crew are the only ones who've seen that coffin with our own eyes, anyway."

"Well, then." The man's bright eyes crinkled with deep laugh lines at the corners, clearly returned to his original good spirits. "Sounds like we're all in this together. We'll keep mum on the whole ting. You have my word."

"Thanks." Halsey wondered what their next steps were supposed to be after this conspiratorial conversation with someone who wasn't technically an Ambrosius by either blood or marriage. Still, Patrick was probably the only regular human and "outsider" she trusted.

At least we don't have to worry about him reporting back to the Council. He'd only end up on the chopping block with us.

"So!" Patrick clapped his hands together, rubbed them vigorously, and spun before waving them after him down the hallway. "Let's get you looking at what you came here ta see. And if you happen ta figure out how in the world that casket got disappeared on our end, I'll float yer drinks at the pub."

Halsey snorted as she and Brigham followed him

through the acquisitions warehouse. "And if we can't, drinks are *still* on you."

"Ya have yerself a deal."

They let him get ahead before Brigham leaned toward his cousin and muttered, "You weren't kidding about his disappearing accent."

"Yep. If only that coffin reappeared as easily."

CHAPTER TWELVE

The first thing they tackled, with Patrick's help, was a quick but thorough inspection of the warehouse's entire security system. Entrances, locking mechanisms, cameras, electrical panels, bay doors, and various access codes given out to his crew members. The man had been accurate in his assessment when he'd told Halsey and the Council there had been no signs of forced entry or a break-in. No hint that the coffin had even been taken from its private, locked storage room.

This time around was no different. Though it was disappointing not to find a single blemish, footprint, or dent that might lead them to the casket, Halsey was satisfied with the initial results. It proved Patrick and his men hadn't missed anything, and this wasn't a result of negligence or distraction on their part. Not that she'd suspected them of anything, but now they could be sure.

Which means somebody actually stole from us. From this facility. That's gonna make finding the damn coffin harder than any of us want.

Though Brigham had assured Patrick they didn't need to see the security footage right away, the end of their security-check tour landed them at the control room, so that was where they stopped next. Sure enough, the team kept immaculate records of everyone who entered and exited the buildings, plus incredibly well-organized backup files with date- and timestamps.

They watched the footage of the night in question three times before being forced to conclude it was another dead end.

"Nothing," Brigham grumbled as he pushed away from the control desk housing the security monitors. "Not even a twitch."

Patrick raised an eyebrow and sniggered. "That sometin' ya folks generally see with technology when sometin' funny happens?"

"Ha. About as much as you generally get robbed without being able to figure out *how*."

"Thanks for taking the time to find these for us." Halsey nodded at Patrick, then rolled her chair away from the control desk before standing. "I know you already knew it was a dead end, but we're trying to look at this from every possible angle."

"'Tis the least I could do, Hal. Major screw-up like this had me on pins 'n needles for weeks. If takin' the time ta go through a few hours of absolutely nothin' with ya means the lads and I all get ta keep our jobs, and nobody's payin' a steep price for what happened, I'm happy ta do it." He smiled, then looked at Brigham, waiting for one of them to say something else. When they didn't, Patrick gestured toward the door. "Last ting I can think of is the storage unit where we kept the ting. You still wanna inspect that, too, right?"

"Definitely."

He led them halfway back down the warehouse and turned down a short, narrow hallway into the west half of the building. Which, apparently, was designated for storing unpredictable, potentially volatile items their acquisitions team picked up after completed Ambrosius Clan missions. This area looked more like a regular storage facility than anything else, with individual garage doors securing units of all sizes.

Unsurprisingly, the missing silver coffin wasn't the only issue Patrick and his crew had to deal with today, even while giving their unexpected guests a tour of the facility where the casket had rested for all of twelve hours. Patrick was called away for some other project only he could handle, but he introduced Halsey and Brigham to three employees who had personally been with him on the Cliffs of Moher to collect the coffin.

"Yer in good hands with these blokes," he'd told them before playfully shoving one of the men aside on his way out. "Don't let 'em fill yer heads with any o' their nonsense, though. Lord knows Brigham's got enough in his already."

That made everyone howl with laughter, then the cousins' new guides led them down another short series of twisting hallways. They talked and laughed together as one of them flipped through an enormous key ring with hundreds of keys to find the one he was looking for.

"All these units have a few levels o' extra security," Mickey told them as the group stopped outside the unit. "Bottom rung o' the ladder's yer good ol' key 'n padlock system. Simple, sure, but most o' the time, it's enough ta keep out the desperate, panicky bloke who decided five minutes ago he wanted ta try his hand at robbery. Takes a special kinda eejut and a special kinda metal clippers ta cut through a lock like *that*."

He nodded at the padlock as he finally found the key he wanted. The lock itself was enormous, the metal so thick in places that it would need to be melted down or blown up to open without a key.

Mickey inserted the key, unlocked it with a metal click and a jingle of keys, then removed the padlock and handed it to one of his buddies. "After that comes the access code."

"What is that, like a different code for every sector of the warehouse or something?" Brigham asked.

"Try fer every individual unit."

Brigham almost choked as the man demonstrated by flipping up the plastic lid covering the keypad and started punching buttons. After he'd entered the series, the keypad flashed green and beeped.

"Hal," Brigham murmured. "He didn't even have to look for the code." He glanced at Mickey and spread his arms. "You didn't even have to look for the code!"

"Trust me, boyo. When ye've got sometin' tricky as that glimmerin' silver box o' yers, ya remember the code real quick."

That's the second time somebody's mentioned the coffin acting up. We definitely missed that the first time around.

When she met her cousin's gaze and lifted two fingers, Brigham nodded in understanding, then shrugged.

Yeah, that's something we'll have to ask about afterward.

"Finally," Mickey proclaimed as yet another security

panel opened beside the unit's garage door. "Ye've got yer good old-fashioned biometric scanner."

Brigham snorted. "Holy shit."

The man positioned an eye in front of the panel built inside the wall beneath two metal segments that had slid apart to reveal a scanner. A red light flashed across his iris, then a green light and a happy little blip emanated from the system.

Mickey turned and grinned at the cousins. "That's the best part. Don't try it if yer not in the system, though. The alarms aren't the only tings that go off for a security breach."

"What else?" Brigham's eyes were wide and eager as he turned in a slow circle to scan the floor, walls, and ceiling of the hallway with a new perspective.

One of the other crew members, a ridiculously short man named Kyle who couldn't have been much older than Halsey and her cousin, chuckled and pointed at the floor. "Tink giant taser, aye? Yer standin' on it."

"No way." Brigham glanced down, backed up a step, and broke into a wide grin.

"After that, there's—"

"No, that's totally cool, man. I don't need to hear anything else." He lifted both hands in surrender. "You had me at giant taser."

"Of course he did," Halsey murmured, rolling her eyes.

The guys on Patrick's crew laughed at that, then the pressurized locking system *around* the garage door clicked, hissed, and flashed with green light.

"Wow." She peered at the top of the unit, trying to get a look at the mechanism that kept this insanely high level of security functional. "I feel like we should be wearing hazmat suits for this."

"Ya know, I tink some o' the boys said the same when we had that ting in here," Mickey replied. "Our system doesn't give a damn 'bout what's inside it, o'course. A little more protection goes a long way ta feel safer, 'specially wit sometin' like that old casket. If that's even what t'was."

"Fair enough." Halsey watched the men grab the handles on the bottom of the garage door. All three of them had to haul it together to get it off the ground. After that, the wheels on the metal tracks took over, and the door opened easily. Yet, while she watched them, her mind was somewhere else.

They're not gonna tell us what it was doing in here that freaked them out so much, are they? They're joking about it now, but everybody's still too scared to call it what it is. Shit, I hope nobody got hurt.

The loud bang of the garage door reaching the top of the unit jerked her from her concerned thoughts. The sound echoed through the narrow hallway.

"Here we go." Brigham rubbed his hands together and peered into the large, dark storage unit. A ridiculous amount of top-level security hadn't kept one slippery thief from getting their hands on one incredibly important artifact. Hopefully, something was left inside the unit the Ambrosius cousins could use to move forward. If not, the acquisitions warehouse was a dead end, and they'd be running out of options.

As Mickey headed toward the open unit, Brigham nodded. "Show us what you got, gentlemen."

"If ya say so." With a tight, hesitant smile, Mickey

reached around the corner of the doorframe to feel along the interior wall. There were two sharp clicks, and bright overhead lights flipped on in sequence to illuminate all that was left of the incredible, potentially deadly discovery they'd made on the Summer Solstice under the light of the full moon.

Of all the things they expected to find, what greeted them wouldn't have even made the list.

CHAPTER THIRTEEN

Halsey's immediate instinct was to ask the three Irishmen under Patrick Graham's employ what they were trying to pull here. Fortunately, she didn't say a word. She was too confused by the empty storage unit mixed with the startlingly potent energy of a new kind of magic she'd never felt before.

That residual energy pulsed across her face, neck, and arms in gentle waves, neither harmful nor benevolent. Simply different.

It was coming from inside the unit.

"Huh." Brigham folded his arms and cocked his head. "I don't know why I thought that would be less anticlimactic."

"See?" Mickey shrugged and leaned against the thick doorframe. "Nutin'. There's no way an amateur or even a fairly decent professional could burgle this unit without leavin' so much as a scratch. Nawt even a bit o' explosive or anytin'. As ya saw wit our somewhat complicated system."

"Ha. Somewhat, yeah."

"Whoever t'was didn't come through the walls, the

ceiling panels, or the floor. Trust me. We all checked once we found out t'was missin'. Multiple times. Absolutely nutin' left behind."

"'Cept fer the sand," the third crew member said in a low, rumbling voice as he nodded inside the unit. "Not all that surprisin', considerin' we picked that ting off the beach. Was damn heavy, too."

"Sand." Halsey shot the employees a distracted glance. "It was still covered in sand when it got all the way inside and locked up here?"

Mickey shrugged. "Must have. Pat said not ta touch a ting in there until he heard from yer family, and none of us had a problem wit followin' those orders ta perfection. I suppose now that the two of ya came by, we'll have ta clean up whatever's inside and get it ready for the next weird ting you Ambrosiuses feel like sendin' our way."

Brigham laughed. "Well, if it's only a little sand, it can't be that bad."

"Ye'd be surprised…"

"You said *no one* has been in here since the coffin went missing?" Halsey asked, though even she could tell she didn't sound interested in the answer. She was. Except it required a staggering amount of effort and focus to prevent being overwhelmed by the calm yet somehow energetic pulsations of the strange new magic wafting from the unit.

"Aye." Kyle nodded. "Soon as we heard, this unit got sealed off entirely. Do Not Touch, aye? Not sure how much of a difference that makes now, but yer welcome ta step inside an' have a look around if ya want."

Brigham frowned at the group of guys standing around

a storage unit that had given them all the creeps a little over a month ago. "How did y'all check every crack and crevice in there if nobody walked inside?"

Mickey laughed. "We still got a few tricks up our sleeves. Can't give away industry secrets all at once, mind. Next time yer in our neck o' the woods, pop on by again, and maybe we'll tell ya. Maybe."

The other two chuckled along with him, and Brigham stroked his chin, pretending to think about it. "Hmm. Not sure that's enough of an incentive for me. Tell you what. Throw in a few pints, and you got yourself a deal."

"Oh, aye? And what's in it fer us?"

Brigham spread his arms and grinned. "Getting to drink a few pints with *this* gorgeous face. Obviously."

The men fell into gales of laughter, and Brigham spun to join Halsey outside the unit.

"Hate to say it out loud, cuz, but it looks like we hit another dead end," he mused. "Probably time to *call* it a dead end and move on to Plan Havalon, right?"

She blinked, turned toward him, and tried not to frown as deeply as her instincts demanded. "I think we should step inside and check it out for ourselves."

"Really?" He chuckled as he swept a glance around the inside of the unit. "Come on, Hal. Bare floors, bare walls, and a bit of leftover sand. There's nothing here."

What's his game right now? If he's trying to keep this weird magical energy a secret, he doesn't have to worry about these guys overhearing. Everyone who works for Patrick knows the Ambrosius family dabbles in weird shit, as far as regular humans are concerned...

She raised her eyebrows at her cousin, trying to reinforce that she wasn't backing down from this decision. "Maybe. Still, it's one more road we can't afford *not* to follow to the end. *Don't you think?*"

Apparently, her cousin had no clue what she was talking about. His only response was to laugh again and fix her with a strange look.

No way. There's no way he doesn't feel what's in here.

"Ya know what?" Mickey called from behind them. "'Tis 'bout that time anyhow for me an' the lads ta take a quick fifteen. Think that's enough for yas ta take a good look 'round ta yer full satisfaction?"

Brigham shrugged. "It's not really—"

"Absolutely," Halsey interrupted with a nod and a grateful smile. "That's plenty of time. Thanks."

"Don't mention it. We'll be in the break room at the end o' the hall. Can't miss it. Just don't…try ta pull anytin' apart in there, aye? That'll set off the breach alarm, and nobody wants yas gettin' fried ta Kingdom Come fer bein' a little overzealous."

"Good thing I left my sledgehammer at home, then."

The guys laughed and waggled their fingers as they headed toward the aforementioned break room.

Brigham sighed in exasperation and stared at the ceiling. "You know what I don't get?"

"That's a long list, cuz." Halsey waited until she couldn't see Mickey or his team down the hall, then she carefully stepped into the empty unit. "Why don't you narrow it down for me?"

"I don't get how you make me feel like I did something wrong with all your wink-winks and nudge-nudges without actually saying anything to make sure we're on the same page. Then two seconds later, you're cracking jokes with everyone else, like that's what you've been doing the whole time." He spun to face her, then groaned when he realized she wasn't standing in the same place. "Oh, come on, Hal. What is it this time, huh? What'd I do?"

"Well, unless you're the person who broke in and stole the casket, this has nothing to do with what you or I or anyone else *did wrong*."

"All right, fine. I can explain. First, will you—wait. What?"

She glanced over her shoulder and shook her head. "Not your fault. I'm only…surprised you really don't have a clue what's going on right now."

"Ah-ha! So *that's* what I did. Being clueless." He stuck a finger up like he'd discovered the secrets of the universe before his eager smile folded into another confused frown. "Okay, we've covered why you're giving me those weird looks. Any chance you feel like fillin' a cousin in on what the hell you're talking about?"

Halsey walked to the edge of the sand littering the storage unit floor and stopped when her boots reached the furthest line of tiny, thoroughly scattered grains. Now she felt like she was standing in another open doorway, only this one was invisible and led to the source of the strange magic. "Are you being serious right now?" she murmured as she scanned the unit.

"Ha. Listen, I know sometimes it *seems* like I'm joking about everything because I can, but yeah. Right now, I'm serious. What did I miss?"

For some reason, her attention kept getting drawn back

to the grains of sand. The longer she studied it, the more she noticed something not quite right.

The grains closest to her boots were a bright, glittering off-white color, as close as sand got to actually being white in Ireland. It was the same color as the beaches of Moher where they'd found the coffin. Halsey remembered it well because she'd spent her first few days back in Texas after that trip washing the same sand out of her hair.

That only made it easier to follow her original assumption that something was off about this sand. She followed the train of thought all the way to its unexpected end.

"You gonna give me an answer I can work with, or what?" Brigham chuckled again, but his cousin ignored him as she stepped over the first thin line of almost-white sand that had a real, normal explanation for being here. "Uh, Hal?"

Halsey stopped at the next ridge of grains that looked like they could have fallen off the coffin like all the others. At least, it made the same pattern one would expect from a large amount of transported sand falling off a huge, heavy, rectangular object. It simply wasn't the same, though.

She frowned at the thickest part of the ridge that formed the general outline of the silver coffin and squatted to examine it better. When she hunkered down, there was no denying the surges of new, powerful magic she'd felt in the hallway were coming from directly beneath her.

This sand, which formed a rectangular outline almost impossible to detect when standing, was obviously a different kind. Different color, different size, different thickness, slightly different shape.

Halsey reached out and almost brushed her fingers

along the ridge before she paused and thought better of it. "Two kinds of sand…"

"Okay, listen. If we were gonna find the thief's footprints in here, Patrick and his guys would've found 'em first." Brigham approached her from behind, his footsteps echoing through the unit. "Unless we're dealing with *invisible* footprints, in which case I'm gonna go ahead and say it right now. We're still screwed."

"Actually, I don't think 'invisible footprint' is that far off the mark here."

He sniggered and turned in a slow circle, inspecting the unit again. When he realized his cousin was still crouched in front of a bunch of sand and acting like they'd come to the most logical conclusion in the world, he started toward her again. His smile flickered in and out because he wasn't sure whether to laugh at Halsey's quirks or get seriously concerned. "Hal, I love you, but that makes no fucking sense."

To make sure, she reached behind her toward the scattered sand she knew was from the beaches. She also reached out with her magic, searching for the earthen life force that existed in every grain, as it existed in all the dirt, pebbles, stones, and minerals of the Earth. The light, tickling zap of the white sand's energy flickered up her fingers, and that was when she knew.

It was nothing like the magic rippling off the darker sand in front of her like an ocean of its own.

A slow smile spread across her lips. "Two types of energy."

Brigham stared at her, then turned to double-check that the hallway outside the unit was still empty. "I know

I've been asking you this a lot lately, but are you feeling okay? 'Cause honestly, I can't tell." He walked aimlessly across the unit, heading in her direction again. "One minute, you're Hal. We're cool, and I'm behind you, and we're doing our thing. The next minute, it's like you fell into a well and got dipped in some kinda—"

"Whoa." She extended an arm and tapped her cousin's shin to stop him.

After five years of working closely as partners on monster missions, especially those that required a solid foundation of open communication and mutual trust, Brigham knew what that subtle gesture meant.

He froze instantly, arms spread to maintain his balance and didn't even put his foot back down. "What are we looking at here?"

"The sand, Brigham."

"Are you—" He scoffed and gaped at her. "For real?"

Halsey looked up at him, finally convinced they weren't on the same page for this part of their unsanctioned mission. "You don't feel that?"

"I'm about to feel a cramp in my leg if you don't tell me where to step—"

"Behind you."

He did as she said, then dropped into a squat behind her and to the left to gaze at the sand for himself. "And the sand is…"

"Not the same kind that hitched a ride from the beach. At least, not the beach where we found the coffin."

"What?"

"Invisible footprint, Brigham. Like you said. Only not

one that comes from an actual shoe. More like a magical footprint, I guess."

"Yeah, that's real deep," he replied, heavy on the sarcasm. "Seeing as how magic would *have* to be involved to make it invisible."

Halsey shook her head. "All right, if you can't feel it, that's not on you. I have no idea why *I* can, but we'll figure that one out later. Look at this." She leaned forward slightly, careful not to touch the ridges of new sand that made her think of a high-voltage electric fence, whether or not that was accurate. She pointed at the center of the negative-space rectangle on the floor. "We thought all this came off the coffin, right?"

"Uh-huh. 'Cause that's…what sand does."

"Okay, smartass. What do you see in the middle?"

Brigham smirked and peered at the spot where she was pointing. "Yeah… Sorry, Hal. I got nothing."

"That's the point." Halsey drew her finger back and forth across the air, pointing from one end of the rectangle to the other. "There isn't a single speck of sand *inside* the coffin's outline. That's not an exaggeration. I mean literally."

He shrugged. "Well, yeah. That's where the bottom of the coffin was. Keeping the sand from getting under it."

"When the coffin disappeared, wouldn't there have been at least a little bit of sand left behind, like there is everywhere else?"

"Yeesh." Brigham rolled his eyes, pushed to his feet, then gestured toward the empty rectangle. "It's sand. Sand brushes off. Pretty damn quickly too, when it's dry. That's probably what happened. Patrick's guys transported the coffin over here, and the sand from the beach got brushed off in the process. Simple explanation, cuz, and you're making a whole lotta nothing out of trying to turn it into something else."

"Right." She propped a forearm on her thigh so she could twist to look him in the eye without falling over and touching this more-than-sand before she was ready. "Tell me, *cuz*. When was the last time you brought home something from the beach covered in *this* much sand, but only *one* flat surface was completely brushed off and immaculate?"

Brigham clicked his tongue and lifted what was supposed to be a condescending smile. The expression only lasted a few seconds before he realized he couldn't come up with an answer. Instead of writing off everything his partner said, he understood she was leading this pointless conversation toward something he needed to pay attention to right now.

"What are you saying? Somebody broke into this triple-secured storage facility for weird Ambrosius Clan crap, sprinkled a bunch of sand around the coffin for fun, then took the whole damn thing without anybody noticing?"

Halsey raised her eyebrows and couldn't resist a small smile as she and her cousin put together the pieces they had, one by one. "I think somebody broke into this triple-secured storage facility for weird Ambrosius Clan crap, stole the coffin with *magic*, and *this* is what they left behind."

"Aw, shit. On purpose?"

"I don't think so. It takes a hell of a lot of magic and probably even more skill to do something like this. Obviously." She nodded toward the darker sand again. "Plus, the energy radiating off this stuff is...intense."

"Again, I got nothing on that."

"This is proof, Brigham. Hard to find or even pay attention to if you're not looking closely? Yes. It was seriously well-hidden, that's for sure." Halsey scanned the raised ridge of magically energetic sand. "Which means whoever pulled this off knew what they were doing. They wanted the coffin so badly they were willing to risk being caught. You know..." She shot her cousin a sidelong glance. "By leaving an *almost* invisible footprint."

"Two different kinds of sand," he repeated. "Are you sure?"

"Oh, yeah. I'm sure." Halsey stood and stepped backward to join him, then pointed at the off-white sand along the outer ring. *"That's* from the beach. All this over here? It's something else entirely."

They stood in silence, considering the implications of two different kinds of sand. Then Brigham scratched his head and crinkled his nose. "I don't know, Hal. Yeah, I believe you when you say you can *feel* the difference or whatever. I do."

She snorted and closed her eyes. "Why do I have the feeling there's a 'but' coming after this?"

"*But* you're also the only one of us who feels other things, too. Like weird empathy for monsters—"

"Dude."

"And that one time you were, like, a thousand percent positive there was a gremlin living in my mom's kitchen cabinet above the fridge. Remember that?"

Halsey laughed. "We were *eight*. Plus, it was actually a

gremlin, thank you very much. It happened to move out the day your mom took me seriously enough to check for herself."

"Maybe she wanted you to quit talking about it all day, every day."

"Now you're just making excuses."

"Some excuses are real, Hal. That's all I'm saying. Nobody ever saw the gremlin in the cupboard. *I* can't feel the magic in this weird sand, if that's what you think it is." He jerked a thumb over his shoulder toward the open unit door. "None of *these* guys are gonna be able to feel it, either. We both know that much."

"Okay. I get it." She took a few steps back for breathing room, spread her arms in concession, and shrugged. "You're still in 'Halsey might not be all there upstairs' mode."

"That's not what I'm saying."

"That's exactly what you're saying."

"I'm saying... Maybe you want to find this damn coffin so badly that you're kinda pushing a little too hard."

She sighed and stared at him. "*I* wanna find it so badly. Meaning you don't?"

"*No!*" Brigham shrank into himself when his unintended shout echoed through the unit and escaped into the hall. He got himself back under control with a soft chuckle as he shook his head. "I'm right there with you when it comes to finding this crap and making sure the whole Clan's prepared for what's coming. Hell, I *know* there's something coming. I only mean... Okay. You know how when you're sittin' on the john, trying to drop the kids off at the pool?"

She chortled. "Really? That's where you're taking this?"

"Yeah. And you want it out so bad that you'd do anything to get the job done. Then sometimes, you know, when you push a little too hard, you start seeing stars and hearin' funny noises, and your face gets all hot—"

"Whoa, whoa. Nope." Halsey shook her head and raised both hands for much-needed emphasis. "Stop."

"Aw, come on. It's a good analogy."

"I'm not *pushing too hard*, Brigham. I'm not hallucinating, either, but nice one trying to hide the 'Halsey's crazy' bit inside a story I didn't need about whatever you do on your own time."

Her cousin looked thoroughly reprimanded for half a second before he snorted and smiled sheepishly. "It's a *really* good analogy."

"Fine. You don't think I'm onto anything here. I get it."

"Nah, that's not—"

"Hey, you don't *have* to say it. I know you." She smiled anyway because she also knew there was no way she was wrong. "It's fine, cuz. You don't think there are two different kinds of sand here, and you definitely don't think one of them is infused with so much magic that it's basically not sand anymore. Did I miss anything?"

Brigham's gaze flicked between her face and the rectangle of sand. He shrugged. "That was pretty thorough, actually."

"Good." Halsey faced the sand, wiggled her fingers, and steeled herself for the powerful energy of the not-sand's magic she was about to engage. "Now I'm gonna show you exactly why you're wrong."

CHAPTER FOURTEEN

"Wait a minute..." Brigham examined his cousin, then clicked his tongue. "You did that on purpose."

"Well, I sure as hell didn't bumble into it on accident."

He narrowed his eyes as a suspicious smile flickered. "You were waiting to say that the whole time we were talking, weren't you?"

"Not gonna lie. It has a certain ring to it." Halsey squared herself toward the sand and reached out slightly with open hands. "Didn't wanna waste it."

"Uh-huh. Okay." He looked at her hands. "What are you doing?"

"I already told you. Now, will you please shut up so I can put my magic where my mouth is?"

The muffled click of his back teeth meeting filled the unit, and she couldn't help a smile.

Here we go. If it's sand, it's sand. If it's something else... Well, we'll know that when I'm finished, won't we?

It wasn't only the tips of her fingers tingling now like they had when she'd first reached out. Energy like nothing she'd felt before surged up her fingers, swirled through her hands, and waited for the young elemental to tell it what she wanted. Beneath the foreign magical buzz, though, she felt the life force of the sand.

Technically, it *was* still sand.

Which meant she could call it, manipulate it, and control it like every other natural substance.

So she did.

The darker grains forming the ridges responded instantly. Faster than instantly, even. It was almost as if the sand's magic had anticipated what she'd wanted before she made the conscious decision to form a command.

The first layer of sand leapt from the top of the ridges and into the air, swirling around the rectangle's perimeter once before the next layer jumped up to join it. A soft copper light, so faint it was hardly visible, flared from within the tiny grains. In seconds, the empty storage unit looked like an amateur planetarium with glowing grains of sand swirling around and above the rectangle before being joined by the next layer and the next.

With all her concentration poured into controlling the strange sand without letting the power of its inherent magic consume her, Halsey vaguely noticed Brigham ducking his head and lifting a finger to the corner of his eye. Whether he was joking or it was a natural reaction to flying sand, she didn't know.

She *did* know that none of the sand made it anywhere close to her cousin's face. She could feel every grain individually as if each was a separate extension of herself.

It was the strongest connection she'd ever had to something as simple as minuscule chips of stone heaped together in an endless sea. Part of her wanted to stay here forever.

The other part of her, the one that knew who and what she was, including all the responsibility she carried, knew that was a terrible idea.

Finish it, Halsey. Then you won't have to worry about what's inside the damn sand.

First, she wanted to give her cousin one more demonstration he wouldn't be able to ignore.

When she'd lifted every speck of sand, she'd felt something else as well. An energetic block in the air, which also fit her invisible-footprint analogy perfectly. This one wasn't a mark of what had been left behind, though. It was the mark of what had been taken.

Halsey brought her hands together and urged the sand to do what she wanted. A gentle, clicking rush filled the unit. If she hadn't known what was making that sound, she would have found it difficult to pinpoint where it was coming from.

Brigham certainly did.

He turned in a slow circle, looking at the unit walls and finally dropping his gaze to the floor. "That's not the breach alarm, is it?"

"Forget the security for one second, Brigham." Halsey's tone was more irritated than she'd intended, but it was hard to split her focus between thousands of grains of sand *and* her highly distractible cousin. "Look at that. You're seeing what I'm seeing, right?"

Brigham stared without expression at the swirling, slightly glowing sand that moved in a thick, curving wall around the perimeter of the rectangle. His eyes widened when he saw it.

The noise wasn't part of the warehouse's security system. It came from individual grains of sand smacking against a hard surface. If there had been a glass coffin in the center of the unit, it would have made sense, but there was nothing. It should have been thin air.

That didn't change the fact that the sandstorm surged everywhere *except* where the silver coffin had been. Once more, negative space illuminated the energetic leftovers. Everywhere the grains of sand couldn't touch was perfectly visible because it left the same shape as the coffin.

As soon as she knew Brigham had caught on, Halsey was ready to be done with the whole thing. She brought her hands closer together and glanced down to see them glowing with the same faint copper light.

Again, the strange sand responded to her intentions before she knew what they were.

The next thing she knew, a stream of glowing sand whizzed across the storage unit toward the small, hot space between her palms. Her hands shook as the sand kept coming as if she held an incredibly strong vacuum between her hands.

Really, it was only her powerful connection to her own elemental magic and whatever this type of magic was. It definitely did not belong to an Ambrosius elemental.

After the last trailing flicker of copper grains zipped into the space between her hands, the magical energy grew so hot that Halsey thought she wouldn't be able to finish it. Without warning, all the energy and mass let out a blinding flash of copper light.

Brigham sucked in a sharp breath and flinched away to

avoid the worst of the glare. Yet Halsey couldn't look away. Her own magic wasn't too bright for her, and there was no point missing the incredible thing she'd done. She wanted to watch it all. Watching it, doing it, and *being* it was like nothing she'd accomplished with her magic before. It felt so…right.

The glow faded quickly, and a bright copper sphere the size of a baseball hovered in the space between Halsey's palms. The energetic heat faded too, which made it easier for her to breathe now that she'd completed this strange new thing she hadn't known how to create. It was easier to smile now, too. Especially when she noticed Brigham gaping at the sphere, his jaw unhinged.

She brought her hands together around the sphere and plucked it from the air. Her fingers and palms pressed onto solid, cool metal, which only made her smile widen. The sphere still pulsed with a faint copper light, but somehow, she knew that would fade too.

She arched an eyebrow, faced her cousin, and waited for the orb's internal light to disappear. Then she tossed it up and caught it with a hollow smack. "You ever see regular sand do *this*?"

Brigham's reaction time was slow when she tossed the sphere toward him, but he recovered and fumbled to catch the thing, cradling it against his chest. He tossed it once as she'd done and swallowed thickly. "Holy shit."

"I know."

"I've never seen regular *Hal* do that, I can tell you that much. Hell, I've never seen any elemental pull this kinda trick outta thin…" He paused, turned the sphere over, then tapped it with his knuckles. Sure enough, the orb elicited a hollow *ping* that could only be described as metallic. "It's copper. Legit freaking copper."

"Uh…yeah. That's what it looks like, I guess." After waiting patiently for all of five seconds for him to return her creation, Halsey flicked her fingers for the sphere. The thing ripped itself out of her cousin's grasp, whizzed through the air, and smacked into her palm.

Brigham whipped his head up. "What the actual…"

She playfully shook the orb at him. "Not regular sand. Like I've been trying to tell you this whole time."

"Well, *now*." He gestured in exasperation. "Jesus, Hal. You should've led with that."

"You believe me now, right?"

"Come on. I believed you before." Though he was clearly impressed by her recent demonstration and its surprising new product, his attention was pulled elsewhere. Toward the center of the unit, where now there was only slick tile floor and empty space. "Hey, something about that feel funky to you?"

He nodded toward the space. Even if he hadn't, Halsey would have known what he was referring to.

Don't lay it out for him. Let the guy make one discovery on his own. Especially after giving him such a tough act to follow.

Halsey cradled her sphere and forced herself not to smile as she stared at the space. "A little, yeah. Maybe you should—"

"Oh, yeah. Totally. I got this." He rolled his shoulders back, nodded confidently, then strode across the unit until he stood where the edge of the rectangular sand line had been. Once there, he didn't look too confident. Which probably had something to do with his preferred method of investigation being to reach out with his bare hand.

Halsey cleared her throat.

"What?" He paused and retracted his hand a touch.

"You're not noodling for catfish, cuz. You sure you wanna do it...like that?"

His signature grin flashed, and he followed it up with a bonus wink. "I got this one, Hal. Trust me."

He turned back toward the nothingness and continued reaching out.

Fortunately, he'd given this new investigation his full attention and didn't have any left to notice his cousin's muffled snort.

Teamwork. That's what this is. That's what we're gonna keep calling it.

When he was satisfied, Brigham snatched a deep breath, straightened his back, and nodded. "See? All good."

"And?"

"There's...absolutely nothing there." A frown dampened his good mood, and he withdrew his hand to study that instead, turning it over this way and that. "Total zilch. Which is super weird, right?"

"When there was definitely something there two minutes ago? Yeah, I'd call that strange."

"Right." He studied the clean, empty space on the floor again, then grunted. "Man...and here I was thinking I had the whole thing figured out."

"Really?"

"Yup. Look." He turned his flat palms sideways and chopped each of his points on an imaginary cutting board. "First, we had coffin and no sand. Then, zero coffin and all the sand that isn't actually sand. Maybe, like, some kind of magical residue that…fell outta the guy or something."

"Oh, yeah." Halsey nodded and pressed her lips together as she fought to keep from laughing. "Yeah, that's a highly professional assessment."

"I know, but I'm not done." Oblivious to her sarcasm, Brigham chopped with both hands and added, "So the zero-coffin, hella-sand stage also comes with a glass case, right?"

She choked and muttered, "Of emotion?"

"What?"

"Nothing."

"That case was *here*, Hal. I saw it. You saw it. Hell, I *felt* it when those little pieces of sand knocked against the thing like they were trying to get somebody to open the door. It was like the creepy weirdness crawling over my skin when we first found that coffin. I know you know what I'm talking about."

"I do." With that, at least, Halsey didn't have to hold anything back. "I feel it here now, so we're on the same page there."

"Finally." Brigham dropped his hands against his thighs and heaved a breath. "What's the deal with that, huh? One second, the coffin-shaped case of disappearance is here in our faces, getting smacked by loads of sand. The next? Shit. *You* pulled the sand into your freaky little ball there, which isn't even technically supposed to be metal after what you did to that sand. It should be glass." He stared at the orb, then added, "Or much smaller amounts of metal with a bunch of burn-off and a shitload of extra byproduct. I'm guessing there wasn't a whole lot of magnetite involved, or we'd be telling a different story."

Halsey frowned at the pure copper sphere, then chuckled. "Wow. Somebody's been brushing up on their chemical reactions."

"*Al*chemical, Hal. It's basic metalworking." He pointed at her but stared at the orb. "Which is so totally *not* what you did there. At all."

"I know. This was…something else."

"Uh-huh. You felt an outside thing, you called it to you, we discovered a glass coffin-shaped shield or whatever the hell we're calling it, and now… I mean, now everything's gone."

"Not gone." She spun the copper orb in her hand and noticed odd, segmented lines and etchings that *almost* looked intentional, though there was nothing she recognized. "Definitely not gone, dude. It's…transmuted."

"Huh. *Now* look who's getting fancy about it."

"If you have something better to call it, by all means. Throw your ideas out there, dude."

Brigham rolled his eyes. "Nah. Transmuted works. Except I have even more questions now."

"I have no idea how I felt the magic in the sand, and you didn't." Halsey met his gaze and shook her head. "I have no idea how I transmuted probably-not-sand into pure copper because I *do* know it doesn't work like that. Trust me. I have all the questions too, but I'm telling you that you're not getting answers from me, okay? If I had them, I'd tell you."

Her cousin gawked at her, blinked once, then popped

his lips. "Actually, I was gonna ask whose magic you bottled up there in a neat little ball."

"Oh. Well, I don't know that either."

"Yeah, obviously." They shared a wry laugh, then Brigham gestured at her copper ball. "What're we gonna do with that thing?"

"Keep it. Obviously."

"Yeah…" Brigham scratched his head and glanced into the hallway again, which was fortunately still empty. "I don't think Patrick and his guys play by the Finders-Keepers rule."

"If it has anything to do with the coffin, they'll be happy it's gone. No questions asked."

"True. Still, maybe we should—"

A door creaked and banged open somewhere in the hallway, followed by the echoing laughter and conversation of the three men as they headed out of their break room.

CHAPTER FIFTEEN

"Okay," Brigham stated. "Next question is what the hell we're supposed to tell these guys when they find this unit looking like we double-timed it with a steam cleaner."

Halsey scanned the floor. "There's still a little sand in here…"

"Yeah, like one percent of what there *was*. You don't think it's gonna make anybody suspicious?"

The conversation in the hall grew closer by the second. It sounded like Mickey and his guys were right outside the open door.

"They might say something to Patrick about it after we're gone," Halsey suggested. "Still, if he says our little visit stays between us, it'll stay between us."

"Yeah, and how many times do regular humans see things they can't explain and actually keep their mouths shut about it? You remember that one time we had to crash Annie Peyton's birthday party because of all the—"

"Well, look who's still here."

They turned to see the crew standing by the open storage unit. Mickey folded his arms and smiled at them. Kyle stood without expression, working a toothpick between his teeth. The third guy, who Halsey thought someone had called Merl, noisily sipped something hot from a foam cup.

"Find what ya were lookin' fer in there?" Mickey's raised eyebrow and easy smile made him look more amused by the cousins' attempts to search an empty unit than anything else.

Halsey returned the smile and shrugged. "More like what we didn't find, actually."

"Sure. That's ta be expected." He stepped toward the door and swept a glance inside. Kyle and Merl briefly studied the unit as well, though neither looked excited about moving any closer, so they didn't. When nobody said anything else, Mickey looked between the cousins, and his smile disappeared. "The two o' yas didn't get up ta any funny business in there while we were out, did ya?"

Brigham's thick swallow was loud in the ensuing silence, and he glanced at the copper orb resting in Halsey's hand. "Listen. We can only explain so much, and it probably won't make much sense anyway. But—"

He was interrupted by Mickey throwing his head back and roaring with laughter. Kyle and Merl chimed in with sniggers and soft chuckles. Brigham frowned at Halsey when she joined them.

"I'm takin' the piss wit' ya, boyo. Look at this place. O' course ya didn't do anytin' to it." He glanced at his two buddies, who looked only slightly less amused. Merl kept staring into the storage unit over the rim of his cup.

None of them want to stand in front of this thing any longer than they have to. Totally fine by me.

"O' course..." Mickey turned back toward the cousins. This time, his smile held wariness, and he added in a conspiratorial voice, "If ya *had* gotten into anytin' funny while we weren't lookin', go ahead an' keep that ta yerselves, aye? We don't wanna know."

Halsey leaned toward him and murmured, "Deal."

"Ha!" Mickey's laugh broke the tense air of suspicion, then he waved them toward him. "Come on outta there, then. An empty unit, sure, but it's the only empty unit we all want locked up tight and probably forever. If I had my way, I'd throw away the key, but Pat's got a bunch o' rules 'bout not tamperin' with company property and all that. And a job's a job."

Halsey took off, walking quickly but not too quickly out of the storage unit. Kyle and Merl stood back as much as they could without looking afraid of the empty unit that had once housed the magically unpredictable silver coffin. Brigham, on the other hand, seemed frozen to the spot. He looked over his shoulder at the thin but still visible scattering of natural white sand and shook his head.

"Yer cousin have a death wish?" Kyle asked as he pulled the toothpick from his mouth.

"I think he's a little confused," Halsey replied, trying not to laugh. "And disappointed. Looks like we hit another dead end."

"*We* could've told ya that. Been a dead end since the day we brought that creepy box 'ere. Sometin' not right 'bout that ting."

"O' course there ain't nutin' right wit it," Mickey called

over his shoulder as Brigham stepped out of the storage, though he still looked confused. "The ting up an' disappeared itself in the middle o' the day, and wit none of us the wiser to it."

Merl slurped his hot drink and mumbled, "He's talkin' 'bout what happened since."

Halsey nodded, her eyes wide with interest. "What's been happening since?"

The garage door released a loud, metallic rumble as Mickey pulled it shut, which was apparently easier than opening the thing. "Don't go fillin' their heads wit all your superstitious junk, now." The lights on the keypad and the biometric security scanner flashed red as he knelt to reapply the enormous padlock. "Waste o' time, if ya ask me."

"Well, nobody asked ya," Merl responded curtly. "And t'isn't superstition, Mickey. You know as well as the rest of us that tings 'round 'ere have—"

"That's enough." Mickey straightened, dusted off his hands, and gazed firmly at his coworker. "I won't tell ya again. These two didn't come here ta listen ta yer country-laid fairytales, and Pat's not payin' the rest of us nearly enough ta listen to it day in and out. Besides, we got an incomin' shipment to meet on t'other side, an' Jimmy's always early. Let's go."

Merl sipped out of his to-go cup, then sighed and headed toward his apparent supervisor.

Mickey extended a hand to Halsey. "Good meetin' ya. Sorry we couldn't help ya more."

She shook firmly. "We got what we came here for,

anyway. Even if it was only confirming what Patrick's already told us. Thanks for taking the time out of your day."

"Don't mention it."

Mickey and Brigham shook next, and only now did Halsey's cousin look recovered enough from his shock and confusion to pay attention. "See you around."

"If we do, it better be fer sometin' other'n that box." Mickey chuckled and added, "Kyle'll walk ya out. Unless there's anytin' else here ya wanted ta get yer eyes on before ya call it a day."

"No, I think we've seen everything," Halsey confirmed. "Thanks again."

"All right." With a casual wave, Mickey turned and headed down the hallway toward the break room. Merl slurped his drink again, then lifted it in a farewell salute as he followed his boss.

Kyle hooked his thumbs through his jeans belt loops, clicked his tongue, and turned in the opposite direction. "We're off this way. Ya sure there's nutin' else ya wanna look at?"

"We're good here, man." Brigham stared at the enormous padlock. "Thanks."

He and Halsey fell in line behind the employee who'd mentioned a curious subject before his coworker had gotten in trouble for agreeing with him. That was the only thing on Halsey's mind as they followed Kyle down the narrow hallway and through the twists and turns of the facility's complicated layout.

Before she could say anything to get Kyle talking,

Brigham coughed, glanced at the copper orb in her hand, and muttered, "Really?"

"What?"

"Right out in the open like that?"

She snorted. "Did *you* bring a purse, cuz? 'Cause I didn't."

"Very funny." He looked at Kyle walking ten feet ahead of them, then lowered his voice. "For real, Hal. Doesn't feel like a good idea to walk around Ireland waving a magic-stuffed copper ball around, don't you think?"

"Well, where do you *want* me to put it?"

"I don't know. Tuck it into your jacket or something."

She snorted at her thin, green canvas jacket, the only appropriate outerwear for Dublin at the end of July. "Right. A giant lump right here isn't conspicuous at all."

"Oh, *now* you care about being conspicuous."

"Says the guy who's suddenly worried about every little thing. What's going on with you?"

"What's going on? With me?" Brigham scoffed before actually considering the question. "I have no idea what's happening here, Hal. *That's* what's going on. Disappearing coffins, sand that isn't sand, and you being some kind of… transmutation whisperer back there."

She laughed, then covered it up when he shot her a scathing glare.

"Listen, I don't like being the voice of caution here—"

"Or paranoia."

"—but none of this falls in our wheelhouse. You get that, right? Hell, the last five weeks have been one crazy thing after the other, and I don't know which way is up anymore. Now my best friend's making toys out of someone else's magic, and I... It's..."

After waiting for him to finish, which he never quite managed, Halsey smiled reassuringly. "I'm starting to understand why the Council's been treating this the way they have."

"What?"

"I'm pretty sure they've been freaking out as hardcore as you are right now. Only for a lot longer than a few weeks."

"Hey, I didn't start freaking out until you went all elemental-wildcard back there."

She opened her mouth, paused, then shot him a crooked smile. "Okay, that's fair."

When she tossed the copper orb in her hand and turned it over to admire the strange thing she'd created out of her own magic and someone else's, Brigham's scowl returned. "You don't think that thing's gonna draw more trouble to us than it's worth?"

"Honestly? I don't know."

"Great."

"Brigham, relax." She couldn't help laughing at this odd, overly cautious side of her cousin she hadn't seen before. "Think of it this way. We collected a bunch of residual magic lying around inside a facility operated by regular humans. This way, we're keeping everyone safe, right? Nobody is gonna walk into that storage unit and accidentally start something they don't know how to deal with. This is a good thing.

"Besides, I don't think any of this will be an issue with

regular humans, anyway. You heard Mickey. He basically said the unit looked exactly the same as the last time he'd bothered to check it. I don't know about you, but that makes *me* think regular humans couldn't see the extra sand anyway."

Brigham scrunched his nose and scanned the ceiling. "You forgot potentially volatile."

"Huh?"

He dropped his gaze to the copper sphere again. "Residual magic, sure. Still, if it did all that as a byproduct of someone else's weird-ass disappearing spell, that thing could explode at any second."

"I feel like you didn't hear what I said."

"Well, you're entitled to your feelings, Hal. *I* feel like this doesn't gel with our long and fairly successful history of *making good choices*. You know, as a team."

She pressed her lips against a laugh.

He's seriously freaking out. I don't think he's gonna calm down until I prove this thing isn't gonna explode the second we turn our backs.

Telling her cousin that the transmuted orb wasn't dangerous because she simply *knew* wouldn't go over well. She'd already tried that. Brigham was still trying to wrap his head around how everything they thought they knew about the supernatural world they'd sworn to keep hidden was changing faster than they could keep up with. It wasn't only monsters acting differently.

Now, apparently, they were dealing with changes in their own magic. Or at least Halsey was. Whether or not that meant anything was still anyone's guess. For now, trying to change his mind or reassure him about the orb was a lost cause.

That meant she had to change tactics. And if that didn't work on her cousin, she could at least turn her attention to something that had equally piqued her interest but wasn't as irritating.

CHAPTER SIXTEEN

Halsey clasped her hands behind her back, conveniently hiding the orb from view, and picked up the pace, leaving Brigham to figure out his magically existential crisis on his own. "Hey, Kyle."

The man leading them out of the warehouse slowed, looked over his shoulder, and widened his eyes like he'd forgotten the two of them had been following him. "Ma'am?"

She huffed laughter and caught up to him. "Call me Hal."

Brigham realized he was considerably behind. "Dude, what is she... Oh, come on," he muttered. With a frustrated growl, he picked up the pace so he wouldn't miss anything.

"All right, then, Hal." A tiny smile flickered across Kyle's lips. "What can I do fer ya?"

"Hopefully, answer another question, if you don't mind." He nodded, looking uncertain but willing to help, and she dove in. "Back at the unit, when you and Merl were talking about what's been happening since that coffin showed up at the warehouse—"

"Naw." He shook his head. "Sorry ta bother ya wit all that. I wasn't plannin' on sayin' anytin' else, but Merl's got a bloody big mouth on 'im. Best ta forget about it, aye?"

"That's the thing, though." Halsey hoped her small frown looked more apologetic than frustrated. "I don't want to forget about it."

The man looked like he would start talking, then he sighed. "'Tis nuthin', really. And Mickey'll flip his shite if he gets wind o' me tellin' ya a bunch o' tall tales."

"You think they're more than tall tales, though. Don't you?"

Clearly conflicted about opening his mouth, perhaps because he couldn't bring himself to lie to her, Kyle looked ahead and bit his lower lip.

Damn. It must be bad if he can't say it out loud in an empty hallway where no one will know.

She looked back at Brigham, who had caught up and fallen in line on her left, while Kyle set a slow, thoughtful pace on her right. Her cousin also looked interested in the tall tales that probably were more than that, but he wasn't saying anything, either.

Really? She gave him a look, but he shook his head and shrugged one shoulder. *Okay, so the guy who can weasel information out of anybody with a friendly conversation feels like taking a break today. Awesome.*

What she wanted to do was grab Brigham by the shoulders, haul him in front of Kyle, and force him to ask the right questions. Unfortunately, people didn't work like that.

After drawing a deep breath and releasing it slowly, Halsey turned the copper sphere over behind her back and smiled sympathetically at the warehouse employee. "Listen, Kyle. We know there are a lotta people out there who'd say the same as Mickey about all this stuff. That it's only a bunch of stories, right? Things people tell themselves because they can't come up with any other explanation, but none of the stories are ever worth their weight."

That seemed to get the man's attention. For the first time, he looked at her as if she was an interesting person and not some random relation of the company's owner.

Yep. Now he's listening.

Finally, Brigham caught on to her ploy and beat her to the next part of the conversation.

"We're not those people, man," he claimed with a smile. "Promise."

"We get it," Halsey added. "Mickey's your supervisor. You wanna listen to him. Looking at it from his perspective, I'm sure he was trying to save Brigham and me from what he thinks is more trouble and frustration than it's worth. Especially after everything that happened with the coffin, right? He's not *our* supervisor, though." When Kyle looked up in surprise, she knew she had him. "Mickey doesn't call the shots on what we do and don't want to hear."

Brigham snorted, which made Kyle blink.

"True story, bro," Brigham agreed. "Who are *we* gonna tell? Not anybody who doesn't wanna hear it. That's for damn sure."

Kyle's hesitation fractured. He chuckled as if he couldn't believe he was being roped into this by a couple of

Americans his own age who were technically two parts of his employer's larger whole. "Right. Ya had me at Mickey doesn't call the shots."

Bingo.

They all laughed, then Kyle turned right down the next intersecting hallway, stopped, and waited for them to catch up. Once they rounded the corner, the man looked up and down the next hallway to make sure they were alone, then grinned. "Feels like sneakin' 'round wit Mary Higgins out the back o' her pa's shop so he wouldn't see us together."

"Only better." Brigham spread his arms. "This time, you get *both* of us."

Halsey choked on a laugh, and Kyle frowned at Brigham before slowly nodding.

"Not sure I'd call that better, lad."

Brigham sniggered, then blinked when he caught Halsey staring at him. "What?"

She didn't have time to make fun of him anymore, because Kyle dove right into storytelling mode. He lowered his voice further and ducked his head like they might be discovered by someone above them at any second.

"Now, I'm not gonna say Dublin doesn't already have its own strange happenin's from time ta time. The whole o' Ireland's got tales of magic 'n beasties 'n the like. Ya know, the ones that've been 'round for hundreds o' years."

"Pooka. Banshee. Changelings." Brigham nodded briskly. "We get the gist of it, yeah."

"Aye, but this? This is sometin' different. Started up 'bout five…nah. Six weeks ago. Ya already know that, don't ya? Same day the lads brought in that box or coffin or whatever ya wanna call it. Now, that ting was crazy enough on its own. Flashin' and shimmerin' like it had some kinda fairie inside it fightin' ta get out. Never could tell *when* the ting was 'bout ta start actin' up, but when it did..." Kyle released a low whistle. "Makes it real hard ta tink o' anytin' else, and that's not helpful in a warehouse full of valuable tings 'n heavy machinery."

Halsey and Brigham nodded, watching the man intently for cues about where he was taking this little story.

Let's get to the point, Kyle. If you don't have anything to say that isn't about how creepy that coffin is, we're wasting our time.

The man glanced down the hall again out of reflex. This part of the warehouse was so silent and so empty, they would have known the second anyone else headed toward them. He nodded for a few seconds longer like he was trying to reassure himself. "That's when the weird shite kicked up. Started wit a bad feelin' here in the warehouse, right? Everybody felt it. When that silver box up and disappeared, we thought fer sure that was the end of it. 'Twasn't.

"Next day, I kept feelin' sometin' watchin' me, aye? Sneakin' 'round. Spyin' on me. Like t'was crawlin' through the walls 'n waitin' fer the right moment ta pounce. Thought I was losin' me mind fer about a week before Merl finally said sometin'. He'd been feelin' it, too. Then a few more lads started talkin' in the halls and the break room 'bout the same ting. Brian Maguire tried ta convince us all t'was a company-wide curse after handlin' all the weird shite we pick up fer ye 'n yers and bringin' it back here. Fer doin' our jobs."

Brigham snorted. "Don't worry, man. There's no such thing—" He grunted when Halsey elbowed his ribs but didn't say anything else.

Kyle continued. "Be that what 'tis, it weren't only the creepy-crawly feelin' we got 'round 'ere every day o' the week and Sundays. Nah, it started spreadin' a lot farther'n right 'ere at the warehouse. It moved ta…other tings."

Halsey raised her eyebrows and leaned forward, trying to telegraph her intense interest in what came next. *This guy knows how to tell a story. Points for suspense, but let's get to the part that might be useful.*

Kyle, however, seemed to have gotten lost in his own memory of what had been happening here. He stared blankly at a spot on the wall behind his avid listeners until Brigham stepped in.

"What other things?"

After sucking in a sharp breath, Kyle blinked and came back to the present. "Aye. Tings I never thought I'd hear and see and carry wit me ta keep me up at night. Not as a grown man. And I came up in Donegal. Way out in the country. Spent hours wit my Gram scourin' the flowerbeds fer fairies and hangin' up wreaths and talismans over the door ta keep the pookas out o' the house. Steppin' wide 'round fairy circles and the like. Thought I heard a leprechaun laughin' at me from out in the fog a time or two. So the strange and the inexplicable hasn't even been all that strange and inexplicable fer me.

"Yet there's no name for the shadows movin' 'cross the walls in the bright o' day. Or the growlin' laughter that followed me all the way home from the bus stop after my shift, only whenever I turn 'round, there's no one there. For two weeks. Had ta change my route after that 'cause I was startin' ta lose sleep over it."

"Yeah, I would, too," Brigham offered with a serious frown.

Halsey didn't have anything to say. *Could be monsters, sure. Except this sounds like a guy who's into folklore and fairytales was already losing too much sleep and found another magical explanation for it.*

Kyle nodded like they were all on the same page and in this together. "Sounds mental. Believe me, I know. Talk ta any o' the other lads on Pat's crew, and ye'll hear more'n enough o' the same. Then talk ta anyone outside the city, Galway or Clare or even Sligo, and they'll tell ya more. Aye, then they'll tell ya 'bout the howlin'."

The cousins shared a knowing glance, and Halsey forced herself not to cheer because he'd finally gotten to something good. "The howling?"

"Aye. There's always been a few here and there. Mostly the real wolves, but sometimes they don't *quite* sound the same. This isn't that. This is dozens of 'em at once, roamin' t'rough towns and villages, out in forests and fields. My cousin Thomas swears he saw a *wolf-man* out his bedroom window 'bout five nights back. Whatever t'was, sometin' had ta have spooked the horses, and the chicken coop was empty the next morn. Whole ting looked like they were housin' bombs in there, not birds."

Brigham wrinkled his nose. "Damn."

"That's it. Right on the nose. *Damned.*" Kyle glanced between the members of his two-person audience. "I haven't breathed a word o' this ta anyone, but about tree, almost four weeks ago, I tink I've seen the same. Not only one wolf-man but dozens of 'em. I know 'bout all the movies and books and fun, entertainin' tings ta keep the kiddies shiverin' in their boots, but this weren't that, either. Weren't my imagination. I saw a whole damn pack of 'em racin' 'cross the field behind the house. Half the time on four legs, t'other half on two. One o' those nights, there was a woman with 'em."

Yes. There it is.

Halsey's lips parted and curled until she was grinning at the man clearly disturbed by retelling his own stories. "A woman…"

"Sounds bloody ridiculous, doesn't it? One woman, all on her own, walkin' across a field at night under the dark moon. Not a single one o' those beasties paid her any attention. She weren't even afraid. Just kept walkin' and walkin'. I finally got up the stones ta open my door and tell her she shouldn't be out in the dark like that with all the crazy tings poppin' up out o' nowhere. Would've offered her my extra bed, but I didn't have the chance. She was there one second, gone the next. Up and disappeared on the wind. 'Twas an awful lot like yer vanishin' silver box, come ta think of it."

"What did she look like?" Halsey asked. Brigham frowned at her, but she ignored him.

"The woman?" Kyle scrunched his features in an effort to remember, then shook his head. "She wasn't anytin' more'n a dark figure walkin' across a dark field. All's I can say is she had long, dark hair. Or at least it looked dark from t'other side of my window. Wearin' some kinda shift. Ya know, a night-dress or the like. And I tink she was barefoot. Which, ya know, made me wonder fer a bit if she was all there upstairs ta begin wit. Nobody in their right mind would be walkin' 'round like that wit all the howlin' and snarlin' and strange voices comin' out o' dark places lately. All of it since that box o' yers got locked up here and vanished, anyhow."

"That's..." Brigham stared at the concrete floor in front of Kyle's boots and shook his head. "A lot to take in."

"Ya don't believe a word o' what I said, do ya?"

"Oh, we believe you," Halsey insisted. "Trust me. We've seen more than you can even imagine—"

He laughed bitterly and stepped back, waving his hands. "Don't tell me any more'n that. I don't need someone else's stories takin' up space in my head wit all the rest o' my own. But I do have ta ask..." After clearing his throat a few times, he looked back and forth between them. He made Halsey think of her younger cousins, who already knew about monsters, asking whether Santa Claus and the Tooth Fairy were real. "Either of ya have any idea what all this is?"

"Nope." Brigham stuck out his lower lip and elbowed Halsey for good measure. "Not a clue, bud. Honestly, it sounds like you had a few Wanderers passing through."

"Wanderers?"

"Oh yeah. Spirits, you know?"

"Like kelpies 'n banshees?"

"More or less. They're all a little different, right? These aren't native to Ireland, though. When you're dealing with a Wanderer, there's no telling exactly where they came from 'cause it could honestly be anywhere. Which makes it hard to help them or figure out what they're looking for. Most of 'em aren't even looking for anything, really. They just...move."

"Is that right?"

"Yep." When Brigham folded his arms and lifted his chin, he looked every bit the serious professional coughing up free advice. "They're harmless for the most part. Still, I'd stay inside and not try to interact with 'em anyway, you know?"

Halsey shifted and leaned against the wall to observe her cousin. *If I didn't know any better, I'd call that highly impressive.*

"Well, now." Kyle stuck the toothpick he'd been holding onto back in his mouth and rolled it around with his tongue. "Can't say I've heard o' those, but I'm... Ha. Not in the business of knowin' all there is ta know, am I? I'll tell ya what. That takes a bloody big weight off me, hearin' that somebody else knows what's happenin' 'round here. Tanks fer that."

"Don't mention it." Brigham shrugged and laughed self-consciously. "Best not to mention it to anyone else either. Unless one of your buddies has already seen these things for themselves, obviously, I'd say it's safe then. You never know how people are gonna react when they hear about stuff like this and aren't ready for it, though."

"Oh, aye. Ya don't have ta tell me that. Reckon I won't even be tellin' Merl 'bout this one, either. He'd be runnin' his mouth halfway to Roscommon and back 'bout tings he hasn't even seen wit his own two eyes."

"Good idea."

"Last question," Halsey cut in before the guys could seal the deal with a handshake or something and never talk about this again. "Have you seen the...wolf-men again since that first time?"

"Nah. I only hear 'em every couple o' nights. Some

nights closer'n others, o'course. Still far too close fer my likin'."

"Right. What about the woman? Have you seen her again?"

Kyle shook his head and thoughtfully scraped his teeth with the toothpick. "No sign o' her after that first time. Glad of it, too, now that I know what she is."

"And you know to steer clear and let them do their thing," Brigham reminded him with a warning finger.

The other man laughed. "Aye. I promise I won't forget. Was there, uh…anytin' else ya wanted ta know?"

The cousins made a show of looking at each other in consideration, then Brigham shrugged. Halsey smiled at their guide and shook her head. "I think that's it. Thanks."

"Oh, hey." Brigham pulled his wallet from his back pocket and flipped through its contents. "If you hear or see anything else, more wolf-men, the woman, or any other kinda creature your Gram wouldn't have a good explanation for, give us a call." He produced a plain white business card between two fingers. "Always a good plan to help each other, right?"

"That's how I try ta look at it." Kyle studied the card, which only had Brigham's name and cell number on it, then turned it over to find nothing on the other side. He chuckled. "All right. Huddle's over. Let's get ya outta here."

CHAPTER SEVENTEEN

It would have been easy to tell Kyle they weren't in a hurry because where Halsey and Brigham needed to be next depended on the response they were still waiting on from the Havalon Clan here in Ireland. That wasn't Kyle's business, so they followed him back to the warehouse's front door and hit the road again.

Only after they'd settled in their two-room hotel suite with beers in hand did they start discussing everything else they'd discovered in the acquisitions warehouse. Almost by accident.

The only reason Halsey brought up Kyle's fantastic story was that Brigham wouldn't stop checking his phone. "Still no word from the Havalons?"

He scoffed and shook his head. "Nothing. At all. Like not even one of those automated replies. You know, 'Thanks for contacting the Havalon Clan. We try our best to respond to all emails within forty-eight hours.' How hard is it to let another elemental know you got the message?"

She looked away from him before she could laugh. "Maybe they only check emails once a week or something. I can't imagine any elemental Clan has a need for a prompt and attentive customer service department."

"Yeah, but I left a voicemail and sent at least three texts to three different numbers. And yes, Hal, I double-checked they were the right numbers."

"Okay, first of all, we're here. They know that now. Someone will get back to us. Second, you need to put the phone down."

Brigham rolled his eyes and refreshed his email inbox.

"Now."

"Damn it. It's not like I asked them to meet with us for kicks." He tossed his phone onto the cushion beside him and slumped back on the couch. "I was very clear. 'An urgent matter affecting all elemental Clans.' You can't misinterpret that."

"Hey, instead of complaining about what somebody else *isn't* doing, why don't we focus on our wins today?"

His gaze dropped to the copper sphere she'd set on the coffee table between them. "Yeah, I'm still not sure I'd call that thing a win, Hal."

"I'm not talking about the ball." She pulled her legs onto the armchair, crossed them beneath her, then sipped her ice-cold beer. "I'm talking about Kyle."

"What? Why?" Brigham sniggered as he lifted his own drink to his lips. "You give him your number or something?"

"Here we go…" Halsey rolled her eyes and drank again. "His *story*, Brigham. The things he said have been happening here since we found the coffin. Specifically, since the coffin *disappeared*."

"Right. That was a good chat. Hey, maybe I started a new thing, you know? Wanderers. Every monster story's gotta start somewhere, right?"

"I think that only applies to stories about real monsters."

"Yeah, but I sold the hell out of that fake-monster story." He grinned and raised his beer in a toast. "Here's to thinking fast and talking faster."

"Dude, I'm trying to have a serious conversation with you."

"I know, I know. Just..."

Brigham ogled her drink. She begrudgingly raised the beer and drank with him, unable to disagree that he *had* come up with a convincing explanation on the spot for what Kyle had seen.

When their toast was over, Brigham sighed, smacked his lips, and crossed one leg over the other. "Okay. We're looking at...what? Local superstitious Irishman spots a werewolf pack migrating across his back yard? Mysterious woman makes a ghostly, barefoot appearance?"

Halsey raised an eyebrow and smiled crookedly. "You know it was more than that."

"I don't, actually."

"Fine. We both know there's an *incredibly* high probability it's a lot more than your half-assed summary. He said dozens of werewolves. Two weeks *after* we left Ireland the first time."

He shrugged. "Yeah, well, when your partner's opposed

to *eradicating* certain troublesome monsters, they're gonna come back. Not that surprising."

"True. If you ignore all the details he gave us about *when* he saw them."

"What details?"

"He said 'under the dark moon.'"

Brigham shook his head. "Yeah, and? Shit gets dark at night."

"A *new moon*, Brigham. New moon. As in zero moon in the night sky. The opposite of a full moon." Halsey stared at him in disbelief. "Lemme know when you start receiving the signal, cuz…"

For a moment, she truly thought he wouldn't figure it out on his own. Finally, he gasped and snapped his fingers. "A full moon, which is the only time werewolves turn."

"*There* we go."

His proud smile lasted two seconds before the implications dawned on him. "Aw, shit. Are you telling me werewolves are turning every damn night of the month now? That was the only way to predict when they'd show up."

Halsey nodded. "It definitely fits the bill by not fitting the bill. All the monsters are doing what they aren't supposed to, and we have an eyewitness account from a *normie*. Werewolves running around under a new moon. Not ideal."

"Yeah, no shit." Brigham upended his beer and guzzled it like it had personally offended him.

She waited until he finished to dive into the second almost-unbelievable thing Kyle had mentioned. It would have been completely unbelievable if they hadn't already suspected it. "And the woman."

"The woman." Her cousin rolled his eyes. "There's always a story about a lost, confused woman floating in the darkness like a wraith to lure in unsuspecting victims or get help with her unfinished business. You name it, it's been seen before."

"In the middle of a pack of werewolves under a new moon?"

"What? When did the werewolves come back into this? No, Hal. Those are two different things."

"No, they're *not*." She chuckled and leaned back, propping her beer on one knee. "Wow. You were so freaked out today that you can't even remember the guy's whole story."

"I wasn't *that* freaked out…"

"Well, either that or you took way too many painkillers this morning, and now I'm paying for it."

Brigham looked everywhere except at his cousin, then growled in defeat. "Okay, fine. Your weird little séance with the magical sand gave me the heebies for a bit. I admit it. Still, are *you* sure you aren't mixing up different parts of the guy's story?"

She didn't even have to think to recall Kyle's words. "'Sounds bloody ridiculous, doesn't it? One woman, all on her own, walking across a field at night under the dark moon, and not a single one of those beasties out there paid her any attention. She weren't even afraid.' You can quote me *and* Kyle on that one, cuz. It's verbatim."

After gaping at her for several seconds, Brigham cackled. "Shit. How do you *do* that?"

"Raw talent, I guess. Don't worry. There are plenty of things you can do that I can't."

"Yeah, but that one would make a helluva party trick."

Halsey smiled tightly. "Can we try to stay on track here?"

"Sure. If that's what he said, it means you think he saw the Matriarch out there."

"You don't? Come on, Brigham. One woman, all alone, walking across a dark field at night in the middle of a *werewolf* pack that turned under a *new moon*. Does it scream cause and effect? Not really. There's a certain suspension of disbelief we have to take here, though."

He pursed his lips and dipped his head toward her. "Something tells me you don't know what that means."

"Shut up. We all know you're the logic-and-reason guy, but there *is* none anymore. That got tossed out the window when monsters started deviating from *what they are*, and a giant silver coffin washed up from the ocean. Open. Empty. With a giant slash mark across the lid, and don't tell me you've changed your mind about what could've made a mark like that on a huge hunk of metal."

"Werewolf," Brigham muttered. "Yeah, I remember."

"Good."

"That's only assuming his story matches up with what he actually saw, not to mention what actually happened."

He had a point there. Halsey countered it with a few minor details she hadn't expected to be so useful in their brainstorming session. "He said his Gram taught him how to look for fairies, pookas, and leprechauns, right? Checking flowerbeds and rotting logs and mushrooms growing in a circle, more or less. I bet Kyle's Gram is old-school. Attentive. I bet she taught him how to scrutinize everything, assume nothing, and look for the tiniest sign in the tiniest details. *Specifically* for supernatural creatures.

Somebody who grew up like that wouldn't forget what they saw or mix the days together until the waters got muddy."

"Huh." Brigham frowned as he considered her counterpoint. "Well, shit. Again."

"So, yes. I do think our buddy Kyle happened to see the Mother of Monsters walking through a pack of her lunar-challenged children. A week after we found her coffin and lost it again."

"Keeps getting better, doesn't it? You think she's still here?"

"There's no way to make that call right now." She nodded at his phone. "If we can get a meeting with the Havalon Clan and figure out what *they* know without setting off any panic alarms, I think we'll be more prepared."

Brigham grimaced, stared at his phone, then snatched it and stabbed at the touchscreen, bouncing from incoming call and text notifications to email and back. When he was finished, he tossed it even farther away. "It's like the whole world wants us to sit back and do nothing."

"Hey." Halsey gave a passably accurate version of Brigham's cheesy grin. "Nobody ever did great things because the world dropped them into their lap, right?"

He scoffed and raised his beer for another toast. "There *is* that."

Neither of them expected to spend the next three days whiling away the time in Dublin and waiting for a response from the Havalon Clan. Admittedly, most of that time was spent holed up in the dark, musky pub closest to their hotel. That wasn't Halsey's first choice for how to spend their time, but she changed her mind after their first hour in that pub.

The gossip rings among middle-aged men crowding in for their daily pint after work were unreal.

A good deal of it consisted of airing their complaints about bosses and supervisors or making bets about the upcoming soccer season. Yet within the daily conversation the Ambrosius cousins sifted through as they drank their own pints and listened were frequent mentions of "strange occurrences."

The stories they overheard sounded a lot like Kyle's personal account. Moving shadows in the daytime. Strange voices. Noises from creatures they'd never heard before and couldn't name. Howling, growling, hissing, clicking. Whatever the beastly sound, Halsey and Brigham could bet on it being described in detail among the huddling clusters of men enjoying pints, hot meals, or both.

However, none of those stories mentioned a dark-haired woman in a plain dress walking barefoot with packs of nocturnal beasts.

Still, what the cousins gleaned in a few days of acting like barflies on the pub wall told them more than they could have learned by personally questioning the locals or going in search of these "strange happenings." Most importantly, it became clear there was definitely something strange going on in Dublin and the surrounding areas. Maybe even farther away from the center of the city, where there was more open land and fewer bright lights and loud noises.

That alone convinced Halsey they'd made the right

choice by staying in Ireland, whether or not the Havalon Clan contacted them before it was time to return to Texas.

Fortunately, Brigham got a reply on their fourth day in Ireland.

"Yes! *Hell,* yes!"

Several of the pub's regulars turned on their barstools or poked their heads over the top of their booths to cast wary glances at the American making noise in their favorite establishment. None of them said a word, which wouldn't have mattered anyway. Brigham Ambrosius was focused on only one thing now.

Halsey sipped her lager and stared at him over her pint glass. "Somebody sounds happy."

"As a pig in shit." He grinned as he scanned the message one more time, then pumped a fist. "Listen to this. 'Faolán's Inn. Four o'clock. Tonight.' *Tonight*, Hal. We finally broke through on this damn thing."

"Great. Where's Faolán's Inn?"

"No clue. Hold on, I can find it…" He pulled up a search engine on his phone and typed in the name of the pub. "Wait, what?"

"Problem?"

"Yeah. Big one. Nothing comes up."

She grabbed a fry from the basket on the table and popped it into her mouth. "Check the Wi-Fi."

"It's not the Wi-Fi, Hal. There's no search results. Nothing. How are we supposed to find a pub called Faolán's Inn when there isn't even a listing for one?" The end of his outburst got too loud for appropriate pub conversation *without* the intention of getting into a fistfight before the night was over.

Halsey glanced around with a hesitant smile, but her cousin didn't seem to notice anyone or anything else existed.

"How is that possible? It doesn't make any sense."

"Well, it obviously exists…"

"Not helpful, Hal."

The deep rumble of someone clearing their throat beside the booth made the cousins look up at the same time. The bartender, whose name they'd learned was Liam, smiled at them as he whipped a bar rag over his shoulder. "Not tryin' ta pry, here, but I couldn't help overhearin'. Yer lookin' fer Faolán's Inn?"

"Well, I thought so," Brigham grumbled. "According to the internet, it doesn't exist."

"Aye. And accordin' ta Faolán's Inn, the internet doesn't exist." When he caught their dumbfounded expressions, the lines around his eyes deepened as he chuckled. "Meanin' yer not gonna find it lookin' like that. Local spot right outside Limerick. Off the grid, as they say."

"Wonderful." Brigham set his phone down and smiled tightly. "Can *you* tell us how to get there?"

"Sure. Ye'll wanna take the M7 road all the way down, then the 464 on up past Whitehall. Right on the first dirt road, an' after that, ya grab the third dirt road after the yella barn. That's 'bout, oh… Hey, lads!" Liam leaned away from the table to eye the patrons seated at the bar. "Yella barn out in Limerick. How many kilometers is that once ya turn onto the road?"

Several of them grumbled and buried their faces in their drinks again. One old man with a shock of curly white hair raised his pint glass. "That's two."

"Five," another man called from the end of the bar. "If yer drivin' slower'n normal."

A round of laughter rose at that comment, immediately followed by a third man slapping the bar and booming, "Tree-point-six kilometers exact. I know because I helped Mrs. Kenny put up the sidin' on that yella barn meself. Might not be so yella anymore, though."

The pub filled with more raucous laughter than seemed possible for the small number of patrons sitting there at two o'clock in the afternoon.

Liam clapped his hands and grinned. "There ya have it, straight from the old goat's mouth hisself. Tree-point-six kilometers, and ya turn left at da yella barn. Keep goin' 'til ya can't go no more, and that's Faolán's Inn."

"Great." Halsey laughed with the pub's occupants as she nodded at Liam. "Thanks for the directions."

"Pleasure." The man dipped his head, then paused. "I should probably ask how yer plannin' ta get down there. If it's by anytin' public, it'll be a little harder."

"No, we rented a car," Brigham informed him. "Thanks."

"Any idea how long it might take us to get out there?" Halsey asked before smirking toward the bar-warmers. "If we're *not* driving slower than normal."

"Ha. Well, I'd say 'bout…two, two and a half hours. If ya can follow directions the first time 'round—"

"Fuck!" Brigham lurched forward so forcefully that the table screeched across the wooden floor. "We gotta go. *Now.*"

The bartender stepped out of the way as Brigham threw himself out of the booth and raced toward the pub's front door.

Halsey pulled her wallet from her back pocket, counted out a number of British pounds she thought would be enough, then slapped them on the table. "Really, Liam. Thanks."

"Anytime." He watched her race behind her cousin, then called almost as an afterthought, "Make sure ya mind the bridges, too, lass. Lotta nasty tings out there these days."

Halsey flapped a hand but didn't bother turning as she shoved the door open. "Thank you!"

After the Ambrosius cousins were out of the pub, Liam reached across their vacated table and swiped the bills Halsey had left into the front pocket of his apron with a chuckle. "Gets 'em every time…"

"What'd ya go and do that fer?" Connor Flannerty said from the bar with a high-pitched giggle. "Those kids've been 'ere all day every day for the better part of a week. At least they're tryin'."

"Aye, well. Never hurt a young person ta try a little harder'n they thought they were capable." Liam patted his apron and headed back behind the bar with a smile and a nod for anyone who looked his way.

And life in the Horseshoe Tavern went on as if Halsey and Brigham Ambrosius had never been there in the first place.

CHAPTER EIGHTEEN

Though Brigham was the one who'd been freaking out about the new discoveries and unknowns during this trip, both in and out of their control, he could drive like hell. And he did.

The directional advice they'd received from the pub patrons was surprisingly accurate, and in under two hours, Halsey pointed out the yellow barn coming up on their left. "That has to be it, right?"

"You sure?" Brigham squinted through the windshield and slowed from his previous breakneck driving pace, lurching them both forward in their seats. "I wouldn't exactly call that yellow."

"Yeah, but it *used* to be. There isn't anything else out here but grass and fence, anyway." She pointed at the odometer. "Plus, I've been keeping track of the distance."

"Okay, fine." He grunted in frustration and pumped the gas again. The car skidded across the dirt as he slowed in time to make the sharp left turn.

Halsey hissed, grabbed the oh-shit handle on her left,

and hung on tight as the rental fishtailed down the next dirt road with the cousins wobbling inside. "Seriously, Brigham? You already cut half an hour off this drive."

"And it's already three fifty-two."

"Driving like a lunatic on dirt roads isn't gonna take us back in time, so maybe cool it."

"Hal, the guy at the pub said we had to keep driving until we couldn't anymore. That's it. If it's another hour down this road—"

"Then we're already an hour late. Which sounds a hell of a lot better than being stranded in the middle of nowhere *without* a car or lying dead on the ground next to it."

He scoffed and shot her a sidelong glance. "Do those have to be the only two options?"

"Slow down."

Despite his urgent frustration, Brigham pumped the brakes and took them to a safely normal speed. The enormous wave of dust that had been trailing along behind the vehicle for the past two miles still hung in the air, filling the car's interior with a dusty, sandy odor tinged with freshly mowed grass.

It was hard to tell where this road would lead because it seemed to disappear over the rolling hills before them and reappear to take them in a completely different direction than they expected. Ten minutes later, the road made a sharp right-hand curve after they crested the next hill, which took them around the border of the thick woods that had stretched beside them on the right the whole time.

As soon as they rounded the bend and whizzed past the first few trees, a single building came into view at the end of the road. It was nestled in a little clearing at the edge of the woods with a large, cleared area behind it for a storage shed, a wood pile, and the maintenance machinery required to keep a pub up and running where there was literally nothing else.

"That's it." Halsey smiled at the sight of the two-story building with ancient siding and a real thatched roof. "Has to be."

"Only if we can't keep driving past it."

"Brigham, there's nothing else here." She laughed and gestured at the rolling green hills on their left that seemed to go on forever and the thick, lush forest walling them in on the right. "Are you expecting some secret road to pop up out of thin air?"

"I have no idea what to expect." Her cousin stared ahead, focused on the pub with grim determination. He inhaled deeply, released his breath, and smiled in concession. "It does look like this is it, huh?"

Halsey rolled her eyes. She rested her head back and enjoyed the incredible view of the greenery and wild nature around them. If not for the dirt road and the little plot of land occupied by Faolán's Inn, this area would have looked untouched by human hands.

Finally, they arrived at the pub's front parking lot, and Brigham slowed to navigate their rental as close to the entrance as he could get.

There were four other vehicles parked here. A dented and rusting antique motorcycle, two motorized scooters, and a bicycle.

"Local place is right. Look at that." Brigham snorted as he rolled to a stop and put the car in park. "All they're missing is a horse and carriage. Then they'd have every known mode of transportation."

"Stop." Chuckling, Halsey unbuckled her seatbelt and opened the passenger-side door on the left side of the car, which she still wasn't used to. As soon as she climbed out, she had to stop and breathe in the warm, fresh, sweet-smelling air. "Wow. This is so much better than Dublin."

"I'm convinced anywhere in this country smells better than Dublin." Brigham popped the driver's-side door and checked his watch. "Damn. Six minutes late."

"You honestly think the Havalon who wanted to meet us is gonna call off the whole thing because two foreigners couldn't make it out here at four on the dot?"

"Probably not. I just don't like being late." He shoved his hands in his pockets and power-walked across the dirt parking lot toward the pub's narrow front porch.

That was one of his many quirks Halsey had put up with and generally ignored in the nearly five years they'd officially been partners. She had plenty of her own quirks, too, which her cousin had graciously brushed aside in lieu of prioritizing their friendship and almost-perfect working relationship over the years.

Kinda seems like this side mission of ours is poking a lot more of his issues than normal, though. Can't really blame him. There isn't a single elemental on the planet who has the full story of what's going on or understands the scope of what it's gonna mean for all of us. Which sucks when the two of us have more information than anyone else. Other than Meemaw. Maybe.

It felt odd walking up the porch steps of a pub in permeating silence. Birds twittered and rustled in the trees, a few insects buzzed in the summer heat, and the wind whispered through the woods before drawing Halsey's dark hair across her face. With the vehicles parked out front, motorized or otherwise, Faolán's Inn obviously wasn't empty. Yet even if each of them had carried one person, it seemed reasonable that four people gathered in a pub in the middle of nowhere would have made more noise.

Even directly outside the door, the place was way too quiet.

Brigham didn't hesitate to grab the doorknob, turn it, and push the door open. The hinges creaked in protest, which sounded louder than it should have.

Halsey stepped through the entryway after her cousin. For the first ten seconds, she couldn't see a thing.

The pub's interior was so dark that it took extra-long for her vision to adjust after spending the last two hours and change racing down the wide-open highways of Ireland under the bright July sun. It was still unusually quiet, too.

"Who are we supposed to be meeting here again?" she muttered, gazing around as the dim, hanging lights covered by stained-glass shades took on clarity.

"It's, uh… We're meeting…" Brigham frowned and pulled out his phone to double-check. "Well, I didn't get a name. So it's Mystery Havalon."

Halsey peered over the edge of the room divider that doubled as the back of the closest booth. She didn't immediately spot anyone who looked more like a Havalon elemental than the other patrons. "Maybe send him a message, then. Or her. Whoever. Let them know we're here."

Her cousin sighed and wiggled his phone. "No service."

"Right. Of course not. That's fun. Guess we'll have to make ourselves more conspicuous than we already are and see if the right person notices." Halsey raised her eyebrows, then stepped past him to head for the bar.

Her vision had adjusted enough to take in the pub's details, though her eyes felt tired and heavy after the switch from bright to dark. Everything in Faolán's Inn was made of dark wood and brass, which made the place cozier but harder to see in. She didn't even notice the white-haired couple sitting at the booth she passed until they were almost behind her, and she only saw them because the man cleared his throat before setting his pint glass on the chipped wood table.

The three patrons at the bar had spaced themselves out with suspicious evenness. One man on the last stool at either end and the third on the exact center barstool. She didn't bother to investigate much further. Instead, she headed for the bar.

Behind it stood a red-cheeked, middle-aged woman with thinning, colorless hair falling out of an attempt at a bun. She focused on drying a freshly washed pint glass with a rag, and the squeak of the material drawing over the glass seemed as loud as the door creaking open. So did the clomp of Halsey's footsteps across the warped wooden floors. And Brigham's slightly heavier footsteps behind her.

The man at the far left end of the bar, closest to the narrow hallway toward the bathrooms, coughed once. No one looked up from their drinks. The bartender continued to studiously dry the glass.

"Excuse me," Halsey announced with a small smile,

hoping she didn't appear as lost and confused as she would be if this little meeting didn't go the way they hoped.

Still, the woman behind the bar didn't look up.

"Two pints of lager, please," Brigham added, holding up two fingers that their silent, studiously cleaning bartender couldn't see.

The rag squeaked around and around the inside of the glass.

The cousins shared a confused look. Brigham stepped closer and drummed his fingers on the chipped bar wood that had only been stained and polished in certain places. "Love the atmosphere in here, by the way. Wasn't sure what to expect in a place like this, all the way out at the edge of Whitehall. Now I totally get why it's such a well-kept secret."

Halsey fought a laugh. *He's not gonna get anywhere if he keeps that up.*

"Bet you got some of the best brew in the area out here, too, right?" He nodded and smiled like an idiot who'd stumbled into a place that probably didn't see any Irish from the city more than once or twice a year, let alone two Americans. "Can't wait to try it."

That got the woman's attention. Or maybe she was simply finished cleaning her glass and finally had enough bandwidth to focus on the gabbing young man at her bar. The glass *thunked* onto the worn wood, followed by the rag flopping in a wad beside it. She slowly lifted her head and fixed Brigham with watery, bloodshot eyes.

He grinned. Halsey was the only person who would have known her cousin's 'I'm nervous and trying to hide my surprise' smile.

Before anyone said anything else, a door at the far left side of the pub creaked open and banged against the adjacent wall. Slow footsteps moved down the hallway to the restrooms. Brigham continued drumming his fingers and smiling at the lady who clearly wanted nothing to do with him.

This isn't going well.

It took all Halsey's effort not to turn and stare at whoever had come out of the restroom or some other hidden back room.

All that effort was useless when a deep voice boomed with perfect clarity, "Ambrosius!"

Halsey stepped away from the bar and turned toward whoever had called her name. Brigham leaned forward to look at whoever had called his. Even if they hadn't been too dumbstruck to respond, it was clear the two foreigners in this very local, very private Irish-country pub were the Ambrosiuses in question.

The man standing at the mouth of the hallway was around six-foot-three, wearing jeans and a gray sweatshirt that fit his broad shoulders but bagged around the rest of his torso. He'd pulled the bill of his dark-gray baseball cap down over his face, making it impossible to tell what he looked like or how old he was. Yet the creased lines around his mouth and the dimples in his clean-shaven cheeks when he grinned and exposed straight rows of startling white teeth marked him as friendly enough. For now.

"See ya got me message," the man rumbled. "T'ought ya might've been a mite tardy gettin' yerselves out here, but ya made it quick enough anyway."

Brigham chortled and rapped his knuckles on the bar. "Sure did."

"Let's take this somewhere a little quieter, eh?"

Halsey almost laughed at the phrase. It was hard to imagine anywhere inside Faolán's Inn quieter than this.

The man didn't wait for a reply before he stalked across the front room of the pub. He didn't lift his hat so his American visitors could see his face. He continued past the bar, his dark-brown work boots clunking across the wooden floor, and lifted three fingers toward the bartender. "Tree pints 'o the lager, Maeve, and tank ya fer it."

For all her concentrated effort, Maeve moved like a sloth as she lowered her head and reached for the pint glass she'd been squeaking dry for who knew how long.

The Havalon Clan representative, since he couldn't possibly have been anyone else, stopped at a narrow door in the opposite wall and opened it with a skittering creak. Only then did Halsey and Brigham kick themselves into gear and move to join their elemental contact in Ireland.

Halsey flashed Maeve another smile before heading off.

Brigham knocked on the bar one more time and grinned at the woman who may or may not have heard the order for three pints. "Appreciate it, Maeve."

She didn't respond. He nodded, pushed away from the bar, and hurried after Halsey with renewed pep in his step.

CHAPTER NINETEEN

The man who'd called the Ambrosius cousins in shoved the narrow door all the way open, then stepped aside and swept his arm toward the small, dark room on the other side. Halsey could only see his face below the nose, including his crooked smile as he declared, "After you."

She tried to keep a straight face as she passed him, which was harder than expected when the door was so narrow, and he stood so close that she almost brushed against his baggy sweatshirt. The fact that she also got a nose full of fresh soap and a faint hint of cologne only made it worse. Biting her lower lip, she slipped into the dark room and hoped the guy's lowered hat kept him from seeing how it affected her.

Great. I come all the way out here for a meeting with another elemental family's representative, and I'm giddy over some Havalon member's aftershave. The guy's gotta be as old as my dad.

There wasn't any evidence to support their new friend's age, but him being sent to meet the Ambrosius cousins narrowed it down to one generation older than them or less. She hadn't expected him to be so tall or slender, at least as far as she could tell by the bagginess of his sweatshirt from the chest down. When she'd first heard his deep, booming voice, something like her dad's physique had come to mind.

Not like all the elemental families come from the same place. There aren't a lot of men anywhere built like Aiden Ambrosius. Plus, we're in Ireland.

After stepping into the room, she had a few seconds to take in the layout. One long, continuous built-in bench covered in faded green cushions lined the back and right-hand walls. Other than that, the room contained two small tables with room for one person on each side. One had been shoved into the far left-hand corner against the back wall bench with a chipped wooden chair beside it. The other was in the far right-hand corner where the bench intersected. It had two chairs, neither of which matched each other or the third chair.

Because the second table appeared less squashed, Halsey headed toward it and slid onto the right-hand bench. That left the parallel bench beside her open, plus the two other chairs, making this a cozy, private, slightly cramped meeting place for the three of them.

The narrow door shut with a click, and she looked up to see Brigham and their still-unintroduced Havalon contact standing inside.

"Brigham, aye?" The man extended a hand toward her cousin.

"That's me." They shook, and the other man's perfect teeth flashed from beneath the bill of his hat.

"So yer the one who likes ta bombard people wit all the messages at once."

"Ha." Their hands released, and Brigham spread his arms. "Only when it's important."

"Ah, sure. Ya made that clear enough."

They shared a light laugh, then Brigham faced the table and gestured toward his cousin. "And this—"

"Must be Halsey."

Halsey chuckled. "I didn't know he was mentioning *me* by name."

"He didn't," the man replied.

At the exact same time, Brigham said, "I didn't."

The Havalon elemental, who still hadn't given them his name, laughed softly, then dipped his head and self-consciously lifted the bill of his baseball cap. "That's because we've heard o' *you*. Both o' yas, o' course. As an awful good team."

"Right." She caught her cousin's gaze. Judging by his wide eyes and shocked mouth, she knew they were having the same thought.

The Havalon Clan of Ireland's already heard of us. Halsey and Brigham Ambrosius. Shit, I hope it's more good than bad.

"Take a seat." Their contact gestured with one hand toward the table where Halsey was seated and grabbed his hat with the other. "Sounds like we have a lot ta talk 'bout."

"You could say that, yeah." The chair on Halsey's left scraped across the chipped wood floor when Brigham pulled it out. He sat and folded his arms. "And let *me* say we're glad somebody on this side of the ocean felt like listening. It's been…"

Whatever her cousin said next went in one ear and out

the other without registering. Maybe he kept talking because his seat put his back to the door and their new acquaintance was standing in front of it. Or maybe he was only being Brigham and following up with friendly conversation to get the ball rolling.

Whatever the reason, he had no view of their Havalon contact peeling his hat off his head.

Halsey did.

Her assumptions about the guy had been utterly wrong.

He was her and Brigham's age, maybe a little older, with pitch-black hair and the most striking blue eyes she'd ever seen. When he smiled, his eyes lit up like fireworks and made him look strangely boyish.

It was only strange because when she thought of *boyish*, she thought of Brigham. Of course she did. He was her cousin, her militia partner, and the guy who could crack jokes as much as he could charm his way into and out of anything. Yet there was nothing similar between Brigham and this man.

She couldn't stop staring.

No way is he on their family Council. He's not old enough.

Halsey didn't actually know a thing about how the other elemental families handled their business, including who filled their Council seats or how many seats each Council held. Still, thinking about him as a Council member, even a potential one from a different Clan, felt wrong too.

The man swung his cap in a carefree gesture as he headed across the small room. He caught her staring at him when their gazes met, and his brilliant smile widened further.

She quickly looked away and tried to appear interested in whatever Brigham was saying. Her cousin's mouth made noise, and she heard vowels and consonants in his familiar voice. Yet, for some reason, not one of those noises made sense.

Get it together, Halsey. He's a pretty guy with a great smile, and we're here to talk about a war. That's it.

She thought he'd take the chair across from her and beside Brigham. But he kept walking, and she could have sworn she felt him watching her as he tossed his hat onto the faded green cushions, slid onto the bench along the back wall, and settled across from Brigham.

Next to her.

"...perfect timing, too," Brigham continued. "Honestly, I was close to—"

"Glad ya made it all the same," the man interrupted. Still smiling, though not as brilliantly, he glanced at the narrow door leading into the main pub area. "No offense, Brig-o, but it's better ta save the serious talk fer after we have our drinks."

Did this guy just call my cousin Brig-o?

"Oh." Brigham straightened in his chair, cocked his head, and shrugged. "Yeah. Totally. Those *are* coming, right?"

At the same second, the warped, echoing, barely coherent bubble in which Halsey had spent the last fifteen seconds popped. Color and sound snapped back into her awareness, and time started moving again as she turned toward the beautiful Irish elemental on the adjacent bench so she could smell his cologne again. Or aftershave. Or soap, whatever it was.

She plastered on a pert smile and casually dropped her forearm onto the table. "What did you say your name was?"

His blue eyes roamed over her face, and his smile flickered. "Ah didn't."

"Yeah, sorry about that one," Brigham interjected, oblivious to the staring contest between his best friend and their new Havalon ally. Probably because he was too busy scrolling through the text and call history on his phone. "I know I reached out to a bunch of different numbers. Let's see, uh…email to Cillian. One call to Fiona and a voicemail, of course. A call *and* a text to Fiona. Then I had this other number saved as Havalon Clan, which I think was probably supposed to be a general, like, hotline or something. Sometimes a Clan needs a hotline, right?" He sniggered at his own joke, still not looking up from his phone, then shook his head. "I don't have *your* number in here, though. Not saved or with a name… Actually, I'm not sure how that happened."

"Most likely it's 'cause ya didn't send a message ta my personal number."

"Huh. Well, that explains it." Finally, Brigham set his phone down, thumped his arms on the table, and regarded the other two people sitting with him. "So. What do we call you, then?"

The words were out of his mouth before he caught on to the fact that his companions weren't remotely interested in what he had to say. Halsey had shifted in her seat, one forearm propped on the table, so her back was basically turned to him. The black-haired, blue-eyed smiler wouldn't stop staring at her.

Brigham waited a moment longer, then cleared his throat. "What was that? Sorry. I couldn't hear you."

That got the Irishman to stop stargazing into Halsey's eyes. He dipped his head and swung it lazily toward Brigham. "Nutin' wrong wit yer hearin'."

Brigham snorted. "Well, you got *my* number and texted me the time and place. Normally, I like to have a person's name when I'm sitting down with them for a meeting. If that's not your jam, I'm sure I can come up with a placeholder instead. *Champ*."

The unnamed stranger released a harsh laugh, volatile enough to make Halsey sit back against the bench for a good look at her cousin. Brigham was slouched in his chair with his arms folded and a challenging smirk on his lips.

Seriously? We don't even know the guy's name yet, and they wanna start off by whipping out and comparing sizes? Come on, Brigham...

She didn't want to consider the possibility that her partner had both seen and understood the way Halsey and their new friend had been staring at each other.

She didn't even want to admit that was what happened.

They were momentarily saved from further awkward exchanges when the door squeaked open, and a fourth person joined them.

Maeve the bartender turned sideways in an attempt to fit through the narrow opening. Briefly, it looked like she might not make it through. She grunted and squeezed the rest of the way inside, then headed for the table without a word.

It wasn't odd that she carried three pints in her hands instead of on a tray. Yet the first glass she set down happened to be the one carried on its own, and it also happened to thump onto the table in front of Halsey, sloshing lager and foam down the sides and onto the chipped wood.

What did strike Halsey as odd and simply unsanitary on multiple levels was the way Maeve fit the remaining pints in her other hand. She'd pinned the rims of both glasses together with her thumb inside one and her index and middle fingers inside the other.

Directly into the lager.

Now with a free hand, she rearranged her transportation method and placed the pints in front of both men at the same time. She stepped back, licked the beer foam off her fingers, and stared blankly at the black-haired Irishman. "Anything else?"

"That'll do it fer now, Maeve. Tank ya."

Without another word, the bartender turned and headed back through the door. This time, it was apparently easier to squeeze through without carrying three full drinks.

The Havalon man pulled his pint closer across the table.

Brigham stared at the foam dripping down the side of his glass, clearly trying not to make a scene over some random woman's fingers all up in his beer. That quickly became too much for him, and he turned toward Maeve. "Excuse me? Maybe it's an American thing, but I'm pretty sure I saw your—"

The narrow door slammed shut, and that was the end of that.

With a heavy sigh, Brigham turned back and tried not to grimace at his drink.

Halsey watched him with an empathetic smile and didn't touch her own lager. She absolutely would've traded drinks with her cousin, knowing he sometimes had a thing about germs but only with *some* people, but the undeniable gulping sound from the other side of the table distracted them.

Their Havalon Clan counterpart knocked back half his pint in one breath, staring unblinkingly at Brigham the entire time before setting his drink back on the table. He sighed in contentment and nodded. "Seamus Havalon. It's a real pleasure."

"Yeah, you're telling *me*." Brigham snatched his drink without looking at it and glugged as much as he could in one go. Which happened to be slightly more than the half-pint Seamus had easily managed.

Halsey watched him with a deadpan expression, then glanced at Seamus and found the guy still staring at her cousin.

Nice. Now it's a drinking competition. This'll be so much fun...

When Brigham finished, he slammed the glass down and swiped the back of a hand across his upper lip. "Damn. That's really good."

"Made right out back, if ya can believe it."

"You know what? At this point, I might believe anything." Brigham slung an arm over the back of his chair and nodded, apparently satisfied that he could drink more lager with less oxygenated blood flow to his brain. "Let's get down to it, then."

Seamus dipped his head, then smiled at Halsey. "I'm listenin'."

She chuckled and hoped her return smile looked amused and unaffected instead of uncertain and mortified.

This did not start out well. No matter what we say now, it's all gonna sound like a bunch of crazy from a couple of foreigners. I probably would've said the same thing if an elemental from a different family showed up on our doorstep for an urgent meeting about being on the brink of war with the Mother of Monsters. Super fun.

To give herself more time to collect her thoughts, Halsey picked up her pint glass and joined the unspoken challenge. The pub's small, private room filled with the sound of her gulping Faolán's Inn's actually delicious in-house lager, and neither Brigham nor Seamus said a word.

When her pint glass clinked onto the table, all that remained was a stream of beer foam sliding down the inside of the cold glass.

Seamus' smile broadened.

Brigham raised his eyebrows and snorted.

Halsey folded her hands and met their contact's gaze. "Guess we should start at the beginning."

CHAPTER TWENTY

For as much story as there was to tell, Halsey made quick work of giving Seamus Havalon the pertinent details without skimping on the intrigue. Of course, the tale had grown longer since the last time she'd told it.

The silver coffin on the beach disappearing from the insanely secure acquisitions warehouse. Monsters switching up everything about their usual MO and causing serious trouble for elemental monster hunters. The night she and Aiden handled a gang of nine corpse-eating ogres by chopping off their blood-rune-embedded hands. And, of course, the evidence they discovered in the warehouse that pointed to an outside party having stolen the coffin in an as-yet-undiscerned fashion.

She added the stories they'd heard from Kyle about what he and his coworkers had been experiencing lately. She also threw in a few anecdotes of what they'd overheard in the pub by their hotel.

It felt important to give the impression that they weren't a couple of Americans aimlessly poking around in a country that had its own Clan of elemental monster hunters.

The only thing she left out of her summary was what she'd done with the sand inside the storage unit. For now, that part felt better left perpetually ignored for as long as possible.

Turning sand into copper doesn't have anything to do with the disappearing coffin and the Blood Matriarch running around with her screwed-up little monster children. Right?

By the time she finished, Maeve had come and gone with another round of drinks. Halsey gave herself permission to start her second pint. Apparently, that was a clear sign she was done talking.

Brigham smirked. "That was...*incredibly* thorough."

"Aye." Seamus raised his pint. "I'll second that."

The guys drank to each other, then Brigham nodded. "So. We're trying to figure out what the hell went wrong and what we need to do to fix it. Part of that included reaching out to your Clan to see if your family knows something ours doesn't."

The black-haired elemental snorted and stared at his drink, failing to hide a smile. "That's likely ta be a long list, Brig-o."

"Specifically about the things we've heard, seen, fought with our own hands," Brigham clarified. "This is your home turf, right? Kinda feels like the best idea is to team up and share resources now before the monster shit hits the fan."

"Ah. That it does." Seamus sipped his lager and didn't offer anything else.

We're gonna be here all night if we keep going like this, and if

Maeve treats a plate the same as a pint, I don't think I wanna stick around for dinner.

"Now you know everything we do," Halsey added to nudge things along. "We're hoping you and the rest of your Council have something we can use. Even confirmation that what we've told you about is happening in Ireland, too. Frankly, we're running out of ideas."

"Time to jumpstart the brainstorming power, right?" Brigham gave their new friend two thumbs up. "Go ahead, bud. Hit us with some Havalon Clan knowledge. We can take it."

The man took his sweet time enjoying a long draught from his pint before he spoke. It was the complete opposite of what they expected to hear. "I suppose now's the best time ta tell ya I'm not actually...*on* the Havalon Council."

"What?" Halsey croaked.

"Dude." Brigham pinched the bridge of his nose and sighed. "Okay, I didn't have *your* number, but I know the numbers I *do* have belong to Council members."

"Ye'd be correct in that." Seamus dipped his head, looking incredibly calm for having thrown a massive wrench in their plans.

"Then...what?" Halsey shook her head. "They got his messages and figured it wasn't important enough to send a Council member?"

"Eh...that's one way o' puttin' it, sure."

"So why did they send *you*?"

Seamus pressed his lips together. His smile was tight, irritated, and nothing like the carefree grin he'd worn all evening. "Actually, now that ya mention it, they didn't send me a'tall."

Brigham's eyes bulged. "Awesome. Perfect. We asked for the support of another Clan, and we get rogue…whatever he is instead."

"Huh. Now I'm wonderin' what that makes the two o' *you*, then? Certainly not a pair o' rogue whatevers actin' outside yer own Council's knowin'." Seamus cocked his head. "Or is there some other ting that makes ya so special?"

"As a matter of fact—"

"All right, that's enough," Halsey interjected. "Both of you."

Her curt tone worked, and they shut their mouths without another word, though they didn't stop glaring at each other.

In the interest of time and actually getting somewhere with this conversation, she addressed Seamus and did her best to keep the hopelessness out of her voice. "To make sure I've got this, *your* family doesn't know about this meeting either, right?"

Seamus absently spun his half-empty second pint with one hand and looked bashful before he met her gaze. His startling blue eyes almost distracted her again, but she forced herself to focus on why they were here.

"No. They don't know I'm here. Ta tell ya the truth, they probably don't care."

Brigham snorted. "Why? Because you're too much trouble to keep track of on a regular basis?"

Halsey shot him a warning glare, and he shrugged before taking another long drink to keep from mouthing off again.

"Listen, I'm not tryin' ta pull the wool over yer eyes, all

right?" His statement felt completely genuine. "My family thought 'bout what ya said in yer messages. Had a little sit-down 'bout it, too. Fer the most part, everyone figured it was some kinda shite joke the Ambrosius Clan was playin' after all these years, and the general consensus was that it weren't worth its weight ta reply. That it'd be a waste of our time and we were better off leavin' each other be, the way we have been. Yet ya piqued my interest, Brig-o. Hafta say."

The cousins' matching frowns would have been comical if not for the strange revelation their new friend had given them.

"Hold on." Brigham shook a finger at the man. "I went through all the trouble of finding those numbers and emails. I reached out more than once to make sure I wouldn't get lost in the notifications pile. And your family thought I was kidding. Like to make everybody laugh?"

Seamus' reply was to raise his jet-black eyebrows, shrug one shoulder, and raise his pint glass to his lips.

"That doesn't make sense." Halsey laughed bitterly. "The only person who has a consistent streak of playing jokes on anyone is Brigham, and half the time, *I'm* the one on the receiving end."

Her cousin jerked his chin at her with a self-satisfied smirk. "Because you know how to take a joke, Hal."

She ignored him and focused on Seamus. "The rest of our family? Hell, I haven't seen anyone on the Ambrosius Council so much as crack a smile in years."

Except for Dad after we finished cleaning up ogre parts that night. And I bet that was only because we were alone.

Brigham scratched the side of his face. "Yeah, our family doesn't do humor. As a general rule."

"That's …" Halsey still couldn't get over the idea that anyone would think the Ambrosius Clan elementals would make up such an intricate, complicated, and terrifying story. Anyone *outside* the family, at least. Her own family Council had resisted believing anything until they literally couldn't keep pretending anymore. "How the hell would that be their first logical conclusion?"

Seamus finally realized they weren't pulling his leg for fun. He gaped at her, then shook his head and chuckled. "Ya really don't know, do ya?"

"I wouldn't ask if I did, Seamus."

"Fair. Honestly, I'm not sure I have all the details myself, but as I've heard it, there was some kinda trouble stirred up a few decades ago. My family reached out ta yers, and the only Ambrosius ta call back was Greta. That'd be yer Gram, aye?"

Halsey glanced at her cousin and was relieved to see Brigham wondering the same thing. *Did the Council seriously kick Meemaw out because she wanted to be friends with another elemental family?*

"Yeah," she replied softly. "That's her."

"Right. So." Seamus shrugged again. "There was some sorta kerfuffle 'bout the whole ting. Went back and forth fer a time, and I don't know what came of it after that. I *do* know there's been a feud wit Ambrosius on one side and Havalon on t'other ever since. We're not big fans o' yers. 'Cept when it comes ta Greta, I suppose. The tings I've heard 'bout *her*? That woman knows what she's doin'.

Other'n that, though... Well. Let's just say Havalons tend ta have long memories, if ya get my drift."

"Trust me, man." Brigham nodded slowly. "We know all about long memories and *certain* people holding grudges."

"Why did you decide to get involved, then?" Halsey asked. "By the way, I'm hoping it has something to do with you wanting to see if the legends are true."

"What, ya mean about yer family bein' a bunch o' lunatics wit sticks up their arses?"

Brigham snorted halfway through a swallow of lager, which made him choke until he fell into a fit of coughing.

A smile flickered across Halsey's lips. "Well, I guess there's *one* thing our families agree on."

Brigham finished coughing and burst out laughing.

Seamus looked confused, but he went with it and smiled at the joke he didn't understand. "Everytin' ya said 'bout yer own family holds true ta that, maybe, sure. It doesn't look like *you* have any sticks up yer arse."

"No, I'm just a lunatic, right?"

"Not what I said. Actually, you comin' all the way out here ta talk ta us makes me tink yer more like yer Gram."

Halsey rolled her eyes and dropped her gaze to her drink. "You definitely aren't the first person to tell me that."

"That's perfect!" Brigham guffawed. "*Perfect!*"

Seamus raised an eyebrow. "*He* might have a few loose screws, if ya ask me."

"If he does, so do I," Halsey replied.

Her cousin pointed at her. "*His* family thinks we're all insane. *Our* family thinks you and Meemaw are nuts.

You're the only one of us who's crazy enough to transmute a bunch of—"

Halsey kicked his shin under the table, and Brigham choked on his words. Whether his next fit of coughing was real or forced, at least he got the picture.

We're not bringing the magic sand into all this. Not after things got way more complicated than I could've imagined.

"Transmutation?" Seamus leaned closer and eyed her sideways. "Now I'm intrigued."

"It's an alchemy thing," she replied, the lie rolling off her tongue as naturally as if it had always been the truth. Probably because it had much of the truth wrapped inside it. At least, she thought it did. "One of those family secrets, you know?"

"Aye." He scrutinized her, then trotted out that brilliant white grin again. "I'd bet ye've got plenty o' secrets."

"Hey." Brigham slapped the table in protest. "Whatever secrets she has, she's not giving 'em up to you 'cause you have the most perfect smile I've ever seen, okay? Give it a rest."

Seamus threw his head back and roared with laughter. His deep voice was startling enough, but hearing it bounce around the tiny private room felt like being inside a soundproof booth with a raging thunderstorm.

It made Halsey jump, which he didn't see because he was busy laughing. Brigham shot her a half-grimace, half-smile and shook his head.

Uh-huh. Maybe we're all a little insane. We have to be to do the things we do, right?

CHAPTER TWENTY-ONE

When Seamus calmed down enough to continue the conversation, tears shimmered in his eyes. "Here's the ting. Real honest. The tings ya sent in yer messages, Brig-o? Aye, they did sound insane. I didn't expect my family ta write it off as complete shite, but when they did… Well, I couldn't help myself. Had ta see what might happen if one of us followed this ta the end. I snagged yer number and told ya to meet me here. Wasn't expectin' ya to show up, but I'm tickled ya did."

"Tickled." Brigham pressed his lips together and nodded. Clearly, he struggled to hold back whatever wry comment sat on the tip of his tongue, but at least he and Seamus had stopped trying to one-up each other. "You know what, Hal? I think our new friend's the Havalon version of us."

"Maybe." She couldn't look directly at Seamus because he was still grinning, and she wasn't sure she'd be able to focus on the discussion. Instead, she grabbed her pint glass and raised it for a toast. "Here's to the new generation of elementals shaking things up. For both families."

"Aye. Ta trouble." Seamus raised his mug and nodded.

"To…" Brigham scoffed. "Really? You're gonna be *that* guy?"

"Ya don't like it, Brig-o? All right. Ta shakin' tings up, then. 'Cause we *have* ta, wit everytin' goin' on lately, don't we?"

"Hell yeah, we do." Brigham stood to lean across the table and clink his glass against Seamus'.

They both extended their lagers toward Halsey, but she'd already lowered hers. "Hold on."

"Finish the toast, Hal," her cousin insisted. "Not finishing a toast is almost as bad as toasting with water. You know that."

"What do you mean 'with everything going on lately?'" she asked Seamus.

Brigham sighed, rolled his eyes, and drank anyway.

Seamus waited with his pint glass raised, then gave up and drank too. Halsey didn't stop staring at him until he answered. "I was plannin' ta get ta this part, anyhow. Looks like now's as good a time as any."

"It certainly is."

When he set his drink down, Seamus' playful, *boyish* amusement had vanished. "Yer not the only ones who've been dealin' wit strange happenin's in yer everyday, Halsey. Believe me."

Now she had no problem staring into those blue eyes of his because this had gotten serious. She could feel it. "I want to," she replied evenly. "First, I need to know if you believe *me*. Us."

He dipped his head in acknowledgment, then reclined against the built-in bench, once more adopting his casual slump. "Aye, well. Can't say I know much of anytin' 'bout silver caskets and the Mother o' Monsters. That's not fer me ta decide. The rest of it? Sure. Strange tings. Changes in the monsters, aye? 'Specially wit those werewolves."

"Yeah." Brigham clicked his tongue. "We've been hearing a lot about those lately."

"Believe you me, Brig-o. We've been tryin' ta get those tings under control fer weeks. Then I heard the two o' *you* were comin' out ta put in extra firepower, and I thought fer sure a pair o' Ambrosius elementals would've figured out how ta get the job done. Bloody surprise ta see all those messages from ya weeks later wantin' ta meet up. I figured ya came back here ta clean up yer own mess before anyone noticed. Lemme tell ya, though. We definitely noticed."

The cousins shared a look.

How the hell did he know we were out here driving back the werewolves? That was almost six weeks ago. It wasn't a little meet-and-greet like this trip, either. That was an actual mission.

There was no point acting like she had no idea what he was talking about. Halsey gazed at Seamus and asked, "What mess is that?"

He sniggered, then realized she was serious and wiped the smirk off his face. "Yer not kiddin'? Well, shite. Ya weren't blowin' smoke either, talkin' 'bout the rest o' yer family."

"Not even a little," Brigham replied flatly. "And now you're gonna tell us why that surprises you so much."

With a heavy sigh, Seamus nodded as if he'd finally realized they truly needed help. "All right. Tings've been topsy-turvy wit dozens of the beasties here for well over tree months. Fer the most part, we were able ta handle it on our own. Then the werewolves started gettin' outta control. Showin' up where they weren't supposed ta and never had been before. Startin' way more trouble wit the locals. *Turnin'* more'n they should've, and on all the wrong days. New moon. Half. Crescent. Ya name it, they were doin' it.

"We tried everytin' we could ta drive 'em back, but they kept *comin'*. Like some kinda bloody exodus from wherever the whole lot of 'em came from, an' they all picked Ireland as the place ta go next. Got too much for us on our own, and that was a hard enough pill ta swallow. We didn't much have a choice. My Council reached out ta yers. Asked fer help. All the pride in the world wasn't worth lettin' the tings take over here in *our* home. So yer Clan sent ya."

Halsey thumped back against the bench and stared at the opposite wall. *What?*

"Ta tell the truth, we were fairly relieved. Looked like the rift between Ambrosius and Havalon was on its way ta mendin'. Then a few days later, we get the news that the both of ya packed yer bags and headed back 'cross the pond with nutin' ta show fer it."

"Whoa, man." Brigham spread his arms. "*Nothing?* That's harsh, don't you think?"

"I'm callin' it like it is, Brig-o. From where my family's standin', all we could see was hope landin' on our shores, two elementals from another Clan reachin' out and givin' a hand, only ta strip it away without actually fixin' the problem." Seamus shrugged. "If we're gettin' *real* honest, ya made it even worse. What else were we supposed ta think?"

"We *what?*" Halsey blinked and whipped her head around to look him in the eye. "What do you mean we made it *worse?*"

"*Now* I know it wasn't intentional on yer part, but it sure seemed like cause and effect at the time. The second the two of ya hopped back on a plane, sometin' in those beasties changed again. For the absolute worst. Not only droves of 'em runnin' 'round the fields and turnin' on their own in dozens upon dozens. They took ta the villages and towns. Left nothin' but trails o' blood behind. We can't tell one way or t'other if the bastards turned the normal folk into some o' their own or if they ripped 'em apart 'til there weren't nothin' left. We *still* can't drive 'em back enough ta convince ourselves the folks we're here ta protect are actually bein' protected."

"Shit." Halsey inhaled sharply and glanced at her cousin. Brigham's face had lost its color, and he ran a hair through his messy auburn hair before pressing a fist against his mouth. "Seamus, we had no idea," she added.

"How could ya? Ye'd already left."

"Which we absolutely wouldn't have done if we'd known it wasn't a regular mission." She shook her head, her mind racing. She wanted to stay here and do everything in her power to fix the massive mistake they'd made that wasn't their fault. She also wanted to hop on the first flight back to Texas, storm the Ambrosius Council room, and give every one of them a piece of her mind. This time, it wouldn't be contained to words and a few severed ogre hands. "I'm so sorry."

"Ya didn't know…" Seamus studied her gaze, which was apparently genuine enough to surprise him. He looked at

Brigham and saw the same thing. "Neither one o' ya? We asked *yer* family fer help, and they didn't tell ya a bloody ting 'bout it?"

Brigham's scowl deepened. "Wouldn't be the first time, man."

"It *is* the first time anyone else was involved," Halsey pointed out. "Especially another elemental family. Seamus, if we had *any* idea there was something going on here, we would have stayed, met with the Havalon Council, and done everything we could to help you. We didn't even know the werewolves were acting different until we got here. Then that…silverback. The alpha? It called them away before we could even *begin* to wonder if there was anything else happening. We figured it was…"

"A fluke," Brigham intoned.

"Then we found the coffin, and I had my head in the clouds, babbling about ancient legends and the Blood Matriarch. I didn't even stop to think about what—"

"Whoa, there." Seamus placed a hand on the table in front of her. "Look at me."

She frowned and pressed her lips together. *Why is he saying that like we know each other?*

He glanced at Brigham instead and chuckled. "Is she always this hard on herself?"

Brigham stared at his cousin. "Only when she actually thinks she screwed up," he muttered.

"Halsey."

The way Seamus said her name made her freeze. His voice held a level of calm understanding she'd only heard from Brigham and Greta. To receive it in a pub in the middle of nowhere from a man who was practically a stranger...

If he keeps going like that, I'm gonna lose it. I'll fall apart.

He laughed and removed his hand. "Listen. Don't fer a second tink any o' this is so bad that ya can't look at me."

Brigham sighed. "Hal..."

"I'm fine." She snatched her drink, downed the rest in one go, then almost slammed the glass down. The beer wasn't so strong that it wiped out everything she was feeling. Not even close. Yet pulling herself out of the dark, lonely place she hadn't seen the edge of in years was all the reassurance she needed. She straightened, met Seamus' gaze, and nodded. "How do we fix it?"

Seamus' heart-stopping grin returned. "I think that's a question better asked o' the Havalon Council, wouldn't ya say?"

CHAPTER TWENTY-TWO

Apparently, Seamus Havalon had a tab at Faolán's Inn. Maybe he simply didn't pay for drinks there. Brigham didn't ask about it either way when Seamus led them out of the pub, and they climbed into their respective vehicles.

It was probably a good thing Brigham didn't have to think about where he was going or pay attention to driving other than keeping an eye on Seamus' car. Neither of the cousins had room in their minds for anything beyond what they'd discovered.

Halsey had no idea how long the drive was, but as they barreled across open Irish countryside surrounded by so much green, it felt like the trip might take days. She couldn't stop thinking about the mountain of lies her own family had apparently been telling her for years, and they kept adding new ones to the stack.

Why wouldn't they tell us the Havalons had asked for help? We're not an island, and we're certainly not the only elemental family out there hunting monsters. They know *that. Why would they send us out here to hunt werewolves when they knew it was so much more than that? Did they really not think Brigham and I would figure it out?*

The more she thought about it, the more likely it seemed this was only one facet of the Council trying to cover their tracks. That thought wouldn't have occurred to her if Seamus hadn't also mentioned Greta Ambrosius as the only elemental in their family who'd answered the Havalon Clan's *last* call for help. Which also made her the catalyst for the ongoing feud between Clans that Halsey had known nothing about.

Is that why they threw Meemaw off the Council? Because she was willing to help somebody outside the family? Or is it something else?

She could not conceive of anything Greta Ambrosius might have done to make the entire family turn against her and cast her out. The woman was a little eccentric, sure. She liked to play games with people sometimes, but only when those people were in the habit of taking everything way too seriously. Greta was like Brigham in that way, or maybe it was the other way around.

Still, there was no excuse for the Council exiling one of their own. Their own *mother*, for five out of the seven who held the Council seats now. Simply because Greta had wanted to help another Clan. Even if she'd taken it too far for their liking and tried to get the entire Ambrosius Clan to hop on board, there was no good reason.

Now she was headed to the Havalons' version of their Clan estate, or whatever they called it, to sit down with an elemental family who'd been spurned by hers.

It felt like a nightmare. One without any *real* monsters,

but her family seemed to have stepped into that role perfectly.

"Hal."

Halsey jolted in the passenger seat, sucked in a sharp breath, and groggily looked up from staring at the dashboard. "What?"

Brigham frowned. "You good?"

"I'm fine, Brigham." It hit her then that they were still in a car, on the road. She almost snapped at her cousin to return his eyes *to* that road before she realized they weren't moving.

"Okay. Well..." He looked out the windshield at the enormous building surrounded by several small houses, their details overshadowed by the blazing sunset behind them. "Maybe put the daydreaming away for a bit? Listen, I know what we heard today is, like, one of the worst things we could've possibly—"

"I said I'm fine." Halsey swiftly unbuckled her seat belt. Without meaning to, she threw it against the inside of her door. The buckle *clacked* against the glass, and the loud noise jolted her back into reality. She inhaled and looked at her cousin. "Sorry."

"No, I get it. That's all I'm trying to say." He unbuckled himself and made a point of carefully setting his seat belt aside. "Whatever happens in there, I got your back, cuz. Don't forget that."

She smirked. "Kinda hard to forget when you're always right there behind me."

He grinned and pointed at her. "*That's* the Hal I was waiting on to show up."

Halsey opened the door and stepped onto the thick,

lush grass stretching in every direction around the Havalon family estate. She started to ask Brigham if he'd forgotten how to park, then she noticed several other vehicles parked in the grass the same way. *Kinda makes me wonder why our family bothered to put roads on* our *property. I bet they have as much land as we do.*

The sound of Brigham's door clicking shut made her turn toward him. He stood beside the car, one hand propped against the closed door and the other on his hip as he surveyed their destination. Then he drew a deep breath, closed his eyes, and froze. "Wait. You meant that as a compliment, right?"

Halsey shut her door without a word.

"You meant because I'm always behind you to back you up, right? Or was that supposed to be some kinda challenge?"

Not far away, Seamus had parked his car in the grass and now stood beside it, waving one arm to catch their attention.

Halsey flexed her fingers, which were sore from spending the entire drive out clenched into fists without her noticing. She headed toward the black-haired Irishman. "Time for another Council meeting."

"Hal." When she didn't stop, her cousin growled and hurried after her. "Seriously. That was a compliment, right? 'Cause I always got your back. Hey, listen. I can kick as much monster ass as you can, and you know it."

She raised her own hand to let Seamus know they'd seen him and didn't say a word.

"For real." Her cousin scoffed as he kept up with her.

"We're grown-ass adults, and you still gotta put in jabs about always being first?"

"Not what I said. Brig-o."

He slowed, did a double-take, then made a face before leaping forward. "That doesn't have the same ring to it when you say it."

"Oh, but you like it when *he* says it?"

"Whoa, now. Okay." Brigham slipped his hands into his pockets and sniggered. "Talk about liking it when that tall, dark…admittedly charming dude does *anything*—"

"Let's not." Fortunately, they drew within Seamus' earshot, and neither cousin was willing to engage in playful banter about him unless it was behind his back.

They were also close enough to see Seamus staring at Halsey again. Maybe he had been the entire time. She'd been sitting in a pub with the guy for hours, but his brilliant blue eyes caught her off guard all over again. She focused on the enormous house across the grass parking lot and nodded. "This is beautiful."

"Aye. Shar is." He kept smiling as she and Brigham caught up to him, and he didn't take his eyes off her as he turned toward the enormous main building and the little cottages scattered around it to walk beside her.

He'd better not keep looking at me like that the whole time we're here.

Though she fully meant the thought, Halsey couldn't help enjoying the attention. Even if it wouldn't get Seamus Havalon any further when meeting with his family to get everyone on the same page.

Brigham inhaled deeply through his nose and sighed contentedly. "*This* is the Havalon Clan HQ, huh?"

"Aye. If ya wanna tink about it that way. Most of us call it home."

"Why would you ever wanna leave?"

Seamus' brows knit together. "Do ye and yers not do the same? Livin' together on the land yer Clan settled?"

"Kind of…" Halsey wrinkled her nose. Talking about the way the Ambrosius Clan had divided themselves when it came to what they called *home* felt like a major bummer right now. "Some of us do, anyway."

"*She* does," Brigham clarified. "Moved right into the old cottage *way* out on the back of the property the day she turned eighteen."

"Aye?"

"Oh, yeah. See, we had this clubhouse kinda thing back there. We built it, actually. A bunch of trees and vines and plants and stuff. Or I guess we *grew* it, right?"

"Just the two of ya?"

"No. No way." Brigham sniggered and shook his head. "I mean, Hal *could have* if she wanted to. That's where we all hung out as kids, you know? What was it? Like fourteen of us or something, right?"

Halsey stared at the enormous main house growing large and closer with the fiery sunset sky behind it. "Probably."

"Yep. We were out there *all the time* as kids. Like, even when we weren't supposed to be. It was…the perfect place."

Okay, Brigham. Time to stop the sappy walk down memory lane. This is not *why we're here.*

Seamus dipped his head as he gazed at her, probably to catch her attention and make her look up. She didn't. "How'd ya manage ta grab the spot everyone else wanted?"

"'Cause nobody else wanted it," Brigham answered for her. Again. "We all grew up. Got our own places. The greenhouse got left behind, I guess. Out of all of us, Hal's the only one who stayed on the Clan property. Only for that little piece of—"

"Brigham, there have to be a hundred other things Seamus would rather talk about right now," Halsey interrupted with a warning look.

"Pretty sure he can decide for himself, either way," Seamus cut in with a crooked smile. "Actually, I like hearin' 'bout it."

"You do?"

He shrugged. "I've heard stories 'bout what yer out there doin' every day. Professionally, o'course. Nice ta get ta know the woman behind 'em a bit."

That surprised her enough that she couldn't think of anything to say. *He wants to get to know the woman behind the stories? Huh. Even if I* was *interested, we don't have time. Not during this trip, anyway.*

"Hear that?" Brigham grinned and wiggled his eyebrows. "He's heard *stories*..."

"Yep, my hearing works fine."

Before her cousin could say anything else potentially humiliating, they reached the front of the main house.

Loud shouts and laughter rolled across the open field, though from the front of the estate, it looked like the place was empty.

Seamus veered right and waved the cousins after him. "Not the front door. We're goin' 'round back."

Halsey paused to eye the main house, then frowned. "Please tell me it's not because you're trying to sneak us in."

He laughed but didn't offer an explanation as he headed around the side of the house.

Brigham puffed out a sigh. "Well, now you *know* this is gonna be good."

"As long as it's better than meetings we've had with *our* Council."

"Can't be that hard, right?"

They headed after the black-haired Irishman, who'd considerately stopped to wait for them along the side. Here, the noise of multiple voices had doubled in volume.

Halsey released a wry chuckle. "We're not interrupting something, are we?"

Seamus looked confused. "What makes ya tink that?"

"Sounds like a party."

"Nah. This is a regular evenin' at suppertime. Come on."

When the three young elementals rounded the house together, Halsey had to force herself not to plug her ears as the noise intensified.

Dozens of people gathered on the sprawling lawn behind the main house. Most of them were as dark-haired as Seamus, though no one was nearly as tall. Seven picnic tables were interspersed around the grass, filled to the brim with Havalons eating, drinking, joking, and laughing. Two large banquet tables were laid out in the center of the lawn with overflowing platters of food. Several small children chased each other around. Some of them stopped at the end of the tables to sneak desserts before they were chased away by laughing adults.

The sight was unlike anything Halsey had seen before, especially when it came to an elemental family. The

Ambrosius Clan had "family meals" only a few times a year, if that, and they were nothing like this.

"Whoa." Brigham's eyes lit up as he scanned the back lawn. "Did anyone *not* show up for this?"

"Not that I know of."

"It *looks* like a party," Halsey added, her eyes wide. "What's the occasion?"

"Supper."

"Obviously." She laughed and gestured toward the dozens of Irish elementals thoroughly enjoying the massive gathering. "There's something else happening tonight, right?"

Seamus grinned. "Only the two o' ya showin' up ta have a chat with the family."

This time, she couldn't hide her surprise. "You mean you guys do this every night?"

"When the weather allows, sure. Sometimes even when it doesn't."

Completely dumbstruck, Halsey turned toward Brigham, who looked ready to throw himself at the feast and all the people without a second thought.

His composure almost broke as he stepped toward the gathering, but they were noticed before he had the chance.

"Well, look who finally decided ta show up!" A tall man with his head shaved bald above a neatly trimmed, white-streaked black beard headed toward them, grinning from ear to ear. He looked like a miniature version of Halsey's dad, except for the fact that he was smiling and still had both eyes. Plus, Aiden Ambrosius wouldn't have been caught dead walking outside in the grass without shoes. "Dragged a few strays in wit ya, I see."

"I wouldn't say that." Seamus grinned at the man and gestured toward the cousins. "Halsey and Brigham Ambrosius."

The other man's eyes flared as he looked them over, then he broke into a gleaming grin and laughed. "Well, I'll be damned, lad. Ya went fer it anyhow, eh?"

"Couldn't help myself." Seamus met Halsey's gaze and shrugged. "Seemed a bit too interestin' ta be true, but turns out they have a bloody lot ta say."

"Nice to meet you." Halsey stuck her hand out, and the man laughed again before gripping it in a firm shake.

"The same ta ye, lass. Cillian Havalon at yer service. And yers." He reached for Brigham's hand, and Halsey's cousin couldn't stop smiling.

"They were hopin' ta sit down wit the Council fer a wee chat," Seamus explained. "And ta get a few answers."

"Aye, well, that's what the messages kept sayin'." Cillian wagged a finger at Brigham. "Seems my lad saw a ting t'rest of us missed. Yer lookin' fer a meet wit our Council, then? Truly?"

"We are." Halsey nodded. "If the Council's busy right now, we're happy to wait—"

"Ha! I can already tell the way the Ambrosius Council handles a ting like this. We're a wee different out here. If a chat wit the Council's what ya want, that's what ye'll get." When neither of the cousins looked like they believed him, the man shot Seamus a knowing look. "If yer waitin' for an okay from the Council Head, ya just got it. Now, go fix yerselves some supper and meet the family."

Without waiting for a reply, he spun and headed back toward the picnic tables.

Halsey blinked after him. "Seamus."

"Aye?"

"You didn't say anything about your *dad* being the head of the Havalon Council."

He chuckled, and she could feel his gaze across the side of her face. "Ya didn't ask."

"Will ya look at what Seamus dragged in?" Cillian shouted to no one in particular as he pointed toward their visitors. "Two genuine Ambrosiuses. Right here on our lawn."

Several of the adults looked up from their meals and smiled.

"Yer that sure they aren't here ta yoke us about all over again?" another man cried out from the next table over.

"Well, if they are, Billy, a'least they'll get in a full belly first!"

A round of laughter rose from the tables, and no one seemed bothered by the fact that their guests happened to be members of the elemental Clan they'd apparently been at odds with for years.

"Well." Brigham clapped his hands and rubbed them. "You heard the man, Hal. Dinner is served, and we're invited."

He took off at a brisk pace toward the banquet table, grinning at everyone who looked his way but not stopping until he'd snatched a plate from the top of the stack and got to work piling on his dinner.

"Yer not hungry?" Seamus asked.

Halsey had to stop herself from asking if he knew what "hangry" meant before realizing it was his accent. She chortled and slowly shook her head. "I don't know."

"We'll getcha sometin' anyhow." He nodded toward the banquet tables. "Trust me. It's loads better'n anytin' Maeve might've whipped up in the back o' *her* kitchen."

"Oh, I don't doubt that." She couldn't stop staring at all the smiling, laughing, black-haired Havalons as she followed Seamus. Then she couldn't stop smiling because the good mood bubbling over from everywhere was infectious.

An elemental family who likes spending time with each other. Imagine that. No way in hell is this gonna be anything like calling a Council meeting back home...

CHAPTER TWENTY-THREE

It quickly became clear that there was no such thing as a formal introduction for the Havalon Clan. Halsey and Brigham barely had time to fix plates for themselves before names were tossed around as easily as if the cousins were merely refreshing their memories instead of meeting the entire family for the first time.

Only a few of those names stuck in her mind. Cillian, of course, because he'd already dropped the bomb about being the Havalon Council Head *and* Seamus' father. His wife Fiona had the most beautiful smile Halsey had ever seen, which made sense and also made her mentally kick herself when she worked out that the woman was Seamus' mother. Then there were Fallon and Finnion, who could have been twins but were born a year apart. Their nearly identical faces stood out because of their auburn hair that looked so bright and out of place among the jet-black claimed by the others in the family.

The young children hardly stood still long enough to get their names, and the adults around them only laughed.

Some encouraged the children or playfully shooed them away. One man reached out toward the grass beneath a group of kids' feet, lifted it like a wave, and sent them tumbling into each other.

Seamus led her toward the picnic tables, where Halsey was enthusiastically invited to sit, meet even more family members, and tell her story all over again.

In the span of two hours, she'd told at least a dozen different variations of the same story she'd given Seamus, with the occasional embellishment from Brigham when he was nearby or Seamus when he felt like it. Not a single Havalon elemental looked at her in disbelief, and no one said anything that sounded like they didn't want to hear what their guests had to say.

In fact, those who stuck around to listen added their own short anecdotes that seemed to support the information Halsey and her cousin had come to discuss. Though none of it was official yet, there were more than a few mentions of the Havalon Clan being ready and willing to face whatever new threat came their way. Provided, of course, they were able to clean up the most pressing local issue these days.

The werewolves.

Every person she talked to about the werewolf problem was calmer, more accepting, and more level-headed about the future dangers than Halsey thought possible. They took it seriously, of course. Yet now that they were discussing it with the elementals who'd been sent to *help* with the werewolf problem, Halsey and Brigham received nothing but warm welcomes and gratitude for returning to share what they'd learned.

That was an instant balm to the guilt and frustration Halsey had been holding onto since Seamus' revelation in the pub. It didn't stop her from apologizing and promising various Havalons that she and Brigham would do everything they could to correct the mistake, even when their hosts made it clear that no one blamed them. Not since everyone knew the whole story and the slate had been wiped clean. At least, it was as far as Halsey and Brigham were concerned.

The open welcome and the willingness to listen was an overwhelming relief, though it was hard to reach much of a conclusion during a loud, rowdy family gathering like this one. Multiple Havalons told Halsey to lighten the load, enjoy herself tonight, and the decision of "what to do next" could be made afterward. It wasn't until the fifth time she'd heard this from as many different elementals that it finally sank in.

They weren't ignoring her. They were choosing to enjoy the time they had together tonight and leave the business part for a better time.

That was the final detail convincing her the Havalon Clan was the opposite of her own family in every way, except that they were all elementals who shared the same duty to keep the world safe from supernatural creatures. After she stopped comparing the families, she relaxed and enjoyed what was admittedly one hell of a dinner.

It didn't stop at the food, either. Beer and Irish whiskey were passed around like candy, and drinks were constantly being refilled. None of the adults tried to hide their enjoyment, or in some cases, drunkenness, from the children running around. At the same time, there was no separation among the Clan by age and status. The teenagers sat, talked, and drank with their parents, aunts, and uncles. The youngest children sat on laps and ate leftover food off the plates of whoever happened to be holding them, which wasn't necessarily their own parents. Adults left the tables to join the kids in their yard games, laughing and wrestling, invested in the fun without caring about the scores or even the rules.

Then someone turned on the music, and it became a different kind of party. Which the Havalon Clan apparently threw every night.

Cheers rose from those sitting at the table. One of the older teenagers with curly, jet-black hair falling down to his shoulders emerged from the back door of the main house and spread his arms. The cheers grew louder, joined by laughter, and the Havalons got up to start dancing.

Most of those who stood first to dance had drunk enough that it wasn't the neatest or most graceful display, but they didn't enjoy it any less. The little ones laughed, screamed, and danced around them in the grass. Then an older couple with graying hair emerged from the crowd of Havalons to show the younger generations how it was done.

Halsey had long since finished her dinner. She'd only been able to eat a few bites at a time through all the introductions and recounting why she and Brigham were here. Now she was enjoying the cranberry oatmeal cookies still on her plate, laughing with everyone else around her.

This would never happen at home. Not in a million years. I don't know if my family's ever had this much fun together unless it was only me, Brigham, and the other cousins...

At some point in the night, probably before the sun went done, Seamus had left her side to talk to his family. Halsey hadn't paid much attention to the fact that he'd been gone for a while until he returned and dropped onto the bench beside her with a grin. "Fancy a go?"

She frowned with half a bite of cookie still in her mouth. "Hmm?"

"Sorry to burst your bubble, bud," Brigham announced from the other side of the table. "Hal doesn't dance. Not in the way *you're* thinking."

"Dude." She gaped at him and hoped her cousin would pick up on the message to quit saying things in all the weird ways.

He shrugged and nodded toward the trampled grass that served as the dance floor. "Hey, put a monster out there that needs fighting, and she'll put on a show like you ain't *never* seen before."

Halsey swallowed her cookie and chuckled. "He's seriously over-exaggerating."

"The hell I am. You're too good to admit it."

"That doesn't even make sense."

"Well, I was tinkin' more like a real dance," Seamus cut in with a mischievous smirk.

She shook her head. "No, my cousin's right about that part. I don't dance."

"Aw, come on, Hal." Seamus swept his gaze across the enormous back lawn. "A lad can only dance wit his cousins 'n aunties so many times. T'isn't hard, if that's what yer worried about."

She snorted and looked into blue eyes that glittered under the strands of outdoor lights strung between the main house and the smaller surrounding buildings. "I never said I was *worried*. Only that I don't—"

"Put the poor lad out o' his misery, lass," someone shouted from the next table over. "Or we'll be dealin' wit Seamus broodin' 'n huffin' 'round all night!"

Several others called out their own version of the same thing, laughing and waving the young people toward the dancing.

Seamus grabbed the plate of cookies off her lap and stood.

"Hey!" She tried to take them back, but his long arms kept them out of reach. He tossed the plate onto the table, then playfully grabbed her hand and hauled her to her feet.

"Seamus, seriously. I don't—"

"I'll be the judge o' that, tanks." Grinning, he pulled her along with him to the sound of several people cheering and laughing, including Brigham.

Unbelievable. I'm definitely counting this as one time my own partner does not *have my back.*

Even then, she didn't try that hard to pull her hand from Seamus'. He only let go when they reached the messy circle of Havalons dancing the night away.

Halsey giggled as several small children raced around them, screaming, bouncing, and spinning in dizzying circles. "You're going to be disappointed."

"Oh, aye?" The corners of his mouth turned down in brief consideration, then he pulled a leather-wrapped flask from his back pocket. "Then I s'pose ya haven't had nearly enough o' this yet."

Her mouth popped open in a surprised laugh as he

unscrewed the lid. When he offered the flask to her first, though, she shook her head. "I'm good."

"Suit yerself." He shrugged, raised the flask to his mouth, and knocked it back. Then he smacked his lips a few times and stared at the container. "Ah. Better'n a whole plate o' me Gran's soda-bread cookies. Ya sure are missin' out on *this* stuff, Hal—"

"Fine. Hand it over." Before he finished laughing at her, she'd snatched the flask and given it a tentative sniff. Whatever face she made was apparently hilarious as his family danced around them and called out jokes.

"Wee bit stronger'n ya reckoned?"

"Actually..." Halsey jiggled the flask. "I was thinking you should've brought more."

That got him laughing again, and she slowly raised the flask to her lips.

Did I really challenge an Irish elemental to a drinking contest? In his own house? What are you thinking, *Halsey?*

Truth be told, she was thinking how nice it was to attend a family gathering where the sole focus was making sure everyone had a good time. Even if it wasn't her own family.

She hadn't even managed a sip before another shout caught her attention, and it wasn't like any they'd heard so far tonight.

"Cillian! Oy! Cut the music!"

She and Seamus turned toward the source of the shout and found the first Havalon all night who didn't look like he was enjoying himself.

"No need ta tell the whole Clan ya were out in the jacks, boyo," one of the others called out to a round of laughter.

"Hold yer tongue or lose it, ya bletherin' eejit," the angry man shouted as he stormed across the lawn.

"Who's that?" Halsey asked.

Seamus watched him with a curious frown. "Me cousin Finn. He's usually the one takin' the piss outta everyone else, not t'other way around."

Finn reached the back of the house. He disappeared inside, then the music cut out. A good number of Seamus' family groaned in complaint, though it took some of the drunker Havalons a bit to notice the music was missing before they stopped dancing to it.

The back door slammed open again, and Finn stalked out. Most of the family had turned to face the house at this point, so everybody saw him shake a finger in their general direction. "Afore anyone says a ting, I amn't too fluthered ta know what me own eyes're seein'."

"Then gah'head 'n say it, Finn," Cillian called. "What *did* ya see?"

Finn couldn't have been much younger than Halsey, Brigham, and Seamus. Now that he had the entire Clan's attention, his paling face made him look barely old enough to be through his militia training. Yet he clearly knew enough to quickly get his point across. "They're on the mountain."

Halsey looked across the trees in the direction from which he'd stumbled out of the woods. The moon was two or three days before full, but its light was plenty to illuminate the outline of several peaks in the distance.

What does that mean, 'they're on the mountain'?

Beecham Havalon, who was either Fiona's cousin or her

brother, thumped a fist on his picnic table. "Say it now, lad. Are ya sure?"

"Aye, go way outta that, Beech," Finn spat back. "Ya tink I don't know when's the right time ta be sleeven and when's no good ta turn the whole ting arseways?"

"I amn't sayin' that, now," Beecham replied as he scratched his chin. He shot Cillian and Fiona a guarded look. "Only that it's a hell of a time ta be actin' the maggot wit somethin' like that—"

"I damn well *seen* it out in the bloody trees!"

As the two men argued and the Clan watched in curious silence, Halsey tried to follow the conversation. Most of it was lost on her. With the flask still in her hand but its contents untouched, she leaned toward Seamus and muttered, "What's going on?"

"Finn tinks he's seen sometin'," he replied in a low murmur. "Yet more'n half o' what Finn says on a regular basis isn't quite as true as most'd hope."

"What, you mean Beecham thinks he's messing with everybody?"

Seamus looked at her in surprise, and the corner of his mouth twitched. "Yer learnin' fast."

"Yeah, well...runs in the family, I guess." It came out harsher than she'd meant, but he only laughed and shook his head.

Cillian called Finn toward his table so they could talk in private without the entire Clan putting in their two cents. Despite the conversation being relegated to only a few Havalons, the entire back lawn remained hushed. Even the children took the noisiness of their games down by a considerable amount, and the elementals all watched their Council Head for signs of what was going on.

"He said 'they're up on the mountain,' right?" she asked.

"Aye. That closest one there." Seamus nodded toward the mountain peak she'd been studying in the moonlight.

"Okay. Who's he talking about, though?"

Seamus grimaced as he turned toward her. The second he opened his mouth to respond, she already had her answer.

An eerie, hair-raising howl shot into the night sky, its high, warbling pitch descending into a low growl she instantly recognized. Several howls echoed the first. There was no mistaking what had made the sound.

Seamus pointed at it anyway. "Them."

CHAPTER TWENTY-FOUR

As the werewolf cries faded, Finn turned from the table, spread his arms, and declared, "Told yas."

"Aye, that ya did, lad." Cillian clapped his kinsman's shoulder and nodded at the Clan members. "All the bairns inside, now. Ciara. Ava. Keep an eye on 'em here, and don't let a one out 'til we're home again. The rest of ya, ta'arms!"

A collective cry of readiness rose from the Havalon Clan as everyone who hadn't been specifically called into the house leapt from their chairs and ushered the young ones toward the main house. They moved with such fluid succinctness that Halsey wondered how many times they'd practiced something like this.

Before she could ask Seamus about the plan, the mission, or whatever came next, the Havalon elementals had armed themselves.

In the best way she'd seen yet.

The rows of weapons racks affixed to the back exterior wall of the main house had caught her attention halfway through the night, and Halsey assumed they were there for practice or maybe for show. Now that the entire Clan was gearing up for a fight, it was clear the racks had functional purposes.

The Havalons reached out where they stood and called their weapons to them the way she often called her own. Axes, swords, bows, and staffs whisked away from the wall and zipped across the yard to land firmly in their owners' hands. Tree roots burst from the ground to grab other weapons and toss them toward those who'd ordered such a thing with their magic. One of the older women used a miniature cyclone to transport a set of daggers to her.

If anyone else had watched from the outside looking in, it would have seemed like complete chaos. Yet the elementals recognized it as a steady, precise, prepared moment of monster hunters arming themselves for the job they'd held as long as their Clan had existed.

Halsey and Brigham recognized it too. Their gazes met across the lawn, and Brigham nodded toward the main house.

"Seamus." Halsey faced him as the back yard filled with metal *clinks* and the rush of moving plants, wind, and earth.

An enormous spear with a gleaming metal tip shot into his outstretched hand, and he snatched it from the air before turning to look at her. "Aye?"

"We're coming with you."

"O'course y'are." His carefree smile had vanished, and he gestured at the edge of the forest behind the last of the Havalon buildings. "Unless it takes ya longer'n tree minutes ta get what ya need and get back out here."

"Yeah, that's plenty. We'll be right back." She took off running toward the side of the main house.

"Hal!" Brigham spread his arms in a wordless question.

"Let's go!" The next thing she knew, she and her cousin were racing around the front of the main house side by side, headed for their rental car.

Brigham flicked his hand toward the vehicle before they'd reached it and laughed. "Never thought we'd be back in Ireland fighting the *same* werewolves—"

All four car doors lurched open, the metal squealing in protest after his magic pulled them a little too hard.

"Watch it." Halsey reached out and felt for the life force in the wood and metal of her throwing ax tucked on the floor of the vehicle's back seat. Her weapon slid out and zipped up, clanging against the inside of the rear door before spinning wildly toward her.

"Really?" Brigham scoffed as he raced around the other side of the car to grab his duffel bag where he'd packed his weapons. "You're telling *me* to be careful?"

"Yeah, I know." She snatched her ax and swung it down at her side. "You got insurance on the rental, right?"

"Uh…"

"Forget it. Grab your gear. We only have three minutes."

Brigham finally extricated the bag and slammed the door shut. Halsey shoved the other three closed with her magic, and they sprinted back toward the main house. "Hey, good thing we kept all our stuff in the car," Brigham remarked.

"You're welcome for that idea, by the way."

They shared a light laugh before rounding the corner of the estate house to find the entire Havalon Clan armed with magic and weapons, ready to go. Cillian and another older man were breaking the elementals into teams and giving instructions for flanking and surrounding the werewolves before meeting them head-on in whatever this enormous battle turned out to be.

Clearly, it *would* be enormous with this many elementals working. By the sound of another chilling howl and the calls that rose in response, there were just as many werewolves to deal with. Maybe more of them than elementals.

Which was something Halsey and Brigham were used to at this point.

"Brigham. Hal." Cillian finally noticed the cousins rejoining the monster hunters and nodded. "Yer wit Beecham's party. He knows these hills better'n most, so stay close unless ya know ya can find yer way back."

"Got it," Brigham replied.

Halsey nodded. After Cillian moved on to give more orders, she let herself take in the full sight of so many hunters in one place.

There's gotta be...what? Thirty of us here? Maybe thirty-five? Damn it, I hope there aren't more werewolves than that.

It wasn't like they could go after the entire pack in the same place at the same time. Werewolves moved. Fast. She only hoped the Havalon family understood how fast *they* needed to move to keep up.

"Movin' out!" Cillian called before turning to lead the charge into the woods toward the mountain where Finn had spotted their quarry.

The individual units the Council Head had assigned split from each other and followed the man into the thick, cloying darkness of the woods. Where the entire family had previously been smiling, drinking, laughing, and dancing, now there was only a grim determination to get the job done. Together.

You'd never see the Ambrosius Clan rolling out like this to tackle a monster, even if it was right on the property.

Halsey and Brigham exchanged another glance as they waited for Beecham's smaller unit to move out, and her cousin seemed to be thinking the same thing. She looked at the duffel back he'd pulled from the car, from which he now removed three holstered pistols.

With practiced ease, he armed himself, checked his weapons, then paused to look at her. "What?"

"Pistols. Really?"

"I'm not an idiot, Hal." He produced three extra clips, then dropped the duffel bag on the grass. "I packed silver bullets, too."

Beecham signaled for his team to move into the woods. The man set such a fast pace up the mountainside that it was impossible to keep up any kind of conversation. That was a good thing, of course. Werewolves could hear for miles, and a team like this had to focus on moving quickly and quietly, watching the woods for signs of monsters. Talking was too much of a distraction and a liability.

Even if conversation *had* been an option, Halsey wouldn't have corrected her cousin's misconception. Brigham assumed she didn't approve of his weapons because regular firearms and ammunition were useless against werewolves. Her real distaste had come from the fact that he'd chosen to bring his pistols in the first place.

Which meant he intended to kill whatever creatures came close enough for him to aim and shoot.

Not that Halsey *couldn't* kill a werewolf with one of her

perfectly sized, wonderfully balanced throwing axes. She *wouldn't*. That was the difference between her and her cousin. It was the difference between her and the others in her family. Now that she was out hunting with a different Clan, she seemed to be alone in not assuming that killing the monsters was the only option.

It doesn't matter. I can drive them back like I've always done because that's why we do this. To keep everyone else safe. If the monsters aren't hurting anyone or threatening to, what's the difference?

Even as she thought it, she knew there was a massive difference. These werewolves weren't merely turning during the full moon and hunting local farms one night of the month. They'd gotten fearless, destructive, and sloppy, not to mention a sudden new ability to turn whenever they wanted.

She brushed that from her mind as they moved through the woods with Beecham's team. Right now, it was time to focus. When Halsey met up with a werewolf tonight, she would do what had to be done. Because it was her job.

The almost-full moon cast streams of light through the branches above as the incline along the mountainside increased dramatically. The group's pace slowed so the elementals could climb without winding themselves and giving away their location, but it didn't matter.

The werewolves knew where they were.

Every elemental in their unit stopped without needing a signal from Beecham when twigs cracked on their right, three trees away. A dark streak moved with unbelievable speed—at least unbelievable to anyone who wasn't an elemental monster hunter and used to seeing this kind of thing.

The seven-man team put their backs toward each other and formed a defensive circle between the trees.

"Don't break unless ya know fer a fact ya can take the bastard down on yer own," Beecham muttered. "Sounds like far more'n a few takin' a stab at our neck o' the woods. Be ready fer anytin'—"

With perfect timing, a violent snarl interrupted his command before a massive shape leapt out at them. The Havalon with the clearest shot blasted the werewolf back with a howling vortex of wind from her fingertips. It caught the monster mid-pounce and sent it crashing into a tree trunk with a yelp.

Two seconds later, the forest echoed with snarls, snapping jaws, and slavering growls as more werewolves closed in. Another dropped to all fours and darted at Beecham in an awkward, half-humanoid run on four paws. The man growled right back and swung an enormous billy club studded with nails at the creature's head. There was a sickening crunch and a yelp before the werewolf's body dropped to the forest floor.

"Yeah, about not breaking formation..." Brigham muttered as they watched at least a dozen werewolves closing in on the seven of them. "I don't think we're gonna be able to do that."

"Then fuckin' give 'em hell!" Beecham roared, and that entirely changed the game.

Werewolves snarled and launched at the elementals. The sound of Brigham's pistol firing over and over wasn't the subtlest of ways to fight off an attack like this, but it sure was effective. Silver bullets did the trick.

By the time he'd shot down three werewolves who'd reverted to their human forms in death and lay on the ground as dirt-stained, naked men, the other monsters around them seemed to get the picture.

Stay away from the guns.

They circled the elementals instead, hiding behind trees and racing around the monster hunters in the darkness. Toying with them.

"Is it me, or does it feel like they're the ones hunting us?" Brigham asked.

"Bloody tings tink they can make *us* do what they want," someone else commented.

"They've gotten smarter," Halsey murmured. "Way smarter since the last time we were here."

"Not smarter'n *us*." Beecham nodded farther up the mountainside. "We keep movin'."

They did, and the werewolves kept moving with them. The beasts didn't try to circle and attack all at once again, but they didn't bother sneaking around, either. The woods filled with the sounds of claws raking tree trunks, branches and twigs snapping, and the snarls and heaving breathing of at least another dozen supernatural monsters. Yet the werewolves *did* remain hidden, which meant the elementals couldn't stage an attack even if they'd wanted to. Their hearing wasn't nearly as honed as their targets'.

Something about this is all wrong, Halsey thought as the team hustled up the mountain. *Why would they let us keep moving through the center of their pack without attacking again?*

Unless this is exactly where they want us to go. Because they know what's waiting for us at the top...

"It's a trap." Halsey tightened her grip on her ax and lifted her chin to call toward the front of the unit. "Beecham, it's a trap. We have to hold."

"Werewolves don't set traps."

"I think these ones do." She scanned the dark shapes between the trees and couldn't tell if they were rustling leaves or rippling supernatural fur. "Why else aren't they attacking right now? It doesn't make sense."

"Too scared ta attack and too dumb ta leave off."

"That's not it. They're—"

"Listen here, lass. I know yer used ta doin' tings a certain way, but what yer sayin' is—"

The air exploded with the sound of gunfire, shouting, snarling, and bodies smashing into trees. Up ahead, the muzzle flares of whoever else had brought firearms to a werewolf fight flashed through the trees. Then someone screamed.

"Move!" Beecham shouted, though his unit was already moving toward the other group, who clearly hadn't scared off anything.

As soon as the unit took off, the werewolves surrounding Beecham's group made their move.

"Look out!" Halsey shouted as the first leapt off an outcropping of boulders and pounced at Beecham. The man turned but couldn't get his billy club up in time.

Halsey was already on it.

She reached out to the closest tree beside the boulder and called it toward her. As if it were a giant fly-swatter, the trunk bowed, and a group of pine branches drew back and bashed the werewolf aside. It flew backward and hit the boulder with a yelp. Brigham lowered his pistol for a single shot to the head.

Two more werewolves sprang from the trees, and Halsey didn't have time to be annoyed with her cousin for his instant use of deadly force. There were furry bodies and fangs everywhere.

Elemental magic hurtled through the woods as the Havalons used wind, stone, and living plants to stave off the beastly attack. Several managed to toss aside the closest werewolves before Halsey had a chance, but a low growl behind her made her turn before an enormous wolf-man with black fur and an elongated snout leapt at her.

She shouted, pivoted away, and brought her ax up and back in a wide arc before slicing it down again. The blade caught the creature in the calf, and it yowled before scrambling away from her and disappearing. No, a nick to the leg wouldn't kill it, but at least she'd driven the thing off for a while.

When she spun around again, she saw Beecham's sister Claire staring at her.

"What was that?" the woman asked.

"What?"

"Couldn't've cut it down by the neck instead?"

Halsey shrugged. "Wasn't expecting it, I guess—"

"Hal!" Brigham shouted before firing another silver bullet at a werewolf creeping up behind her. The thing went down instantly, then another jumped over its fallen buddy's body and swiped toward Halsey's head.

She raised her ax in one hand to parry the creature's debilitating blow with its claws, which streaked across the flat of her blade in a shower of sparks. Gritting her teeth, she shoved the creature away from her and reached out with her free hand toward the boulders lodged in the mountainside above. A large chunk crumbled away from the outcropping in response to her magic, and she swung it at the werewolf's shoulder to bash it down the mountain. The creature tumbled, snarling and yelping the whole time, but it would survive.

The other elementals in Beecham's unit were busy fighting off their own attackers. With swords, silver-tipped arrows aimed at the heart, and tree roots summoned from the earth to wrap around legs, arms, and torsos before pulling their victims apart.

Halsey raced to help Beecham with two werewolves who'd cornered him. The man swung wildly with his billy club, occasionally hitting an outstretched claw or the tip of a snout but not doing any real damage. At least, not any that would hurt a werewolf. While the others unleashed their weapons on the attacking creatures, Halsey ducked a swiping claw before bringing her fist up and connecting with the werewolf's exposed throat. It choked and staggered backward, and she kept running toward Beecham.

She reached for the loose soil and rocky shale lining the mountain and grabbed the earth magic inside. Then she tore it loose and flung it at Beecham's werewolves.

One of them caught a mass of particles in the face that sent it yelping away through the trees. The second werewolf managed to shield itself with a furry arm, then turned toward Halsey and snarled.

Beecham cut the snarl off by whamming his billy club into the creature's skull and driving the werewolf into the ground. The sound of nails wrenching from the dead man's head made Halsey stop short. She swallowed and stared at the unrecognizable head and the gore that came with being clubbed to death by a Havalon elemental.

"What're ya playin' at?" Beecham growled. "Kill the bloody tings and be done wit it."

"Kind of an issue with my cousin," Brigham noted as he appeared beside them, one pistol still drawn as he scanned the trees.

"What d'ya mean, *issue?*"

"Uh…yeah. She doesn't exactly *kill—*"

Beecham drew his arm back and chucked his billy club over Brigham's shoulder. It flipped end over end and buried itself in the chest of the last werewolf trying to sneak up on the unit. The werewolf squealed as it thumped to the ground. It had shifted back into a man before the dirt and dry leaves settled around it.

The others turned to observe the well-aimed kill, but Beecham only stared at Halsey. "Take 'em out, lass. Or ya aren't doin' a ting ta help on this side of it."

He stalked off to rip his spiked billy club from the dead werewolf, then signaled for the team to move out.

No one said a word. Especially Halsey. If she opened her mouth now, there was no telling what her frustration might lead her to say. She'd promised the Havalon Clan that she and Brigham *would* help.

When it came to killing their quarry, though, that would have to be on *her* terms.

The unit swiftly moved through the woods, occasionally reorienting themselves to the sound of movement or another group encountering a pocket of this massive werewolf pack. Yet their team didn't get much farther before a long, seemingly endless howl split the night air and made every hair on Halsey's body stand on end.

Once again, she recognized that howl.

So did Brigham, judging by his wide-eyed look.

Their team stopped in surprise, the Havalons visibly shaken by the sound as well.

"Beecham," one of them murmured. "Is that…"

"The alpha," Halsey supplied instead. "The silverback."

"Yep." Brigham nodded as he surveyed the woods. "That's him, all right."

"Then we're goin' after that one." Beecham pointed in the direction of the howl, and the team took off that way.

At least he's confident enough in his family's abilities to let them take care of their own targets. Still, it's been hard enough for the seven of us to take on a dozen of these things. He can't think the alpha will be easier.

Beecham Havalon did not, in fact, expect the task to be easier. He also understood the importance of taking out an alpha monster whenever one had the chance. Defeating an alpha was like cutting off the head of a snake. Get rid of *numero uno*, and the monsters who followed it would scatter into confusion, chaos, and disorganized desperation that often led to meeting their end without a monster hunter involved.

That was his new objective.

Halsey wasn't so sure it would be that cut-and-dried.

The silverback's not like the rest of them. I could tell that much seeing him on the night we found the coffin.

Plus, she had a strong feeling those two things weren't mutually exclusive. The silverback werewolf had revealed himself on the Cliffs of Moher the same night the Mother of Monsters returned from the bottom of the ocean.

Which made this a different kind of werewolf hunt.

They were chasing the silverback anyway, and Halsey wouldn't let what she knew about the creature hold her back from doing what she was born to do. Assuming they found him before anyone else got hurt.

CHAPTER TWENTY-FIVE

The last time Halsey and Brigham had heard the silverback's howl, the creature had called the pack they'd been fighting *away* into the Irish hills. Tonight, the alpha seemed to have a different plan. His howl rang out several more times, answered by dozens of others from every direction. Still, Beecham insisted that his team ignore the smaller, less threatening werewolves in lieu of going after the top dog, as it were.

The alpha renewed the bone-chilling call every minute or two, repeatedly raising goosebumps on Halsey's skin. The sounds of other units fighting werewolves grew more infrequent and faded until the groups were too far away from theirs to help with the bigger prey Beecham sought.

The next time the silverback's unmistakable call warbled through the air, it sounded like he was right beside their group. The elementals paused, listening for any other sign of the alpha.

"Split off," Beecham murmured, then pointed to indicate the cousins could form their own two-man team. "Nobody goes in alone. Is that clear?"

Everyone nodded, and Claire went off with Beecham while the other three Havalons grouped together and headed out.

Halsey and Brigham moved on, branching to the left and directly up the mountain while the others took different directions. No one said a word now because a single sound could put them all in danger. Not that the alpha couldn't track them, but it was strange that the creature had let them get so close without attacking.

Halsey strained to listen for unnatural movement as she slowly crossed the forest floor. Brigham did the same beside her, sweeping his pistol from side to side but finding zero targets.

Another howl broke through the night, and she spun to the right, tapping her cousin's arm. She pointed at a crevice in the rocks ahead. The sound had come from there.

Brigham tapped her back, meaning he'd seen where she was headed, and agreed to follow behind her. She quietly and carefully stepped toward the vertical fissure that appeared to open into a clearing in the woods. Holding her ax out in front so she'd fit inside the narrow crack, Halsey squeezed into the rock.

The air in here was dank, warm, and musky, but she couldn't turn back now.

The alpha's through here. Has to be. There was no room to turn and share a look with her cousin, but she knew Brigham had her back. He always did. *He's also figured out how to be a lot quieter on his feet than normal. Good work, cuz.*

Before she reached the end of the fissure, the alpha

released another piercing howl. The sound was deafening in the narrow rock tunnel. If she'd had the room to move, she would've covered her ears. Instead, she picked up the pace before shuffling clear of the rock into the clearing on the other side.

The clearing wasn't like the others she'd seen in the woods so far. This one was penned in on the right not only by trees but by enormous boulders rising from the ground like buildings. There was plenty of vegetation here. Moss, trees, and low-growing underbrush. On her left was a wall of stone cut into several moss-covered ledges at varying heights.

Halsey smirked as she scanned the clearing. *All right. This alpha likes to lure folks in and get them alone in a stone bowl, huh? Too bad for him I'm not another clueless normie human. I don't consider this a trap.*

She'd only taken three steps across the mossy ground before claws scrabbled across stone, and a dark, blurry humanoid shape streaked past her on the right. Halsey spun and caught a fleeting glimpse of another werewolf standing on one of the enormous boulders. His shoulders were hunched, his chest rapidly rising and falling with obvious effort. He was looking at her, but only because he'd crouched enough to peer behind him with his back to her.

With no trees to limit the moonlight spilling down on him, she had a perfect view of his hunched back, and the thick streak of silver fur racing from skull to tailbone like it was the creature's spine, glowing silver from within.

Here we go.

Halsey stayed still and watched the alpha intently. His

eyes flickered in the moonlight, catching it so they shone silver, too. He was definitely watching her.

He straightened, threw his head back, and howled at the moon again before racing off.

She darted after him without hesitation, thinking only of the job she had to do and the new knowledge she possessed. This wasn't any old alpha, and he wouldn't leave any of these people alone until he was properly dealt with. She had no idea what that truly meant as she raced across the slick moss.

The alpha's form flashed in the moonlight atop the wall of boulders before it disappeared again. The next time she saw it, she reached out for the rock and gripped the surface with her elemental magic. The stone crumbled, slid away, and would have taken the silverback with it if he hadn't been so damn fast.

Halsey hissed, picked up the pace, and waved for Brigham to keep up. "We have to stay on this thing. I'll keep along the boulders here. If it heads onto those ledges and tries to get away, take the shot."

She already knew how her cousin would reply. Brigham would gawk at her suggestion to kill a monster most elementals wouldn't hesitate to take down if they had the chance.

The only thing that surprised her about his response was that it never came.

"Hey, cuz. I need to know we're on the same page here."

When he still didn't answer, she slowed and turned to see what his problem was. "Brigham, are you—"

No. He wasn't.

He wasn't anywhere.

"Brigham?" Her gaze darted from the massive boulders to the rocky ledges on the other side of the clearing, to the crack in the stone through which she'd assumed he'd followed her. Nothing.

"Shit." Halsey eyed every dark crevice and thick shadow, searching for movement. *No big deal. As long as the alpha doesn't get out and his pack doesn't get in, I can handle this.*

So she did.

She made almost no sound as she walked swiftly across the moss, looking everywhere. She searched the boulders and the ledges, which would have illuminated the alpha beneath the moonlight. The creature didn't show himself again. Which only meant she had to keep going.

The clearing seemed to go on forever without another glimpse of the silverback or any sound beyond the wind whistling through tiny cracks or the occasional rustle and creak of a tree.

As she started to think she'd been duped by a supernatural monster, the penned-in space between the rocks banked to the left. Halsey slowed, pressed her back against the curved wall of rocky ledges, and listened.

Oh, shit. What is he doing?

She'd heard the sound of the alpha's ragged breathing. The same depth and cadence as when he'd paused on the boulder to apparently let her catch up. This time, the monster released a tight, huffing growl with each exhale, which was odd because he *knew* she'd come after him.

Why is he giving himself away like that? Either somebody already got a good shot in, and he's injured enough to need a healing break...or this is one obvious-as-hell trap.

Based on the alpha's reactions to this point, the latter option seemed more likely. She took a moment to assess her surroundings and figure out the best way to move forward.

Halsey slid the handle of her ax into its familiar loop at her belt. It made little sound, but there was no way the alpha didn't know she was there. Clearly, it wanted her to come out.

She heard the creature's next inhale and recognized it as the deep breath before another howl. When the piercing note split the air, echoing louder in the stone clearing than it had anywhere else, she made her move.

She darted around the curve in the rocky ledge and found the silverback crouched on his hind legs on a small boulder in the center of the next clearing. Having already called to the trees, the roots, and the vines climbing the stony walls, Halsey employed their inherent magic as quickly as possible.

Vines shot from the wall behind the alpha and coiled around his throat, turning the end of his howl into a guttural grunt. The tree on his right bent toward him so the tips of the branches could whip around one wrist while another rope of vines lashed out to grab the other.

Halsey stalked forward, connected with the life force of the boulder beneath him, and called the entire mass of rock toward her. It jerked out of the earth to answer her elemental command, simultaneously pulling from beneath the alpha's clawed feet. She swept the boulder aside and crashed it against the rock wall, fracturing it into hundreds of jagged pieces, then called the trees to raise their captive higher.

In seconds, she'd caught the silverback alpha in a snare of vines and tree branches, holding him around the neck and torso while raising his arms far enough apart to let him know she meant business. Without the boulder beneath him, the beast dangled helplessly in her snare.

His only reaction was to snap his jaws and growl before snarling and lurching toward her. Beyond that, it didn't look like he was struggling to free himself.

Like I said. Something seriously wrong with this.

She pulled the throwing ax from her hip in one swift movement and hefted it into her hand, her gaze fixed on the silverback.

What's wrong with him?

He jerked his head toward her again, loosening the vines' grip enough to release a strident howl that made her take a step back.

Halsey tightened the vines around his throat as a warning, but it did nothing to stop the sound.

Almost instantly, several Havalon elementals who must have inadvertently found their way to this rocky clearing shouted in the darkness. Their words were garbled and mostly incoherent, but she heard a voice that made her heart stop.

"It's her," Brigham shouted. "She's in there! Hal's in there with that thing. We *have* to go in! Find the fucking entrance!"

Shit. Halsey grimaced and made her first mistake. She turned to look over her shoulder, assuming her hold on the alpha was enough to keep her safe in that brief moment of vulnerability.

It wasn't.

With a tremendous roar, the alpha flexed every muscle in his larger-than-human body and pulled his limbs toward his center. The vegetation groaned and snapped, either falling to the ground or, in the tree's case, whipping the trunk upright. He dropped and landed perfectly on his hind legs, both clawed hands bracing out at his sides.

Halsey took in the reality of what had happened seconds before the alpha snarled and darted toward her. She was ready enough, though.

The creature dodged from side to side, trying to throw her off. She waited until the last second to move. Five black, gleaming, three-inch claws swiped toward her in the darkness, and she ducked before pivoting and swinging her ax toward the silverback's ribs.

He was too fast. She wasn't fast enough.

Instead of her ax sinking into flesh, Halsey hit thin air. The next second, the alpha's claws pummeled her side. She staggered across the clearing until her shoulder bashed one of the boulders that penned them in. She cried out and immediately pushed away from the wall to assess the damage.

Other than a few bruises she'd sport in the morning, there wasn't any damage to assess.

What? The thing's got razors for claws. Why the hell isn't he using them?

Another snarl made her look up from the hand she'd expected to be covered in blood. She met the alpha's silver gaze as he paced across the clearing, honing in on his intended prey.

Halsey readjusted her grip on her weapon. She flexed

her side, found it relatively pain-free, and went back to the fight.

On the other side of the boulders, she heard Brigham and the Havalons shouting at her, calling her name, or shouting at each other as they searched for the entrance to the clearing. She didn't have time to respond because the alpha charged again.

This time, she met the creature's attack without trying to swing her ax. The silverback's lean, awkwardly lengthy body loomed over her as he threw himself from his hind legs, and she played that to her advantage. When he was almost upon her, Halsey dropped into a crouch and dove at the monster's legs. She wrapped her arms around his grotesquely hairy limbs and hung on, hoping to trip the thing up enough to pin it down with whatever elemental energy she could access in time.

She certainly tripped the alpha. He went down over her shoulder with a grunt. Yet Halsey was too overwhelmed by the thing's stench and the unnerving feeling of hairy thighs pressed against her cheek, so she didn't let go in time.

They both hit the ground grappling. The alpha kicked, scratched, and snapped, and Halsey did much the same. The heel of a clawed foot struck her stomach and knocked the wind out of her, but she managed to shove her ax head under the creature's chin and bash its disgusting jaws shut in return. Something warm and hard clamped around her upper arm. She jabbed her other elbow into whatever part of the alpha was closest, which happened to be soft enough that his grip loosened.

All her instincts and training took over. In the next second, she loomed over the werewolf with one knee on his chest, the other digging into his upper arm, and the gleaming blade of her ax tickling the fur along his throat. Apparently, she'd pinned his other arm beneath his back in the process. Fortunate for her, at least.

Yet the alpha didn't struggle.

Even if Halsey *had* killed a monster on purpose, even if she wasn't ethically opposed to the act, the fact that the alpha didn't even try to free himself would have made her pause the way she did now.

This is wrong...

The beast's muzzle peeled back from his devastatingly long canines as he growled again. This time, he didn't snap, writhe around, or try *anything*. Instead, his glowing silver gaze latched onto her, and Halsey felt the strong, rapid, defiant thump of his heartbeat beneath her knee.

"Do it."

When the growling words left the alpha's elongated snout, she almost leapt off the creature. Instead, she held her breath and pressed her ax blade harder against his throat until it touched flesh.

Now you're hearing things, Halsey. End it or don't. Make a goddamn decision.

The alpha lifted his head, which only pressed his throat farther against her weapon. She instinctively retracted her ax by the same amount, but now there was no denying it when the silverback's lips moved, and he spoke again. "End me, witch."

"The fuck?" she whispered. She hadn't meant to say anything, but it slipped out. *This isn't real. Werewolves can't talk. Must've been something in Seamus' flask...*

Somehow, it didn't matter that she hadn't actually taken

a drink before Havalon Clan's attention had been drawn toward Finn and his talk of werewolves.

"Halsey!" Brigg shouted. His voice sounded far away now. "Say something! We're coming to get you!"

She couldn't say anything. She couldn't move.

The alpha released another tremendous snarl and lurched upward. His head and shoulders left the ground, and he drove the blade against his own throat. The movement almost knocked her off him, but he stopped in time to avoid that and huffed a putrid breath into her face.

"I will beg if I must," the silverback growled. "Too long have I lived with this curse. Now I *welcome* death but cannot take it for myself."

"What?" Halsey was on the brink of hyperventilating, or at least she thought she was. The world was spinning. She couldn't feel her grip on the ax handle anymore, but neither could she look away from the silverback alpha *speaking* to her.

"I thought I ended it. For *centuries*, I bore my burden because I knew she was gone. No longer." His growl sounded more like a groan this time, and his silver eyes pulsed with inner light. "I cannot bear to watch the horrors unfold again. The Mother has returned."

Holy shit. No, no, no, no, this isn't happening...

"Halsey, damn ya! Where are ya, lass?" This time, it was Cillian roaring her name among the shouts of other Havalons.

She couldn't answer. Not yet.

"Tell me what that means," she replied, growling in the alpha's face as much as she could manage. "What do you mean, the Mother has returned?"

"Release me, *galdranorn*," he snarled. "End me!"

Halsey pressed her ax against his throat again but drew it back when she remembered that was what he wanted. "Not until you tell me what that means!"

She probably should have known that angering an incredibly powerful beast while he teetered on the precipice of suicide by monster hunter would make him lash out. In all honesty, Halsey couldn't have said she would end his life, even if he'd told her what she needed to know.

It didn't work like that, though.

With a furious snarl, the alpha pushed off the ground enough to knock her off balance and free his pinned arm. He could have tossed her off at any time but had held back in the hopes she'd grant him the mercy of death, not knowing Halsey had a thing about that.

He didn't say anything else, but his intentions were clear when he clamped his claws around Halsey's thigh where she knelt on his chest.

Not around her thigh.

Into it.

Halsey Ambrosius wasn't the kind of girl who screamed, but she did when the silverback's claws pierced her flesh and dug in deep. She was lucky the creature hadn't aimed for *her* throat because it enabled her to react in a way geared toward survival. Instead of trying to put distance between them, she fought the agony of claws *inside* her leg and put all her strength behind ramming her knee into the underside of the werewolf's jaw.

His stained teeth clacked together with a deafening *crack*, followed by his furious roar and Halsey's renewed scream when the deepest claw in her thigh snapped from his hand to remain embedded in her leg. She rolled off the alpha, crying out again as moss, dirt, and small rocks increased the agony in her thigh, but it didn't stop her.

After she was clear, she immediately pushed off the ground and onto one knee, the handle of her ax clenched defensively in both hands.

The alpha lunged toward her, spit flying from his open jaws.

She didn't even think.

Her ax swung with the force of both arms and all her physical momentum behind it. The impact was dizzying.

Halsey's arms and chest ached everywhere. For a moment, she thought she was done for and simply couldn't feel it yet.

Then the alpha's enormous weight against her subsided. His growl morphed into a heavy, blustering sigh of relief. She was no longer pressed against an awkwardly lean, lanky body covered in fur but a man's enormous chest. And in the center of his chest was the blade of her ax.

He sagged against her, and she cried out simply because this was the last thing she'd expected. When the man dropped away from her, she failed to let go of her ax handle and fell forward with him.

Her arms shook. Her whole body shook. She couldn't breathe.

The man with luminous blue eyes and a braided beard falling to the top of her ax, his upper body covered in blackened and fading tattoos of symbols she didn't recognize, blinked slowly before muttering, "Thank you."

"No." She looked him over, hoping this was a nightmare

and at the same time knowing it was perfectly real. Her weapon had reached his heart. There was no turning back from that.

"Remember Rólfr Orgnussun," he murmured. "The first of wolfkind." His eyelids drooped again, and he exhaled words that barely made it out on a ragged breath. *"Munkurinn hafdi rétt fyrir sér..."*

After that, there was nothing else. The silverback alpha werewolf lay there as a man, unclothed and dirty, with the blade of Halsey Ambrosius' ax planted in his heart.

No, no, no. What did I do?

She whipped her hands away from her weapon and tried to shove herself off the man's chest, but the agony of the werewolf's claw embedded in her thigh brought another scream. She toppled sideways off the alpha's body, clutching at her leg. She couldn't stop staring at the motionless face of the stranger. A face that still looked like it was smiling.

Rolfr. That was his...name?

"Found it! Over here!" It wasn't Brigham shouting, but the Havalon Clan had figured out how to get to her.

Time stretched, thinned, and blurred one second into the next as Halsey's cousin and the Irish elementals flooded into the rock clearing. Whatever they shouted at each other, she heard the sounds but couldn't work out the words. Her hands were warm and slick with her own blood. The shaking had stopped, but now she felt like she was about to pass out.

Someone ripped her throwing ax free from the enormous dead man's chest, but she didn't know who. Everyone was talking at once.

Brigham's face appeared in front of her, and it took her longer than it should have to realize he was grinning.

"Holy shit, Hal. You fucking did it!"

"I…" A groan escaped her, and she looked at her leg to see an entire inch of werewolf claw protruding from the hole in her blood-stained jeans.

"Shit. Let's get you outta here." Brigham slung her arm around his shoulders to support her in standing, but they couldn't go yet. Every Havalon elemental who'd made it into the clearing blocked their way, staring at them.

Cillian stepped forward, his eyes wide before he gestured toward the dead man on the ground. "Ya did this yerself?"

Halsey swallowed thickly at the pain in her injured leg and the fog overwhelming her brain. "I didn't mean to."

The Havalon Council leader gawked at her, then threw his head back and laughed. "And ta tink we thought the stories were notin' but tall tales! Ta Hal, slayer of the last alpha bastard in Ireland!"

"Ta Hal!" The Havalons in the clearing echoed the cheer.

After that, Halsey Ambrosius didn't remember much of anything.

CHAPTER TWENTY-SIX

The trip back down the mountain and toward the Havalon Clan's estate only reached Halsey's awareness in flashes of dark silhouettes, flickering firelight, and *lots* of shouting. When she'd look back on it later down the road, she would swear she'd heard Brigham shouting loudest and most frequently, but that may have been because she recognized her cousin's voice more than anyone else's.

She did remember laughter. Cheers. Dozens of Havalon voices chanting her name as the party of werewolf hunters rushed from the trees across the wide lawn scattered with picnic tables and the remnants of their feast. She remembered not being able to walk with the broken claw embedded in her leg, and she remembered the strong arms of multiple Havalon elementals supporting her down the mountain and through the back door of the main house.

All of it was to the tune of victorious cries and repeated stories of how she'd singlehandedly taken down the most brutal beast of all those that had plagued their homeland for months. Though the entire Clan had returned to their celebratory mood, with good reason, they called out for supplies, tools, and healing ointments with equal fervor to get Halsey the medical attention she needed.

The next thing she knew, she was half-carried, half-supported down a long back hall of the main house and into a simple, spacious room. Halsey wasn't aware enough to recognize or remember which two Havalons helped her into the room, and she didn't have a chance to thank them, either.

It was quieter here, so far removed from the triumphant bustle, rowdy shouts, and raucous laughter of the Clan's militia operatives returned from the hunt. So quiet that she finally had the chance to hear herself think as she lay against a stack of pillows on an elevated hospital bed that looked like the one Brigham had been confined to.

With nothing else to focus on, it also gave her the opportunity to feel the agony coursing through her right leg, up her hip, and into her back.

At that point, the rest of her awareness returned, and she worked up enough morose curiosity to look at her leg.

There was the splintered, broken end of the alpha's black claw poking from her thigh. Her jeans leg was soaked with blood, and she pressed her hands above the wound in a reflexive attempt to put the necessary pressure there. Then she realized someone had already tied a belt around the top of her thigh as far up and tight as it could possibly go.

At least someone *was thinking clearly through all the victory cries...*

To be safe, she further tightened the makeshift tourniquet, gritting her teeth through the pain and biting back a shout before the multiple loops of the belt were tight enough to slip the buckle's pin into the next hole.

The second it did, the door opened, and Fiona Havalon burst in with two younger women at her heels.

"What the hell d'ya tink yer doin'?" she snapped when she saw Halsey's hands on the makeshift tourniquet. "Don't ya dare touch that, understand? I can set ya right, but only if yer still breathin' by the time I start."

Halsey frowned at the woman. Of all the Havalons who could have given her medical attention, it had to be Cillian's wife and Seamus' mother. "I got stabbed in the leg, not the lungs."

The two women Halsey didn't recognize paid no attention to the odd conversation as they hurried around the room, opening cabinets and drawers, pulling out the necessary tools for what would clearly be an at-home surgical procedure.

Fiona stopped halfway across the room and blinked in surprise. Her gaze flickered from Halsey's thigh to the young woman's face, then laughed and shook her head. "No shite, lass. And now I'm startin' ta retink everytin' I've heard in the last five minutes."

Halsey gripped the edges of the narrow bed and forced herself to watch the assistants bustling around the room instead of staring at one of the worst injuries she'd received on the job in a long time. "What did you hear?"

"That Hal Ambrosius doesn't take shite from anyone, even with a hole in her leg." With a snort, Fiona hurried toward the foot of the hospital bed and snapped her fingers. Her assistants rolled two tall, stainless-steel medical trays toward her, each of them coming from different directions. Fiona pulled up a small round stool on wheels, raised the seat's height by at least three inches, then sat and held out a hand toward the younger woman on her right. A pair of surgical gloves slapped into her open palm, and she tugged them on with brisk elastic snaps.

"Did ya really say ya *didn't mean* ta end that alpha up there?"

It took Halsey a minute to remember that had been her response when asked if she'd managed it on her own. She gritted her teeth and nodded once. "Not all that weird in the scheme of things, but everyone here seems to think it's hilarious."

This time when Fiona held out her hand, it was covered in a glove. The neoprene muted the surgical scissors that one of the assistants clapped into it. She leaned forward to study the claw protruding from her patient's thigh, and a tiny smile flickered across her lips. "In the face of all that? Aye. 'Tis hilarious. Ya can relax a bit, lass. I'm only cuttin' up yer jeans. Fer now."

Halsey's grip tightened, and she held her breath in anticipation before remembering there was nothing threatening about cutting her clothing away from an open wound. Her exhale came out in a long, slow, stuttering breath, but she didn't move.

The scissors sliced away at the denim, and Fiona kept talking as if they were sitting together over a cup of coffee. "What the rest of us can't figure out is whether or not ya meant it."

"Well, I wasn't lying about it for fun, if that's what you're wondering." The sharp, snappy tone in her own words made Halsey grimace, but that could've been explained by the two inches of claw stuck inside her.

Fiona sniggered. "Why in the *world* would ya set out after an alpha werewolf witout *meanin'* ta finish the job?"

"That's not what I do," Halsey murmured, entranced by the quick, precise snips of Fiona's scissors as the woman tore through the center of the pant leg and cut a large swath of fabric out from around the claw.

"What isn't?"

"Killing monsters." Halsey sucked a sharp breath when her healer for the evening peeled the blood-sticky fabric from her skin. "I don't know why, but it...bugs me. Always has. So I don't do it."

As she spoke it, Fiona's assistant handed over a cotton swab soaked in an iodine solution and sterilizing alcohol. Before applying it, the woman paused and looked up to meet the young Ambrosius elemental's gaze. The mix of amusement and empathy in Fiona's green eyes surprised Halsey, especially paired with the woman's next words. "Well, ya do *now*."

Halsey wanted to deny the sentiment, but she couldn't. Not really. She'd gone up that mountain to help drive the werewolves away from the Havalon Clan's home, and she'd come back down with the silverback alpha's blood on her hands. Literally and figuratively.

That doesn't mean I kill monsters. It was an accident.

Fiona pressed the cotton balls gently against Halsey's leg to clean around the claw, and the sharp sting of the antiseptic in an open wound made it easier to clarify her own thoughts.

No. The ogres were an accident. Even if I didn't know it at first, this was on purpose. I killed that alpha because it was either him or me. And we both *wanted it to be him...*

The truth in that made her dig her fingers into the underside of the bed. While she gritted her teeth through the pain of this simple procedure that hadn't even touched the damn claw yet, the rest of her body remained still.

Fiona dropped the cotton balls on one of the stainless-steel trays and looked at her patient again. "Yer no stranger ta pain, are ya?"

"Not really."

"Aye. I can tell." The woman nodded at the cleaned area of skin around Halsey's wound, then accepted a pair of pliers from one of the assistants standing dutifully beside her. "Normally, I'd recommend a belt between yer teeth, but ya seem ta have a handle on that. So whatever ya were tinkin' 'bout just now, I suggest ya keep it in mind."

"Right." The reply burst from her in a huff, and Halsey might have laughed if she hadn't been so disheartened by Fiona's well-meaning advice.

Keep thinking about how I killed an alpha werewolf by not even trying. Like that'll help.

Yet when Fiona clamped the pliers around the splintered end of the claw, Halsey was surprised to find that was where her mind went anyway. Not because the pain was unbearable but because the memories of what she'd done tonight *were*. Now she had an excuse to walk herself through them without anyone seeing her reaction and wondering what was wrong.

Her Havalon nurse worked efficiently, with a conscientious awareness of how one did not simply yank a foreign body from a wound like it was a giant splinter. As she did,

Halsey kept her eyes closed and considered the silverback and what he'd said. The fact that he'd spoken to her at all was mindboggling, then it had only gotten more confusing and, admittedly, terrifying.

He wanted me to kill him. Because he knew the Mother of Monsters is back. Because he knew how shitty things are about to get now that she's here. Because he...had a conscience?

That seemed ridiculous, but there was no other way to spin it. The impossible had become possible tonight. Talking werewolves, confirmed proof of the Blood Matriarch's return, Halsey *killing* her first monster. Not by accidentally chopping off its blood-rune-cursed hand but because it was the only choice she'd had, and she'd known what she was doing. Her instincts and her training had done what she'd been forcing them not to for the last five years after hearing what amounted to the alpha's confession before he'd begged her for death. She hadn't given it willingly, so he'd used *his* last resort to force her.

That didn't make her feel better about it.

In fact, it made her feel worse.

"Almost there," Fiona soothed, one hand pressing on Halsey's thigh to create a constant, aching pulse in the muscle while her other held the pliers with perfect steadiness. "One more pull should do it. Then we move quick ta stop the bleedin' and have this whole ting wrapped up in no time."

Whether she was speaking to her patient, her assistants, or both, Halsey decided to open her eyes and look at the woman's work.

The claw had to be more than halfway out by now, with almost two inches jutting from her flesh and the tip nowhere in sight. Fiona nodded without looking away. That was the only signal she gave before pulling on the pliers that gripped the lowest bit of exposed claw like a vice.

Halsey couldn't have said how much the first part of the procedure hurt because she hadn't been paying attention until now.

This part was excruciating. Somewhere in the back of her mind, she was aware of the high probability that it only hurt so much because of everything that came with the wound left by her first real kill.

The only reaction Halsey had was to grit her teeth harder and stare at the last of the claw as it slid free. She didn't realize her own tears were a factor until two of them spilled from the corner of her right eye and rolled down her flushed-hot cheek in quick succession.

The broken claw *clinked* onto a stainless-steel tray along with the pliers, and Halsey got a brief glimpse of the thing a split second before Fiona and her assistants jumped into action again.

Slightly over three inches of razor-sharp alpha werewolf claw lay there, smeared with her blood. Yet it didn't hide the most striking details of the thing's coloring. Pitch-black with a single stripe of glimmering silver racing up the side.

More pressure bore down on Halsey's thigh, and it felt like Fiona and her two assistants were pressing down on *her* all at once. At least, they were a lot closer with a lot more hands on her.

"Still wit us up there?" Fiona asked before glancing at her patient's flushed face. Halsey forced her gaze away from the claw to look into the woman's bright green eyes. Another tiny smile flickered across Fiona's lips. "Oh, aye. Ye'll be right as rain in no time, lass. Ye'll see."

Halsey let them tend to her wound with quick, effective movements as they cleaned and sanitized the gaping hole in her leg, sewed a few stitches, and wrapped the whole thing in gauze and tape to keep everything firmly in place. She didn't say another word, and she didn't bother to wipe the tears off her cheek before they dried.

When it was done, Fiona dismissed her assistants and stayed behind for a short, private moment with her patient. She didn't say that was why she'd stuck around, but there was no other reason for her to send the younger Havalon women out of the room. Especially when she started talking as she tossed bloody rags into a laundry hamper and bloody surgical instruments into a separate tray.

"I remember my first, too, ya know." Once again, the woman spoke as if they were having a casual, everyday conversation. Like there was nothing strange about tending to an elemental capable of taking down the silverback alpha who wasn't even part of her own Clan. "'Course, t'wasn't nearly as impressive as yers..."

Halsey sat on the hospital bed with her bandaged leg stretched in front of her and watched the woman work. *Yeah, super reassuring coming from another elemental who knows all about killing and more killing. I do not need a heart-to-heart right now.*

Finished with the piling, stacking, and throwing away, Fiona stripped off her gloves, dumped them in the trashcan, then faced her patient again with a knowing smile. "T'wasn't anytin' I ever thought I'd set my sights on, either."

The oddity of that statement hit Halsey with perfect clarity, and she gaped at the woman when it finally made sense. "You're not an elemental."

Fiona chuckled and spread her arms. "Come, now. We know you Ambrosius folk've been carryin' the blue ribbon when it comes ta numbers and successes. Don't go tellin' me your kin all tink the Havalons're out here drinkin' 'n dancin' n' marryin' our own."

"What?" Halsey lurched off the pillows, then grimaced at the flash of pain shooting through her leg.

Fiona *tsked* and headed for one of the cabinets along the wall. "That'll be my fault, lass. Tinkin' I could work ya over like that without a little sometin' ta take the edge off."

"I didn't mean it like that," Halsey explained as she readjusted her position to find one that sparked the least amount of pain possible. Unfortunately, there wasn't one.

"I know what ya meant." Fiona chuckled as she pulled out a bottle of pills, then filled a paper cup of water from the small sink built into the countertop. "We all have our own ideas of who we are. As different Clans. As different hunters. As people, aye?"

The dedicated focus and precision on the woman's features as she'd worked was gone, replaced by the same amusement and empathetic concern that had taken Halsey so off guard before. Halsey couldn't help but smile back when Fiona offered her the water and two pills she'd shaken out of the bottle.

"For the pain, lass. Though knowin' the way all ya magical folk handle it, ya won't be needin' any kind o' relief fer long."

"Thanks."

Fiona waited until her patient had downed the pain pills and drained the water, then she pressed the bottle into Halsey's hand and nodded. "Yer right about *me*. Not one bit o' this is magical in any o' the ways we're talkin'. Aye, I married in. I *chose* this. When I also chose ta do my part and head off with the rest o' the huntin' party ta do what this Clan does best, well… First time, I had no clue what I'd signed myself up fer. Still don't have a clue, but that's a whole different conversation."

Halsey glanced at the pills in her hand and wasn't surprised to find the bottle completely unmarked. "My Pappy was like that," she murmured. "Married for love. Stayed for monster-hunting."

Fiona barked laughter. "Oh, aye. Hell of a way ta put it." She stuck her hands on her hips and tilted her head to scan the "slayer of alpha werewolves" with a pert smile. "The point I'm tryin' ta make here is that I never expected ta come home from a hunt wit another creature's life on my conscience. Didn't expect it ta hit so hard, either, and that's comin' from a woman who had ta reinvent everytin' she knew 'bout the way the world works. And about who she wanted ta be in it, aye? I know it hurts, lass. When folks keep sayin' ya were born fer it, like as not that hurts even more. Yet don't go tinkin' all that pain makes ya worse fer it, understand? Just 'cause it hurts don't mean it's not the right ting ta do."

Halsey couldn't think of anything to say. The woman had read her thoughts and emotions in a way almost every person in her life seemed incapable of doing.

I'm not the only person in the world to kill a monster for the first time. Doesn't mean I have to be like everyone else on every hunt after this.

Fiona dipped her head to catch her patient's gaze and widened her eyes. "Ya hear what I'm sayin', lass?"

"Yeah, I hear you." Halsey stared back and managed a small, tired smile. "Thank you."

"Don't mention it." Fiona chuckled and waved off the comment. "'Sides, I did it as much ta save me own skin as I did yers. Can't have the whole bloody Ambrosius Clan stormin' Ireland's shores. All 'cause one Havalon healer witout magic couldn't manage ta put ya back together the right way."

They both laughed, then the woman turned and headed for the door. "Change o' clothes right here on the counter if ya care ta use 'em. Feel free ta grab a crutch from off the wall there, too. Or not. Whatever ya choose, take yer time, lass. Only not *too* long, aye? There's a party burnin' at both ends out there, and this time, it's fer Hal Ambrosius."

She didn't have to respond to that because Fiona shot her a wink and swiftly left the room.

The door clicked shut, and Halsey was left on the hospital bed with a thoroughly bandaged leg and a bottle of painkillers in her hand.

Great. Now what am I gonna give Brigham shit for if I'm as buzzed as he is?

CHAPTER TWENTY-SEVEN

Halsey waited until the pain pills started to kick in, which didn't take nearly as long as she'd expected. The stabbing pain in her thigh had dulled to a bearable pulsing ache. She had no problem sliding off the bed and hobbling around to change into the loose sweatpants left for her on the counter, though she left on her t-shirt and light canvas jacket. After what she'd seen of the Havalon family, she was afraid taking them off would get them swept up and efficiently cleaned before she could wonder where they'd gone.

She didn't think she could handle any more Havalon hospitality without breaking down in gratitude and losing it.

Her jeans, on the other hand, weren't salvageable. She was fine with that.

The only complaint she had was that she moved too slowly, even with the crutch she grabbed from the wall. That didn't matter much when she left the medical room and headed down the hallway toward the center of the

Havalon Clan's giant estate house. It didn't matter that she had no idea where she was going, either. The sound of laughter, cheering, excited conversation, and cups clinking together in toasts spelled out an auditory roadmap, and the path to the "party" was simply following the noise.

She emerged from the hallway more suddenly than she'd expected. When the Havalons noticed her entrance, the noise momentarily died down.

Cillian raised an actual metal tankard and grinned. "There she is! Come grab a drink, Hal. If ya haven't earned it by now, the rest of us sure as shite haven't."

The room broke into rowdy laughter, and Halsey smiled. The expression felt weaker on her lips than she'd wanted.

After a little bumping around and muttering under his breath, Brigham stole away from his seat at a table in the middle of the enormous common room and made his way toward her. "How you doin'? You okay?"

"Oh, you know. Just had two inches of werewolf claw pulled out of me. No big deal."

Her cousin flashed her a winning grin and shrugged. "Well, it's not getting pancaked between a tree and an ogre or three, but hey. Might have a cool battle scar."

"Yeah, that's *exactly* what I've been hoping for this whole time."

They laughed, then he examined her before his gaze lingered on the crutch pinned under her arm. "Come on. Let's get you a drink."

"I took some painkillers already—"

"Right. Yeah. Okay, only *one* beer." Brigham winked and helped her hobble across the room to the closest table.

Several Havalons stood to offer her a more convenient seat despite her protests.

A few more scrambled around at Brigham's instruction to get his cousin *only one beer*, most of them looking confused by the request. Finally, Halsey got her single drink and a sturdy chair under her. Even if she'd wanted to call it a night then and there, it would've been impossible.

It's not like I'd be able to sleep right now, anyway. Might as well stay up and party with the Havalons, right?

Cillian called for another toast. "Ta Hal!"

Everyone in the room echoed the cry, including the children thrusting juice boxes and soda cans overhead. The ribald conversation returned full force, and Halsey tried to relax as much as possible with her injured leg propped on another chair. Everything she heard centered around the recent hunt and everyone's own interpretation of Halsey Ambrosius going up against the silverback.

Brigham got caught up in all the stories until he noticed his cousin wasn't her usual joking, witty self. "Hey." He gently nudged her arm, and his smile faded. "You sure you're good? We can call it a night now. Say the word."

She raised an eyebrow and lifted the beer from which she'd maybe taken three sips. "Painkillers and a giant hole in my leg, cuz. I'm good."

"You're not screwing with me?"

"Promise."

Brigham took her at her word, which made it easier for Halsey to convince herself she was okay.

Fortunately, amid the drunken retelling of tonight's event, no one asked *her* what had happened in that clearing. If they had, she probably would have told them the various versions floating around were way more exciting. Revealing that the alpha had spoken to her, that he'd both begged her and thanked her for death before giving her his *name*, was out of the question. At least for tonight.

Time ceased to exist as the party continued far into the night. Even the young children stayed up later than they were usually allowed. When Halsey noticed the absence of them running between tables, shouting, laughing, and playing on the floor, she noticed a few pockets of small kids curled up in the corners of the room together, sound asleep.

Some of the older Havalons started turning in for the night, which didn't do much to lessen the noise. Yet when the drinking slowed, and the general atmosphere dwindled into murmured conversations and low laughter around the blazing hearth on the far wall, it was clear the party would soon end. Maybe even before the sun rose.

After the final hour of Brigham telling the Havalons at their table all kinds of stories about him, Halsey, and the creatures they'd gone after during past missions, he released an enormous belch and slapped the table. "Well. If I keep talking like this, I won't even be able to drink. First, I gotta…take a quick break. Be right back."

He pushed woozily from his chair, swayed a little, then turned in a slow circle until he successfully found the direction of the bathroom.

"Need help, lad?" someone shouted after him.

"Hell no. But *you* will if you even think about coming with me."

That got everyone laughing before more Havalons realized it was getting to that time of the night, even for a party like this with one hell of a reason to celebrate. Those who'd been sitting at Halsey's table used Brigham's absence as an excuse to call it a night for themselves. Halsey smiled, nodded, and shook hands with everyone wishing her a good night and job well done. In a matter of minutes, most of the Havalons had cleared from the common room, leaving only small, scattered pockets behind.

Part of her was relieved to see so many elementals leaving the room. The other part didn't want the party to be over yet, because she wasn't sure she was ready for what might happen when she got into a bed, including whether she'd be able to sleep even with the painkillers.

When she realized it was only her and Seamus at this particular table now, she didn't know what to think.

He caught her gaze from the other end of the table, smiled crookedly, then stood and walked toward her before taking a seat across from her. "So."

"So." She sipped her beer merely for something to do, though it seemed like her glass had been half-full for the last hour, at least.

"Hard enough ta get a word in edgewise wit the rest o' the family fightin' each other ta talk ta *The Alpha Hunter*."

Halsey chortled. "Nobody's calling me that."

"They are *now*." Seamus laughed with her as he folded his arms on the table. "Apparently, The Alpha Hunter herself couldn't come up wit sometin' better, so I'm afraid it's bound ta stick."

She stared at the table in mock irritation and wrinkled her nose. "Well, I guess it could've been worse."

"Aye, ya tink so?" His blue eyes glittered in the low light, which had been dimmed at some point during the celebration in an attempt to increase the ambiance. Then it seemed the two young elementals had run out of things to say, and Seamus' easygoing smile faltered. "The title could be worse, sure. What about the woman behind it?"

Halsey scoffed and tried to let the question roll off. "She's fine, thanks."

"And talkin' 'bout her own self like she's not sittin' here at the table."

"Well, I can't blame the drinks..." Halsey wrapped a hand around her beer glass but didn't bother to drink more. "I *can* say your mom keeps a hell of a pharmaceutical stash in that surgery room of hers."

"Ah." Seamus nodded sagely. "And she shared it."

"She shared it." That brought another smile to her lips, though she wasn't sure if the heaviness in her body was from the painkillers, sheer exhaustion, or sitting at a mostly empty table with one seriously attractive Havalon who acted like this was what he'd wanted all night.

Minus the short werewolf hunt and a giant hole in my leg, but hey. Can't blame the guy for not having predicted that.

The thought made her snort, and Seamus arched an interested brow. "What is it?"

"Nothing." Halsey shook her head. "I'm fine, Seamus. Really. My new title notwithstanding."

It was a reasonable response, but the black-haired Irishman wouldn't back down. He kept staring at her, his gaze searching her face despite his tiny smile that never seemed to fade.

Why is he looking at me like that? We met this afternoon. In a seedier-than-seedy pub that half the country doesn't know about and never will. He's looking at me like Brigham *does right before he asks if I'm sure I'm not full of shit.*

She might have laughed at that too if Seamus Havalon's gaze wasn't so intense and didn't catch her so off guard every time she looked at him. She figured the best way to end that cycle was to look him in the eye and repeat herself. "You can stop looking at me like that. I'm fine."

"Aye, ye've said that *tree* times now." He lowered his voice so he wouldn't be heard by the dozen or so of his family members scattered around the room. "I'm still wonderin' why ya look about ta pop if ya don't up and say the ting fightin' ta burst out."

"What *thing*?"

"Whatever it is ya wanna say but can't figure out how."

Jesus, does the Havalon Clan specialize in reading minds, too?

Halsey held his gaze a little longer, then glanced at the hallway where Brigham had disappeared to the restroom. There was no sign of him.

Can't hurt to ask a few things, right? As long as I don't include the part that's gonna make me sound like a lunatic.

"Okay, fine." After scooting her chair closer, which was awkward due to her injured leg being propped on another chair, Halsey leaned over the table and asked, "Do you know anything about languages?"

Seamus frowned and glanced toward the bathrooms. "This wasn't sometin' ya could've asked wit yer cousin sittin' close?"

"No. Only because Brigham's a little…sensitive about it." When her off-the-cuff lie only produced more confusion, she added, "That was the only thing he almost failed before we tested out of training. Regional languages. I mean, he *didn't* fail, but it's been a sore spot ever since. Talk about not letting something go, right?"

"Huh. Wouldn't've pegged him fer the studious type."

"Only when it gets him past training and out in the field." They shared a laugh over that, and Halsey forced herself to make it look real. *Sorry, cuz. Though we could probably file this one under 'having my back,' too...*

"Go ahead, then," Seamus invited before sipping his drink. "I know a ting or two 'bout languages. Doesn't have anytin' ta do wit talkin' monsters, though, does it? 'Cause now would be a hell of a time ta bring sometin' like that up."

She almost choked without the excuse of a drink going down the wrong pipe. "Talking *monsters*? Come on. That's ridiculous."

"'Tis." He looked ready to crack up laughing but managed to hold it together. "If ya aren't askin' 'bout any o' that, I reckon anytin' else is fair game."

"Right." She had to clear her throat again to get rid of the tickling feeling, then she relented and knocked back more beer because it was in front of her. That helped before she launched into the question. "This is probably a shot in the dark, but... '*Munkurinn hafdi rétt fyrir sér.*'"

Seamus' eyes widened, and he leaned away from the table. "Beg yer pardon?"

"Shit. If it's something awful, I swear I had no idea—"

His deep, easy laughter cut her off, and she glanced around the common room to make sure they hadn't caught anyone's attention. Not that it would have ruined anything, but she didn't feel like trying to explain herself to any more people. Especially when she was telling what amounted to half a lie.

"It doesn't mean anytin' terrible," Seamus replied as his laughter died down. "Not that I know, anyhow."

"Good." The relief was real. "What does it mean?"

"Honestly?" He shrugged an apology. "I don't exactly know that, either."

"Oh." *Great. Tossed that one up in the air and came back with nothing.* It took effort to hide her disappointment. Judging by his next words, she figured she'd done a decent job.

"I *do* know what it sounds like. Closer ta Icelandic than anytin' else."

"Icelandic."

"Yes, but not quite. My first guess'd be Old Norse, but I'd wonder why yer bringin' a ting like that ta *me*." Seamus' frown deepened. "Ya know what? Forget that last part. Why *are* ya bringin' a ting like that ta me?"

Answering stuff like this was in Brigham's wheelhouse, but Brigham wasn't here. He also didn't know about the talking silverback alpha or what the dying man had said in a foreign language she didn't recognize. Now, she had to think fast about how *not* to make this sound like a cover-up. "It's something I heard a while back during a minor mission. It's been on my mind since then. Plus, earlier in the night, I heard some of your family speaking...Gaelic, I think. I guess I figured you might know more about old languages than me."

"Huh." He scanned the room and the other Havalons keeping the hearth fires burning. "Sure. Probably heard my Gran and Granda havin' themselves a chat in the old tongue. But I don't understand a word of it, or of Old Norse. Sorry ta disappoint, Hal."

"Not a disappointment at all." The tone of her words sounded opposite to their message, and she couldn't help laughing. "Guess it was too much to ask for a major werewolf win *and* a dead-language translator in the same night."

"Ah." Seamus lifted a finger and exaggerated a grimace. "Can't say I had anytin' ta do with one or t'other of those, either way. But I amn't craven enough ta let that keep me from callin' out me own shortcomin's. How 'bout ya let me make me it up to ya?"

His fake grimace melted into that gleaming, boyish grin Halsey had gotten lost in too many times since they'd met ten hours ago. Part of her wanted to take him up on the offer, whatever that might be. Except it was the part that hadn't delivered a mercy killing the alpha had been *desperate* to receive. The part that didn't know a thing about the Mother of Monsters or that every elemental Clan on this planet would have to make serious changes and end their pointless feuds if they were to have the smallest chance of making it through to the end.

It was the part that would have had no problem spending the night with a charming, sexy Irishman who could read her like a book. That part of Halsey Ambrosius had almost zero responsibilities off the clock. Not to mention the extra satisfaction of enjoying another elemental Clan far more than she remembered enjoying her own family.

Yet that part didn't stand a chance against the rest of her. She had too much on her mind and too much left to do before she could relax enough to enjoy something like that.

She fixed Seamus with a knowing smile, drew a deep breath, and nodded. "That sounds good…just not tonight."

"All right." His smile grew, deepening the dimples in his cheeks as he sat a full head taller than anyone else in the room. "Tomorrow, then."

She tried not to laugh. "I meant another time, Seamus. Right now, it's—"

"I get it." He didn't look disappointed as he held her gaze. "The Alpha Hunter has a bloody gigantic heap on her plate, aye?"

"Something like that." She wanted to say more, but her cousin's timing was perfect. At least as far as ruining the moment was concerned.

"Whew!" Brigham staggered out of the hallway and slapped a hand against the wall to steady himself. "How the hell do you guys get around in this place? I swear it took me like fifty minutes to get *out* of the bathroom…wait. No. Fif*teen*."

"Looks like ya still made it in one piece, Brig-o." Seamus chuckled. "As long as yer trouble comes *after* the jacks and not before, I'd call that a win."

"The jacks… The jacks…" Brigham stumbled toward them, then planted both hands on the table and frowned. "Oh, shit! Like hitting the john, right?"

"Oy!" one of Seamus' cousins called from across the room. "Who the hell's John, and why're we hittin' 'im?"

Halsey burst out laughing.

Her cousin shot her a crooked, mostly drunken smile. "I like these people, Hal. *They* know how to take a joke."

"And how ta hold our drink," Seamus added with a smirk. "Don't tell me ya tried ta keep count with Brennan—"

"Yes." Brigham pointed at him as his head bobbed. "Yes, I did."

"And succeeded," Brennan shouted from a group of late-night Havalons, who laughed at the outburst.

Brigham grinned at them, then had to put his hand back down to keep from falling over. "Man. Hate to ask, Shane, but do you guys have a couple of extra beds here? Only for tonight. I don't think I could find our car even if the valet brought it to me."

"Aye? Well, damn. Guess we should've thought o' that *before* all the inns closed down fer the night." Seamus held a fake frown as long as possible, then met Halsey's gaze and smiled.

Either Brigham couldn't decide which one of them he wanted to look at, or he was too drunk to notice the difference. "Seriously?"

"'Course not, Brig-o. I'm takin' the piss. Come on." Seamus stood and grabbed Brigham's upper arm. "Right on up the stairs wit ya, and lucky fer *you*, there's a toilet down the hall... Shite." He paused with a swaying Brigham in one hand and looked over his shoulder at Halsey. "All the beds in the Big House're upstairs. We can make sometin' up fer ya down here, if that's easier—"

"I can handle a few stairs." With a tight smile, she lowered her leg off the chair and grabbed the crutch to help herself stand. "Wouldn't be the first time I've done it with crutches, either."

He nodded and returned his full attention to the inebriated Ambrosius in dire need of support. Halsey was grateful he didn't ask if she was sure this time. No one else asked either.

After saying her tired goodnights to the Havalons, who would most likely still be drinking and talking at dawn, she hobbled across the common room toward the open staircase.

It wasn't difficult to climb the stairs, only slow. Thanks to Fiona's free pharmaceuticals and probably the beer, Halsey didn't feel any worse at the top of the stairs than she had at the bottom. She didn't feel any better, either.

Especially when a door down the hall opened after she reached the top landing and Seamus stepped out. He stopped when he saw her, then pulled the door shut behind him. "Well, yer cousin's taken care of fer at least the next eight hours. Maybe ten, if he really did match Brennan drink fer drink."

"I'm sure he did." She crutched a few steps forward, then smiled sheepishly. "I can make it up the stairs, but finding the right room might be more time-consuming..."

"Ah. Right." He looked up and down the hall, then crossed it to open the door directly across from Brigham's room. "Toilet's down the hall there. Room should have everytin' ya need, otherwise. Unless there's...sometin' I can get ya now?"

"All I need is a bed and to stop thinking. About everything."

"Aye." He waited for her to hobble into the room, but he didn't leave until after she'd lowered herself to sit on the edge of the twin-sized bed. When she glanced at him again, he was watching her with a knowing smile. "At the least, then, I'll wish ya sweet dreams fer the night."

"Ha. I don't think sweet dreams will do much for me now, but thanks anyway."

"Nah. Yer like me that way. One good night o' sleep, and ye'll be mostly back ta normal in the mornin'."

Halsey was surprised to laugh at that, but he wasn't wrong. Havalon or Ambrosius, elementals did heal fast. His face lit up, and it felt like they'd been staring at each other way too long across the small room. One of them had to end it. "Good night, Seamus."

"Sleep well, Alpha Hunter." With a wink, he backed away and pulled the door shut. The last thing she saw in the sliver of open doorway was his glinting smile.

CHAPTER TWENTY-EIGHT

The next morning, Halsey found only one positive change when she realized she no longer needed the crutch to get around. She still felt as terrible as she'd thought she would —physically, emotionally, and mentally. It seemed she was the only one in the Big House who did.

After showering and re-donning the sweatpants Fiona had handed her the night before, she left her small but efficient guest room. The noise from the first-floor common area hit her the second she opened the door. The shrieks of children mixed with the lower booms and hurried shouts from adults. Dozens of voices vied to be the loudest and grab the most attention, which made it impossible to hear anything anyone said.

Yet the laughter and excitement was clear, and the sound only made the knot in Halsey's gut tighten.

Nobody noticed her until she reached the bottom of the staircase. Even then, it took a moment before Brigham leapt up from one of the long tables. "Hal."

Every Havalon elemental in the room stopped what they were doing and turned to stare at her.

It took all her effort to smile and act like everything was okay. She cleared her throat and tried not to stare at any one face in particular. "Morning."

"How'd you sleep?"

"Oh, you know." She gestured toward her bandaged thigh under the loose sweatpants. "Werewolf scratch still kinda stings."

It was supposed to be a lighthearted 'don't worry about me' statement, but the Havalons burst into uproarious laughter like it was the best joke they'd ever heard.

Halsey tried to laugh with them as she crossed the common area to join her cousin, but she needed more than seven hours of sleep in someone else's bed to come to terms with everything that had happened. Everything they still had ahead of them.

They're so happy. We're on the brink of a potential war with blood humans, not to mention their Matriarch, and they're acting like it's just another day with another successful mission under their belts. How do they do that?

Brigham quickly noticed something wasn't right. He excused himself from the long table where he'd been sitting with several Havalons, including Cillian and Beecham, and met her halfway. "Hey. It's loud in here. Wanna take a walk?"

"Can't say no ta a little mornin' constitutional, Hal," Beecham called from the table, which kicked off another round of laughter.

"Yeah, thanks." She shot him a thumbs-up as she and

Brigham headed for the back door. "I'll tell you all about it when I get back."

That got the older Havalons cracking up, and she chuckled wryly as the loud morning noise faded away behind her. *I have to admit, it'd be nice if my own family joked around with me like that. Weird as hell, but nice.*

As the two of them reached the massive back lawn, she couldn't help but wonder what time the Havalons had woken up this morning. It had to have been incredibly early because it wasn't much past 8:00 a.m., and there wasn't a single shred of evidence from either of the massive celebrations the night before. One of which had been interrupted by werewolves.

"Better?" Brigham asked as they walked in a slow, wide circle around the perimeter of the yard.

"Yeah. Fresh air was a good idea. Thanks."

"Good. Now why, don't you tell me what you didn't wanna say in front of the Havalon family?"

She paused, then released a laugh. "Is it possible for a field injury to suddenly give everyone the ability to read my mind?"

Her cousin snorted. "Probably not. I bet it makes it a hell of a lot harder for you to keep that wall up all the time, though." Brigham glanced at her thigh. "No crutch this morning. That's a good sign."

"Ha. I didn't think you'd remember anything from last night."

"Trust me. I'd trade blacking out for no hangover every damn time. No matter how hard I try, though, it keeps not working out that way." They chuckled, and Brigham thrust his hands into his pockets. "Seriously, Hal. What's going on?"

"We need to go home."

"Aw, really? It's so much better *here*. You know what, I bet the Havalon Clan would fall over themselves if we said we wanted them to adopt us…"

Halsey slapped his arm and shook her head. "I'm serious."

"Yeah, I know. You're welcome, by the way."

"For what?"

"I already told Cillian we'd be heading back as soon as you were ready. Consider the awkwardness of becoming another Clan's hero the night before you fly home officially relieved. Mostly. At least *you're* not the one who has to tell 'em."

"That's…actually a big load off." Her smile was crooked but guarded because she still felt like there was something else attached to this. "So, thanks."

"You know I always got your back, cuz." Brigham eyed her sideways as they continued walking, the sunshine warm on their backs and hundreds of birds twittering in the bordering woods. "Plus, you can always tell me what's going on. You *do* know that, right?"

"Totally. Never doubted it for a second."

"Uh-huh. Why does it look like there's something you wanna say but won't? At least not to me."

Halsey inhaled slowly and searched the trees. It was a gorgeous summer morning in Ireland, and she wished they could stay to enjoy it. Yet they had work to do, and that couldn't start until they got back to Texas and the Ambrosius Clan estate. It was still the only place she could think of with a chance of explaining why the silverback alpha had *spoken* to her. Possibly, if she was lucky, who the hell Rólfr Orgnussun had been, too. At least as a human. Maybe she could get Charlemagne to lift her library ban if she asked *super* nicely.

She wasn't ready to talk about it with Brigham, though. Not yet. Being the only elemental in the hunting party who'd heard the alpha talk didn't come with any way to prove what she'd heard. Especially since she'd also been the one to kill him.

Before she said anything about that, she had to figure out how to deliver the information with unequivocal proof that she wasn't losing her mind like their family was so prone to assuming.

"It's not Seamus, is it?" Brigham asked.

"*What?*"

"Look, I know he makes your brain turn to goo or whatever, but I swear. If he did something to piss you off, I'll take care of it. You can tell me."

Halsey giggled and shook her head. "It's not Seamus. I promise. Though you might wanna call him by name at least *once* before we head out."

"Why? *I* don't have the hots for—" Brigham stopped dead, his eyes wide, and stared ahead at nothing. He blinked and sucked in a breath through his teeth. "Yep. Now it's coming back to me. Did I call him…*Shane?*"

She struggled not to laugh. "You called him Shane."

"Damn it. All right, fine. After I make up for that, if you need me to kick his ass, say the word."

Halsey rolled her eyes and kept walking. "My hero…"

When they returned to the Big House, breakfast was in

full swing, with the entire Havalon Clan in attendance. Cillian found them and offered a brief good morning before ushering them toward the banquet table laden with eggs, sausage, pancakes, scones, bacon, blood sausage, potatoes cooked three different ways, and toast. There was also an entire table devoted to hair-of-the-dog refreshments for the adults. Halsey didn't skimp on the food, but she left the alcohol table alone.

Breakfast felt like as much of an event and a celebration as last night, before and after the werewolf hunt. This time, Halsey found it easier to be present in the conversation. Nobody asked her about the silverback alpha, which was a massive relief. Instead, the Havalons only asked what she'd do next, where she was headed, and if she'd come back to Ireland in the foreseeable future.

All things considered, it was the perfect ending to their trip. If she ignored the unanswered questions she'd formed here and got to take back with her to the States.

As soon as the cousins had finished their meals and agreed it was time for their inevitable departure, Cillian Havalon picked that moment to knock a fork against his metal tankard. Probably filled with beer like many of the Havalons' personal cups. The room quieted down instantly so the Havalon Council leader could make his announcement from his seat.

Brigham leaned toward Halsey and muttered, "Is it me, or does it sometimes feel like these folks can read minds?"

"Definitely not you." She shook her head and looked back at Cillian so he wouldn't notice his guests' attention had been split.

"I'll make this short 'n sweet." Cillian's voice boomed

across the common area, reminding Halsey of the first time she'd heard his son speak. "Been one hell of a night 'n mornin', and ya all know what I'm referrin' ta, so I won't waste time spellin' it out. Never t'ought I'd be welcomin' two Ambrosiuses ta our hearth 'n home, and that's only 'cause I spent the last twenty years tinkin' no two of 'em'd be daft enough ta set foot inside."

The common area exploded with laughter and wordless cheers of agreement as Havalons raised their cups, tankards, glasses, and mugs.

Even Halsey and Brigham had a good laugh. They might have been the only two Ambrosiuses with healthy senses of humor.

Once the laughter died down, Cillian graced the cousins with a warm, sincere smile. "'Tisn't only 'bout bein' able ta stand each other. Nor am I only sayin' the words 'cause we had The Alpha Hunter under our roof last night." His hazel eyes crinkled as he laughed, and despite the white streaks in his beard, it made the man look younger. "Most importantly, friends, ye've brought sometin' like balance back inta the fold. Shown us all over again what's possible, s'long as we're all willin' ta kick the past out the door and tell it ta stay there. For that, Hal and Brigham, you have our Clan's thanks. *Sláinte.*"

"*Sláinte!*" The cry echoed from every Havalon as they raised their drinks again and toasted their guests' good health.

"Aw, man..." Brigham muttered. "I don't have anything left to toast with."

"Something tells me nobody's gonna be offended by

that," Halsey murmured in reply, her gaze fixed on Cillian's before she smiled and mouthed, "Thank you."

The man placed a hand over his heart and dipped his head, though his beaming smile kept the gesture from feeling formal.

"Shit." Brigham pushed to his feet and clapped his hands before raising his voice to address the room. "Now I wish I hadn't finished my drink."

"So do we," Finn shouted from the back beside the fireplace. "Ya damn near drank us dry last night!"

Brigham laughed as hard as the Clan members as he wagged a finger at Finn. The noise died down when they realized he wasn't finished. "We wanna say thanks. I know it goes both ways. This just…meant a lot to both of us. And that's saying something." More laughter followed, then he turned toward his cousin and asked, "Hal? Anything you wanna add?"

She gave herself two seconds before replying, "What he said."

The crowd burst into rowdy cheers, startling her enough that she put too much weight on her bad leg. She clamped a firm hand on her cousin's arm to keep from falling. Brigham hissed but immediately realized she wasn't doing it to mess with him. "You good?"

"Yep." She straightened but kept a hold on him. "Still super weird when a whole room laughs, and I'm not even trying."

"Right? Like I said, they'd probably adopt us…"

Halsey gave her cousin's arm an extra-strong little squeeze because she could, which made him wince before he turned a smile on everyone else.

Apparently, it wasn't time for the Ambrosius cousins to take their leave yet.

"Before ya go," Fiona called as she hurried through the crowd with a finger raised. "We have a little sometin' fer ya."

Halsey chuffed and shook her head. "That's not necessary—"

"Fine ting ya aren't the one callin' the shots, then, isn't it?" Cillian boomed as he stood from the table where his wife had paused. Fiona turned, crouched, and beckoned through the gathered crowd at someone Halsey couldn't see.

The bodies parted, soft chuckles rising through the air as the adults moved aside to make way for one small, bright-eyed, pink-cheeked little girl walking confidently past them. She looked like all the other members of her family with dark hair, blue or green eyes, and fair skin. Her tiny lips pressed together in determination as she emerged from behind her older, taller kin as if she were taking part in a formal ceremony instead of a casual goodbye to two visiting elementals.

It was the first sight that made Halsey smile today without effort. *This kid knows what's up. She'll be lucky growing up with this family around her. If we do our jobs, she won't have to fight the things we have coming for us.*

The little girl whose name Halsey had forgotten from the bombardment of introductions yesterday walked up to her, stopped, and extended her hands out and up.

Halsey glanced into those heartbreakingly tiny palms and froze. The girl held a necklace, and it wasn't the kind a child of her age would proudly offer. Black leather thongs, intricately braided with Celtic knots, were strung with tiny silver beads. Interspersed evenly among them were teeth, one to two inches long and sharp as knifepoints at the ends. Two crude pieces of what Halsey first thought were bones dangled from the center of the necklace.

It took her another second to recognize the werewolf claw that had ripped open her leg and cracked in half in the process. The claw pieces had been cleaned and polished, which meant she wouldn't be walking around wearing a werewolf claw covered in her own blood. The sharp end Fiona had pulled from Halsey's thigh dangled at the bottom, the point glinting in the sunlight with a single streak of silver up the center. The other half, removed sometime after her battle with the alpha, had been sanded into a smooth, rounded edge at the top where the leather thongs were fitted through it.

"Wow," Halsey breathed.

The little girl lifted her chin, clearly trying not to smile. "They let me sharpen it meself."

"Did they?" A soft chuckle escaped her, then she realized the other elementals gathered around to see her and Brigham off were doing the same. "This is beautiful."

"It's our tanks," Cillian added, nodding and pressing a hand to his heart. "Ya walked in here talkin' 'bout the end o' days, Hal. But I tink they're just gettin' started. Wit you."

She looked up to see every Havalon elemental smiling at her. Instantly, she was overwhelmed by a mixture of gratitude, remorse, and excitement. The combination brought a flush of color and heat to her cheeks as her eyes stung and blurred. She didn't cry, though. She couldn't.

They hadn't even cracked the surface of everything they still had to do.

Brigham nudged her and muttered, "Take the necklace, Hal. Don't wanna insult the locals, or they'll never let us leave."

The Havalons erupted into laughter, garbled shouts, and playful insults tossed back at Brigham, who took it all in like *he* was the one who'd received a gift.

Halsey reverently lifted the necklace from the little girl's hands. After she did, the child spun and skipped back toward her parents in the crowd. Halsey surveyed the elemental Clan who had so quickly accepted her, no matter how insane her stories sounded, and her gaze fell on Seamus.

It was hard *not* to find him in the crowd when he was the tallest person there.

Of course, he'd been staring at her the whole time. As soon as their gazes met, he flashed her a final dazzling grin and dipped his head.

Yeah, this isn't the last time we see each other. When we figure out how to stop this, we won't even have to ask for this Clan's help.

It was more than she could say of her own family, but somehow, it no longer made her angry. She felt more grateful than she'd expected after not even twenty-four hours with a Clan she'd never met. Yet they were all elementals. In a way, they *were* family. She and Brigham were not alone anymore.

After many waves and smiles, laughter, and shouted goodbyes, the Ambrosius cousins took their leave of the Havalon Clan's home. They'd been on the road for all of two minutes before Brigham snorted and glanced at the necklace resting across Halsey's lap. "Damn, cuz. You took on a fucking *alpha* by yourself. And *won*. That's badass as hell."

"I did what I had to do, Brigham. Honestly, I think doing all this and handing it over as a parting gift was going a little overboard."

"Nah. You *earned* that, Hal. One hundred percent."

"Thanks." She looked at the necklace of werewolf teeth and the broken alpha claw that could have ended her life if Rólfr's aim had been off by an inch. Yet It hadn't been, because the man beneath the monster hadn't wanted to kill her.

Without expecting it, she laughed and shook her head.

"What?" Brigham smiled before returning his gaze to the road.

"It's funny, I guess."

"What?"

Halsey forced her gaze away from the necklace and the memory of what she'd done. She sighed as she dropped her head back against her seat. "First monster I killed was a *werewolf alpha*."

Her cousin sniggered. "I don't think *funny*'s the right word, Hal."

She rolled her head against the headrest to look at him and added, "I only managed to do it because I refused."

"Plus, it kinda felt like he wanted you to anyway, right?"

Shit, how does he know that? Halsey's heart thudded. When Brigham shot her another quick smile, it didn't seem carefree anymore. *There's no way he knows. No way. That has to be...his way of sharing what it feels like. That's all. Total coincidence.*

Fortunately, her cousin didn't say anything else about monsters wanting hunters to put them out of their misery, so they left it at that.

Except Brigham Ambrosius never had been good at ending a conversation on a low note. After adjusting his hands on the steering wheel, he assumed his usual devil-may-care attitude and shrugged. "Doesn't always turn out like this, Hal, but hey. You're special."

She snorted. "Don't."

"Hey, I mean it. This is, like, turning over a new leaf for you." They both laughed, then he stuck his head through the open driver's-side window and shouted across the Irish countryside, "Hear that, you bastards? When you see Halsey Ambrosius coming for ya, you better be damn careful what you wish for!"

Get sneak peeks, exclusive giveaways, behind the scenes content, and more. PLUS you'll be notified of special **one day only fan pricing** on new releases.

Sign up today to get free stories.

Visit: https://marthacarr.com/read-free-stories/

AUTHOR NOTES - MARTHA CARR
FEBRUARY 7, 2023

I've started a project answering questions for my son about my life. I realized after last year's fifth round of cancer, and then chemo this time that he was expecting me to die sooner rather than later. It's been a lot for him to deal with and there isn't much I can do to make it better, except tell him stories that I can leave behind – eventually. Hopefully, a long time from now. I'm going to let you guys listen in as well.

My author notes for this year are going to be answers to questions and all of you can get to know me better, too. Maybe inspire, maybe give you a laugh along the way.

Today's question is: What is the meaning of life?

That's a fluid question that at 63 years old I think I'm just starting to figure out. Hopefully, you're doing it a lot sooner.

I'm pretty sure I didn't ask myself this question when I was younger. I was consumed with trying to get somewhere. My idea of myself was completely made up of outward things. What I did for a living, what I weighed, how was my hair, who was I dating, was my writing any good. I cared far more about what others thought of me because I didn't have the best opinion of myself.

I was always doing my best to ignore that and find ways I could feel better from something I was doing instead. It's a terrible way to live and fluctuates constantly based on other people. Can you imagine? It's like dividing up your life into a thousand pieces and giving everyone a small piece to do with as they will. I wasn't taking any ownership.

Fortunately, I wore myself out. Sure, it took till my forties to really start to work on the simple idea of liking myself as I am (and it's kind of a work in progress), but it wasn't too late. That's one thing I've learned. It's never too late.

Here's some more nuggets I've picked up that I wish I'd known as a younger version, and I'll put out there for the future one. I'm still hoping for another thirty years or more. That's a lot of time.

Don't keep offering advice to someone with the same complaint who is doing nothing to fix it. It's a drain on you with no end in sight.

Do be of service to those who are doing their best, walking forward and do want to change. But wait for the question and answer only that and let their journey belong to them. Don't fix anything.

Seek help for everything all the time and take the help, as much as you can. Do things in community, as a group. Don't be so independent and ditch that rule about doing something yourself just because you can. You'll find out that you didn't know everything, it could be done better in small and big ways, and you created stronger ties with others.

Participate as much as possible, but only in the things you want to do. Don't stay home all the time, and don't sit through things you never wanted to be at in the first place.

Volunteer at something of your choosing. It's as good for you as it is for whatever place is getting your help.

Hang around kind people, kick the others to the curb. Life's too short and see above about fixing people.

Go for your dreams and turn them into realities. Take off the expectations about when or what it will look like and expect the experience to be bigger than you imagined. For those who say it can't be done and want to tell you why - show them the hand and again, kick them to the curb. Gather those who want to encourage you and hang with them.

Modify your dreams as you go along and add to or delete - and stretch for the one you really want. Not the one you think you can get.

Keep moving and instead of doing those exercises you hate, find the ones you love. Remember what it was like as a kid to run or ride a bike. It wasn't exercise, it was just fun. Those things still exist. Find yours.

And last one for now - choose to be happy and if you can't, go find someone to talk to about why. Our job here - and the meaning of life - is to be happy and have fun. If you're not, that's the thing to go talk to someone about until you know why and can feel happy. Then, every day, including the struggles whatever they are, are all worth it. Love you. Love, Mom. More adventures to follow.

AUTHOR NOTES - MICHAEL ANDERLE

FEBRUARY 6, 2023

Thank you for not only reading this book but these author notes as well!

So, what's a monster?

Figure 1 Midjourney based on Author's directions...

Because I can't draw worth a damn.

There is a scene inside the first *Men In Black* movie where Will Smith's character is shooting aliens or monsters and he drills little Tiffany (an eight-year-old girl with blonde pigtails holding a quantum physics book) right through the forehead after NOT shooting obvious monsters in the gallery.

(*Editor's note: I think I saw Edgar the other day, or someone wearing an Edgar suit.*)

Sometimes, I feel like we allow our preconceived ideas of what monsters are to dull our sense of concern in stories. It's easy to pop a monster like the one above into a story so our little lizard brains will go, "Aaahhh! Sharp Teeth! Run! Kill! Destroy!"

For all we know, the character above is a reformed vegetarian (sucks with those teeth) who got lost in his dimensional portal and is trying to ask for directions on how to get off this crazy planet.

I'm just kidding. That asshole above is trying to take over the planet. Shoot away. This is a fiction story. I'm not trying to teach anyone a lesson.

Thank you for reading our stories!

Chat with you in the next book.

Ad Aeternitatem,

Michael Anderle

MORE STORIES with Michael newsletter HERE: https://michael.beehiiv.com/

THE ROGUE REGIMENT

Z Thornbrook and her cousins are like any other Oriceran pixie on Earth. Mischief is their middle name, and for the last hundred and fifty years, that's been their game.

But what happens when a gang of rogue pixies takes the troublemaking just a little too far?

They get noticed. By the U.S. Army. And playtime is over.

Now that they've been caught, it's time for Z, her cousins, and the entire pixie gang to face the music, and they only have two choices. Sign their lives away to enter an experimental new program for magical Army soldiers - or accept a one-way ticket back to Oriceran for good.

For any other pixie, this would be a no-brainer. They don't back down, and they definitely don't take orders from anyone, even other pixies. But for Z and her eccentric cousins, returning to their home planet is a fate worse than death.

It's time to lace up their boots and stand at attention —or not.

Because the Thornbrook pixies are heading off to magical Bootcamp run by humans, and the Army had no idea what they were getting themselves into.

Z, Domino, and Echo must find the acceptable middle ground between being who they are, in all their chaotic pixie glory, and following the terms of their magically binding contract.

But training three Army pixies is no joke—if it's even possible at all.

Can Z and her cousins learn to rein in the chaos as new magical Army recruits, or will they take it too far and be shipped off to Oriceran, where an even darker menace awaits?

<u>**Claim your copy today!**</u>

BOOKS BY MARTHA CARR

THE LEIRA CHRONICLES
CASE FILES OF AN URBAN WITCH
DIARY OF A DARK MONSTER
THE EVERMORES CHRONICLES
SOUL STONE MAGE
THE KACY CHRONICLES
MIDWEST MAGIC CHRONICLES
THE FAIRHAVEN CHRONICLES
I FEAR NO EVIL
THE DANIEL CODEX SERIES
SCHOOL OF NECESSARY MAGIC
SCHOOL OF NECESSARY MAGIC: RAINE CAMPBELL
ALISON BROWNSTONE
FEDERAL AGENTS OF MAGIC
SCIONS OF MAGIC
THE UNBELIEVABLE MR. BROWNSTONE
DWARF BOUNTY HUNTER
ACADEMY OF NECESSARY MAGIC
MAGIC CITY CHRONICLES
ROGUE AGENTS OF MAGIC
CHRONICLES OF WINLAND UNDERWOOD
WITCH WARRIOR

OTHER BOOKS BY JUDITH BERENS

OTHER BOOKS BY MARTHA CARR

JOIN THE ORICERAN UNIVERSE FAN GROUP ON FACEBOOK!

BOOKS BY MICHAEL ANDERLE

Sign up for the LMBPN email list to be notified of new releases and special deals!

http://lmbpn.com/email/

For a complete list of books by Michael Anderle, please visit:

www.lmbpn.com/ma-books/

CONNECT WITH THE AUTHORS

Martha Carr Social
Website:
http://www.marthacarr.com
Facebook:
https://www.facebook.com/groups/MarthaCarrFans/

Michael Anderle

Website: http://lmbpn.com

Email List: http://lmbpn.com/email/

https://www.facebook.com/LMBPNPublishing

https://twitter.com/MichaelAnderle

https://www.instagram.com/lmbpn_publishing/

https://www.bookbub.com/authors/michael-anderle

www.ingramcontent.com/pod-product-compliance
Lightning Source LLC
LaVergne TN
LVHW091708070526
838199LV00050B/2310